SOUL SEER

Book 2 of The Seers Series

Theresa Dale

Paper Doll Publishing

ISBN-13: 978-1-989897-15-7 ISBN: 978-1-989897-14-0 (eBook)

Cover design by: Theresa Dale

For those connections that are my anchors.

CONTENTS

CHAPTER 1 – CYCLE

Pain.

It was ever-present for Ed, and therefore, for Dawn, whose guilt was enough to stop her from blocking it. There were other things, of course – fear, worry, disappointment, frustration – but the pain overrode it all.

And she hadn't even told him about Shya.

Yet.

She wasn't sure if Big Ed would survive the news that the woman he'd loved in silence for years had been lost to them, just as they'd won back the boy. Dawn could barely believe it herself, but all she had to do to have it confirmed again was to gaze at her friends and see it in their eyes. The *how could this have happened?*

Rory was the worst. He wasn't part of the Seers, not really, except as Shya's partner, which in and of itself was a brand-new direction in Shya's life. Indeed, it seemed that the woman had finally found her place in the world, just before she was sucked into another one.

Possessed.

And as the boy whose place she'd taken thrived in his newfound freedom, seemingly growing right before their eyes, Shya's own body lay in her hospital bed, a husk, so much emptier than any possession can render a physical being because, Dawn suspected, of Shya's unique gifts.

When the girl who'd communicated with the dead her

entire life gave in to one of the darker spirits of Hell, she didn't do it half way. Even the twins had declared her to have entirely deserted her earthly vessel, though it breathed still, heart pumping calmly, blood dutifully touching oxygen-hungry structures and fuelling her onward, physically, through life. She was still alive, but even the doctors scratched their heads over her complete lack of response.

Sheila had equated the sight of her body in her hospital bed to that of a corpse, or of one frozen in time. Sleeping beauty.

Sadly, both Sheila and Mel had gone back home. They all should have, by then! The boy was safe, and their day-to-day lives awaited.

But the twins conducted their business from afar, watching Dawn, determined to stay until she would go, too. And Dawn wouldn't leave without Big Ed. At least that was what she said. But she spent as much time in Shya's hospital room as she did in Ed's, though the former had shown no progress where the latter was near release. She could stare at Shya for hours. Mel knew why, but he was the only one. The others assumed she felt just as they did: guilty. Responsible, somehow, despite their efforts to keep her safe. Rory... well, his guilt trumped that of them all, Dawn imagined. And it was *his* job demanding him home the loudest. But it was Rory who would stay, even after the rest of them went back.

What none besides Mel knew was that Dawn saw something more than what the doctors and their machines could glean. Dawn was an empath, and where there was nothing medically to indicate that Shya was still in there somewhere, Dawn knew she *had* to be, because where they saw nothing, Dawn felt everything. Her heart knew Shya's own as though they were as one, like the twins were with each other. Dawn's heart could know *anyone's* that way. That was *her* gift. And when her heart touched Shya's, one thing shouted louder and with more insistence than Big Ed's pain could ever do:

Regret.

CHAPTER 2 – REVEAL

The man they all affectionately called "Big Ed" watched her idly as she paced, then paused at the window, arms folded over her breast, then paced some more. She imagined he watched because Dawn was the only thing that moved in the sterile, stark whiteness of his hospital room. She imagined, too, that he watched *idly* because nothing ever came of her incessant pacing. Not to mention the sheer sense of boredom that hung over him like a pall.

He wanted to go.

He'd been ready, really, since he'd started to show signs of healing, which was very shortly after he'd been admitted. But the doctors, baffled by the extent of internal bleeding in his torso when no source of the deluge was to be found, had insisted he stay. With furrowed brows and tight-lipped frowns, they bent over him in teams, each growing larger by the day as a myriad of specialists were called in to consult. Each asking the same questions over and over again: *what happened that day? What was he doing? What event, exactly, preceded his collapse?* Dawn had answered them all a hundred times. Patiently. Cautiously. Mindfully consistent. Because perpetuating the mystery behind his injuries was the only choice, when the truth was hard for even the witnesses to fathom.

And Dawn hadn't seen it, anyway. Not close-up, like Rory, Shya's childhood best friend, Bethie, and Shya's father had. She'd felt it, though. Shya had, in her frenzied efforts to get to Jordan and the beast that had possessed him, run straight through Ed as though he were made of glass. Or as though he were nothing but a wisp of a veil, as the twins described his abilities as a portal. And while Shya only suffered the event as a soul who'd travelled to another level – her body unconscious, but undamaged as she did – Ed had suffered it in a physical sense, his insides reacting by tearing and bleeding when they were permeated. The blinding pain like hot knives that sliced through his middle. A thousand claw marks of the demon that crossed the portal, too.

"She was fuelled that day," Dawn muttered, and though Big Ed's eyes were still on her, he said nothing.

They'd talked the event into a pulp; she knew they had. But while Ed was healing, Dawn had been looking forward. It nearly killed him this time, but if he could learn to use it... Sheila said he would. She'd seen it. But there was little else to relay of the portent. Sheila saw flashes, bits and pieces of what was to come and what had already passed, but sometimes there just wasn't enough to form a solid idea from. Just enough to glimpse.

The twins, on the other hand, *always* seemed to know more, but only shared what they deemed essential, claiming many things about the future weren't *meant* to be known. Not yet. It set Dawn's teeth on edge, but she knew it was only impatience and frustration that sparked her reaction. She trusted Jane and Anna. And she was secretly grateful they'd stayed, though she'd encouraged them to leave in that mother hen way she had with all the members of The Seers.

Gifted folk tended to put themselves last, and as someone who could glean their feelings before even they were aware of them, she'd always been protective. Always taken care.

"Fuelled by what?"

Dawn jumped, brought back from her thoughts by the

man whose presence she'd all but forgotten.

He chuckled. "We *both* need to get out of here."

She laughed, fluttering her hand at her heart while she crossed to sit on the edge of his bed, and it truly was the edge; the descriptor part of Ed's nickname was no fluke. "Sorry. Lost in my thoughts again," she patted his hand.

"I know. I was going to let you stay in your own little world, but by *God,* I'm bored."

She smiled. "I know."

"I almost want to say it, you know? The next time the doctors come in to ask the same questions and do the same tests. Just tell them the truth!"

"You know that wouldn't get you out of here faster."

He shook his head. "It'd liven things up though, wouldn't it?" His eyes twinkled.

She laughed. "Frankly, after everything that's happened, I'm OK with boredom"

He grinned.

"Give me more boredom!" She gestured wildly with her arms, making him laugh again.

"They can't keep you forever," she sighed, "and the twins told me this morning that they were packing up."

His eyes lit up. "They swore they wouldn't go until I could!"

Dawn gave him a wink. "Exactly."

"Shit, I wish my 'gift' was that useful," he complained, emphatically putting finger-quotes around "gift".

"Me too," Dawn sighed again.

They sat in resumed quiet for a while. Dawn's eyes went

back to the window, to the sky, which was nearly white that day. It was getting cold, too. She shivered as she thought of the oncoming winter. A time for the earth to sleep, just as their friend had succumbed, retreating like the living things did in the cold.

As though he could read her mind, Ed grasped her hand, engulfing it in his and giving it a squeeze. "Tell me what's going on, Dawn."

She looked at him, mock questioning.

He rolled his eyes. "Come on. I know you all think you're protecting me, but all I can think of is her." He touched his chest with his fingertips, bringing Dawn's hand with them. "I still feel her, Dawn, like she left part of herself behind." He let his hands drop as his expression fell. Dawn squeezed his hand, aching with the sadness that shone in his eyes. "And she doesn't feel right," he finished.

She bit her lip. Wondered if his knowing would have the power to rip him apart again. She took her hand back and grasped his shirt-hem, asking permission with her eyes. He frowned slightly, but nodded. She pushed his shirt up over his belly, eyes on the mottled mess of his skin, bruised and bumpy with hematomas. *At least they're improving,* she noted, spotting yellows and pinks where there had only been shades of purple, black and blue before. Still, tears welled in her eyes as she felt them all, like storm clouds brewing on her front and lava roiling like thunder within. She sucked in a breath and pulled his shirt down, then met his eyes. "I won't hurt you more. Not today."

He took both of her hands that time, beseeching her with his eyes. "Please don't do that to yourself. I know you hurt right along with me, and despite your twisted sense of guilt when you try not to acknowledge it, it's not necessary!"

She looked toward the window again, jaw clenched.

"You do *not* have to feel my pain, Dawn."

She knew it. But he was right about the guilt.

"And it blinds you too, you know."

She looked at him again, brow furrowed.

"Every time you connect to it like that, it's new and terrible. It's nearly gone for me, now! It's so much better than before!"

She nodded.

"So much so," he sat up, smiling, "that I rarely think about it!"

She smiled, too. "That's really good, big guy. Really good."

"Which means I have way too much time to think about other things. Like Shya."

She averted her eyes.

"I know she's here."

She froze. Even her breath was still.

He chuckled. "Someone's always here with me. You switch off with Jane and Anna like clockwork, and I know you don't leave. I'm not just a door to other levels of existence, you know." He placed his hands on his hips, regarding her playfully.

She blew out a breath, then inhaled again. *Has to happen sometime,* she thought. The twins had been begging her to tell him for days. "She is here," she said, finally. The humour drained from his face as he rested back against his pillow. *What next? I won't say she's OK.* She sighed, suddenly overwhelmed. "They're talking about releasing her to go home, seeing as how they can't find a thing wrong with her, physically," she said, her voice wobbling on the edge of tears. "And it's what her Dad wants. Rory too, of course. He's struggling keeping up with it."

"Dawn!"

She frowned, surprised at being stopped.

"What's wrong? Why is she here?"

A tear dropped, and then another. And then the dam was broken. Ed patted her forearm as she sobbed, but he said nothing. She knew he wouldn't take the question back again, and could she blame him, really? *No.* She wiped her face, then met his eyes, resolute, finally. "She's gone, Ed. It happened that night, after you two – collided. After the final exorcism. We took her home. She was so tired! And I felt it... I hate myself for leaving her when I could *feel* how..." she shook her head, searching for the words she'd refused to speak aloud, not even to Mel. "How *untethered* to this world she was!" she finished, her voice rising.

"Don't," Ed squeezed her arm. "You couldn't have prevented it, Dawn. Nobody could have."

She watched his face. He was pale, his flesh blanched by the confirmation of what, she realized, he'd already known.

"Can we get her back?"

She shrugged. Her shoulders rose and fell like massive weights on her tiny frame. "They say – the twins – they say it's woven itself through and around her, like roots of a tree."

Ed shuddered.

"What?"

He shook his head. "I don't know. Something about that..." he shuddered again and made a sound of disgust. "I don't know. Feels bad."

She nodded. "It's like – she's there because she feels she has to be."

Ed was silent.

"It's like – the whole time we were focused on Jordan, it was working on *her.* I thought she was handling it – but it wasn't trying to convince her! It was *becoming* her, Ed. And the fact that she could see her mother there, trapped." She sobbed again, reaching for a Kleenex from the side table and ending up accepting one from Ed, whose reach was easier. She blew her nose. "I don't know what we're gonna do. Once she's released, she'll stay with her father. It's the only thing that makes sense."

"And we'll have to go back home."

Dawn nodded.

"We're only a few hours away," Ed said quietly. She heard the defeat in his words, though. Felt it, too.

"We all want to meet as soon as we're back home," she went on, "and I know we'll come up with a plan, but..."

He nodded. "I know."

They sat quietly for a moment.

Ed smiled. "Hey, it's not like we're *really* apart, you know."

She frowned.

"We're The Seers, Dawn. Who better to figure this out?"

She forced a grin.

"No, really," he cupped her jaw in a rare moment of connection, and she felt his heart through her own. His demeanor was gentle. Soft. But the determination she glimpsed – the drive to get their friend back – was at least as strong in Big Ed as it was in herself. "We'll find her, and we'll get her back."

She searched his eyes, seeing nothing but truth, and

feeling it, finally, after missing it when the twins tried to placate her, not finding it with Sheila, whose eyes betrayed her own fear, and failing to spot it through the mire of Mel's own feelings of disappointment, anger, and guilt. Rory had been the closest, but his desperation clouded everything.

But there it was, in Ed's eyes: the truth of the knowledge that Shya would be back with them again.

Thank you, she sent her gratitude up to that presence, the overarching one that many called *God,* but whose name she felt unqualified to fully realize.

"We'll figure it out," she smiled, and Ed's whole face lit up with hope.

"And soon," he added.

And as if on cue, a clap and a booming voice announced the presence of Ed's team of doctors.

They both jumped, Ed's hand going to his heart.

"Whoa, there!" the head doctor approached Ed, palms out. "Don't let us scare you into another crisis on the day we're letting you leave!"

Ed sat up. "For real?"

Dawn laughed, fully enjoying the childish wonder on her friend's face. And knowing Ed was right. It would be soon.

She patted Ed on the arm and gave him a wink before leaving him to his doctors, who were already milling about the bed, eyes roving over Ed while they puzzled over his case, both fascinated and afraid. She dialled Mel as she started for the elevator, thinking of saying goodbye to Shya, for now. The twins appeared when the doors slid open, and she motioned for them to stay in the car. They complied, looking entirely unsurprised.

And suddenly, the lull that had seen them waiting,

helpless to move forward until all were ready, had exploded into a new stage, and Dawn was more than ready for it.

CHAPTER 3 – PARTING

Shya's dark curls appeared darker still against the stark white hospital linens. Today they'd been smoothed and tucked behind her head, someone's attempt at taming them while she slept on, unable to care for the locks that had thwarted her own efforts ceaselessly.

Dawn put a hand on Rory's shoulder and he cast a grateful gaze up at her. She saw the torture behind his smile, saw how frustrated desperation set an edge to his handsome features, but she closed herself to *feeling* it a little. Just an instinctive act of self-preservation; she'd already experienced the full extent of the man's pain and remembered it well. She squeezed his shoulder, then bent to give him a sideways hug. He accepted it, then turned his profile to her, his eyes back on the woman he loved so much it ached in him.

Dawn lingered on his face. Everybody did, to Rory's apparent acceptance and associated miasma of responses. He was a chameleon, changing to suit the circumstances, blending in seamlessly no matter the situation. She imagined he enjoyed such privileges in court; Shya had alluded to his brilliance as a lawyer. But around The Seers, he'd relaxed into himself. He'd charmed them sufficiently, gaining their trust and admiration – and their approval as Shya's partner, which had been a thoughtful effort, on his part – and now was just Rory. Brilliant, yes. Gorgeous? Almost impossibly so. And sad? Painfully.

"You did her hair," she eyed her friend's smoothed locks again.

"Ha!" he chuckled, "I tried."

Jane and Anna came to stand on the opposite side of the bed. Both gazed upon the unconscious woman with intense looks of concentration.

Rory watched them. "Can you see her today? Where she is?"

The women showed no signs of hearing him, though Anna pressed her lips together. Rory sent a helpless look up at Dawn, who squeezed his shoulder in commiseration. She'd been victim to the twins' odd behaviour for far longer than he, and had passed from annoyance and frustration into acceptance and trust. Despite their somewhat... detached methods, they rarely failed to uncover useful bits of information.

"Any news on her release?"

He sighed. "They can't deny that she's not doing much more than taking up a bed here," he muttered, jaw clenched, "but seem too fascinated by her to let her go."

Dawn nodded. She'd heard as much.

He peered up at her again. "I heard them talking about how she and Big Ed know each other, how both cases are mysterious."

"Really?" She remembered a brief suggestion by the hospital's social worker that the police should be involved, but that had faded after the first day of Shya's admittance. She shook her head. "There's no way they'll work out the connection."

"They mentioned Jordan, too."

The twins seem to snap back to the present, both sets of strange, nearly translucent pale eyes widening as they reacted to Rory's statement.

"It doesn't matter," Dawn said, her eyes going to Shya's slack features again. "Even if they suspect the injuries to be the results of an exorcism, what are they to do? Jordan is fine – better than fine!" She looked at Rory, then the twins. "And Ed's being released as we speak."

Rory's eyebrows shot up in surprise.

"Don't get too excited," Dawn laughed. "They didn't say anything about Shya."

The twins were murmuring under their breath.

"How's work?" Dawn asked, to distract herself and Rory at the same time.

Rory shrugged, took Shya's hand. "They've had to give the more urgent cases to other staff, but I've managed the research and some of the interviews for longer-term work from here. I know they need me to either take time off completely, or get back to the office in short order, but I won't make any decisions until Shya's released."

Dawn recognized the failure to mention any hope that she'd get better, that she'd return to them, and her heart sank.

"I think I could do almost everything from home if she were released," he went on, "but it's her care that ranks highest on my list of priorities."

"Maybe staying at her father's house would be best," Dawn suggested, not for the first time.

Rory nodded this time, to her surprise. "If this is going to stretch into weeks or months, I'll need the kind of support he can offer. And has offered, already." He looked up at her, "I hate this. I'd quit my job in a second if I wasn't determined to have a future with her, but it's the only thing that's holding my sanity together right now. I won't let that go." His eyes shone with emotion.

Dawn could only nod, understanding completely, but

having no words of reassurance. Not yet. She looked to the twins. "What did you see?"

Jane, who often seemed to present the thoughts of both women after they'd discussed them, looked forlorn. Anna cleared her throat, instead. "Much the same as always: the rocky shore, the bed floating on the water – quite distant, this time – and the tree." She glanced at Jane, then continued, "Whenever we try to see Shya, we see the tree."

Dawn nodded. "Whatever efforts we make to bring her back, it seems we'll have to untangle her from that tree, first. Somehow it represents her."

"Or how she's joined to it now," Jane said, then added, "The demon."

Dawn remembered a dream Shya had described to the group when she'd started seeing the boy. "Do you remember how she described the tree from her dreams? The one she'd seen the demon hide behind on the path through the woods?"

"I know that tree," Rory mumbled, almost too low to hear.

"She dreamt about the demon as being part of it, intertwining with the branches and sinking into the fissures of the bark."

Jane inhaled sharply. "Maybe the tree is just a comforting symbol the demon's used to convince her she's hopelessly entangled with it, now."

"Are you saying she might not be?" Rory raised his gaze to the pale women again.

"Of course," Dawn cut in, "it may have convinced her they're one soul, but I don't believe it. We *can't!*"

"What does it want her for?" Rory asked, his voice rising. "She has these gifts, sure... but what would the supposed King of Hell do with them?"

Dawn watched Shya, part of her hoping for a reaction, as earnestly as the larger part knowing it wouldn't come.

Rory stood and began to pace, another hint at his time in court. "I mean, is this just something that could go on forever? Does it just want to have her, like she's just part of some sick collection?" He gestured toward the bed. "Her mother first, now her! Are there others?"

"Not there," the twins chorused.

Rory stopped in his tracks. "But there are ghosts, right? Other spirits?"

Dawn recalled the group's first, hurried discussions after Shya had failed to waken the day following Jordan's successful exorcism. They'd all used their gifts to try and discern what had happened, but even their combined efforts could not produce a fulsome answer.

"On the boundaries of where she is," Jane answered, nodding, "but while they seem to want Shya, too, they appear stuck there."

"On the outside looking in," Anna confirmed, looking wistfully back at Shya, "held at bay by something unseen."

Rory put his face in his hands, then ran them through his hair, clearly frustrated.

"Come sit," Dawn touched the back of the chair. Rory complied, seemingly drained of the fight that had fuelled his outburst. That was all he'd had during the first few days after the exorcism – *fight.* Refusing to be daunted by whatever task lay ahead, retrieving Shya had been the one goal he'd honed in on, even when the rest of those who loved her floundered for answers.

"We need to get together," Dawn renewed her gentle grip on Rory's shoulder as she looked to Jane and Anna, "all of us. We need a plan."

Rory nodded as he took Shya's hand up again.

"As soon as we're all home," Anna confirmed, and Jane nodded in agreement.

Dawn looked down at Rory. "We *all* want her back. But we have to recharge. We need to tend to the other areas of our lives: work, family, etcetera, before tackling this."

Rory shook his head. "I can't do that. How can any of us do that when she's like this?" He gestured toward Shya with his free hand, but there was no ferocity left in his words or his actions.

"We *have* to, Rory. Or else she won't have anything to return *to.*" As usual, Anna had said the exact words needed to reach him. And Dawn, too.

"She's right," Dawn said, giving Anna a grateful look. "And we'll keep in close contact. We won't put this aside, even as we go back to our lives. I promise."

Rory leaned forward to rest his forehead on Shya's limp arm, his shoulders shaking. Dawn couldn't help it, she opened up to him, to his pain, to share it, even just to know his torture intimately so he wouldn't be alone in it. And it crashed over her like one of the dark waves on Shya's darkened shoreline, a drowning deluge of melancholia. She bent over him in an embrace of commiseration. "I'm so sorry," she cried, tears dampening the shoulder of his slate-colored sweater like rain on a concrete wall. And then Jane and Anna were behind her, lending their arms, too, and their tears, the white curtains of their hair coming together like a shield against reality, if only for a moment. The four of them bent over Shya in that way for some time, saying goodbye. Preparing to leave even as their hearts were forged together in a shared determination to take her back from the demon who claimed to be called Asmodeus, the fourth demon of Hell.

CHAPTER 4 – GHOST WRITER: REACH

How can it be so still
In conjunction with the quake
A cycle unfulfilled
No ending, no beginning as he in shadow conquests make

How can everything be hollow
With the weight of so much hate
Cracked and furrowed, maggots wallow
Rendered open, raw and bleeding, waiting helpless for my fate

How does the sequence fail
Past and present, early, late
Fall to pieces on horizon's sail
Bending time senselessly as her sickbed on the surface skates

How does it wind into the fabric
The breath of rot that permeates
Layers of death long passed and tragic
Congealing in the empty spaces, sealing madness as my

state

I cannot remember

I am not I; I am fate

Dragged unknowing, torn asunder

Trailing fairy strands of brightness, that he uses for the gate

CHAPTER 5 – WAKE

She bolted awake as the car hit a speed bump, the stark image of a gaping hole ripping the fabric of a sky heavy with the portent of an oncoming storm still at the forefront of her mind. She gasped as she lunged forward, straining against the dutifully-engaged seatbelt.

A hand touched her arm from the back seat. Her instinctive first reaction was to snap her gaze to the left, where Anna sat in the driver's seat, calm but undeniably concerned. Dawn turned, then, and met Jane's strange eyes, which studied her intently through a pink-tinged veil of the palest blue.

"What is it?"

Dawn's eyes darted to Ed, who'd reluctantly given up the driver's seat before promptly falling to sleep in the back, where he slumbered, still. She looked at Jane again. "You didn't see it? The gate?"

Jane's eyes clouded, tremoring subtly as she furrowed her brow, then she shook her head. "I can only see the shoreline, and the tree."

Dawn rested hard against the back of her seat. She wished for Mel, for his calming touch. Or even Sheila, whose empathy was far better expressed than the twins', who were as short on words as they were long on insight. Indeed, Jane and Anna seemed only to communicate freely with each other, unless sharing was deemed (by them) to be essential. And even then, they were quiet. Dawn suspected they were joined in stream of consciousness as closely as they were joined by genetic code, seeming to take that sometimes-eerie twin bond to an entirely different level.

As if to counter her thoughts, Jane added, "And there were... words. Like a passage."

"Like a song," Anna added.

Dawn lunged forward again as the words flowed back. She grabbed her purse and started shuffling madly through it. She was on the brink of giving up when Jane reached around her with a pen *and* a little notepad, which Dawn accepted without a word. She rifled through pages of fractured thoughts and doodles, and then bent over the first clean page she found, singly focused on emptying the words out before they faded again.

When she was done, she held it up and read it silently, breathing slow. "A *poem,*" she whispered, once she'd finished. Tears welled in her eyes. Anna flicked her gaze to the rear-view mirror, no doubt to share a look with Jane.

"Here," Jane reached for the pad, which Dawn willingly gave up, shocked as she was by the eloquence that had flowed from her own hand, yet not of her mind.

Jane read it aloud, stumbling a bit over its unusual rhythm before getting it right on the third verse. Dawn barely breathed as the passage was read, cringing when Jane got it wrong, because she knew it back to front. Knew how to say it right. Could have recited it without effort, she realized when Jane reread a line.

And yet, it wasn't hers.

The realization set her heart to a gallop. But it wasn't she who said it, first.

"That's Shya's," Ed muttered, sleep lacing his words. The three women exchanged glances before Dawn said what they were all thinking.

"Holy *shit.*"

CHAPTER 6 – A CHILD EMPATH

The station wagon shook as Dawn's five-year-old brother, Kenny, dove from the back seat to the wagon's trunk space, where her two older brothers played a game of Old Maid.

"Get back in your seat!" Freddie protested as Kenny landed, sending their cards flying. Jason yelled wordless sounds of frustration, supporting his older brother, and Dawn watched it all from her booster, where she remained belted in, despite the fact that she was a full year older than Kenny.

Her mother turned, her face a mask of frustration. "Let your brother play, you two!" She glanced at Dawn, eyes tired, and smiled. Dawn noticed her chipped front tooth with a pang. She felt it every time her mother smiled: the blow that had sent her slamming into the tabletop. It had both chipped her tooth and broken her nose, if her mother's admonitions toward her father had been accurate. Papa hadn't allowed a visit to the hospital, though, so none of them could be sure, he said. But Dawn knew. She'd felt the starburst shock of pain when it had cracked as surely as her mother had. "How you doin', Dawnie?" She touched Dawn's knee, which was white-stockinged beneath her Sunday dress.

"Good, Mama," she replied quickly, glancing at her father's eyes in the rear-view mirror. It was never easy to tell what was safe to say around Papa. But his eyes were on the road. Sweat beaded on his brow; it hurt him to drive,

Dawn knew that. His back ached, sickeningly hot around his midriff and reaching like fiery tendrils around his hips. But he drove, anyway, because of something Mama whispered as she tucked them in at night when she explained Daddy's actions. Something called "pride." *Stubborn* pride, if it had been a bad day.

Her mother peered toward the boys in the back again. "Kenny? You see how your sister sits? Nice and still! Come on back into your seat, now, hear?" Her brow was damp, too, and her hair was frizzing out of its careful rows of braids. The summer had been unforgivingly hot, even sending the woodland creatures into the cool shelter of the trees more than in any recent years, Papa said. He hunted, so he knew. The animals were coming out later than usual. Hiding, he'd said many times with a frown.

Which made the events that followed stranger than they would have been in any other year.

Dawn's oldest sibling, Cadence, didn't have to go to church. She lived with her boyfriend, to their father's great disapproval, seeing as how she was only seventeen, but on the day she left, she'd screamed that Papa wasn't her Papa, anyway. Not *really*. And so, she could do what she wanted. And somehow, Mama had seemed relieved that Cadence was gone. Dawn saw it in her mother's demeanor as clearly as the boys did, but she felt it, too.

She wondered if it had something to do with the way Papa looked at Cadence. Sort of how he looked at those women on the sidewalks in town, with their brightly-colored hair and short skirts. The ones who burned with a need Dawn couldn't put a name to. Cadence was beautiful; Dawn could see that, too, but she didn't look like those women. Her skin was lighter than the rest of the siblings', Dawn included, but it was unblemished where the sidewalk ladies seemed as troubled with sores as they were with their apparent lack of a place to be.

Cadence would have worn her seatbelt. She would have shown Kenny that the smartest ones played it safe, even if they didn't have to. She'd taught Dawn similar lessons before she'd left. Indeed, she'd spent more time raising Dawn than their mother did, what with all the jobs Mama had to work since Papa got hurt. *Disabled,* Grandma said when she came to look after them after school. But now Cadence was gone and Mama was relieved, and Dawn missed her painfully, especially when Papa started eyeing her like he had her half-sister.

Cadence would have held her arm out across Kenny and Dawn when the deer sprung out of the ditch and onto the highway. Would have protected them when Papa swerved hard with a curse, but she wasn't there, and so Kenny toppled with the boys in the back, screaming, their fear spilling over Dawn like molten lava, and Mama jerked forward just in time to see the buck rear up, eyes wild, and she screamed, too, her arms going up to shield her face instinctively, and that was good, because Mama wasn't wearing a seatbelt, either, and she flew through the windshield when the wagon hit the blue Toyota in the lane beside them at full speed, for Papa had swerved, but he'd missed the brake pedal. It was his right leg that he had troubles with, see. The gas and brake leg that went numb intermittently and sometimes refused to obey altogether. It was OK, though, because Daddy said he could just use his left leg if that happened. But he didn't or couldn't. Dawn would never know which, and when they hit that Toyota, Mama launched sort of sideways and forward at the same time, crashing through the glass on Papa's side and preventing him, as it turned out, from sailing out the window, himself.

And then they were impossibly still, as though time itself had stopped, and there was smoke rising from the crinkled hood, and Dawn's collarbones were broken neatly in two beneath the straps of her five-point harness. She knew it because the feeling was exactly like how Mama's nose had felt when Papa hit the back of her head so hard that she slammed into the table. And she couldn't feel Mama at all, now. For the first time in her life, she recognized the connection she'd taken for granted… because it was gone.

She felt Kenny; he was OK, somehow, alive, though his arm was broken and he had ended up on the floor between the passenger seat and the back seat, unconscious.

Her two older brothers were generally unscathed and exclaiming in shrill voices from the back. Dawn reached out for them, connected, felt their fear and confusion.

Still no Mama.

But there *was* pain, pain that was not Kenny's or her own. She strained to see her father's face, her heart fluttering as panic set in, finally. He was bent over the steering wheel, arms akimbo. Blood dripped from the wheel where it had run in rivulets around it as gravity and movement had dictated. But he was not gone. Not like Mama. He was… sleeping. Sort of. Like he did when he smelled funny and had trouble walking. Like he did when he fell onto the couch and dropped into sleep like a stone, his guttural snoring the only sign he was still alive.

There was pain coming from Papa, yes, but it was more of the usual. Back, hips. Blinding sometimes, dull others. In that moment, though, the *other,* foreign pain trumped it all. It was sharp… so sharp it felt as though the world was cut in two, but there was pressure, too, an explosive squeezing in the guts that felt impossible, felt like death coming, and she knew it: that feeling of dying, for the first time in her young life, she knew it exquisitely because she experienced it as though it was first-hand, and she thought it was she that would succumb, and she wished for it because it was too much. The sharpness, the squeezing, the bursting of vessels and crushing of ribs, and she choked out a scream that was so shrill it brought her father back to consciousness. And he turned and saw his daughter, shoulders out of place and shrieking the place down, red in the face, and knew she was alive and so looked some more and saw his oldest sons and then he was getting out of the car and shouting for Kenny because he couldn't see Kenny, but it wasn't Kenny who hurt, and it wasn't her mother because her mother was gone. And then the smoke was clearing and there were sirens and she saw it, the deer, standing on its hind legs still and screaming, too, for it was sandwiched between the wagon and the blue Toyota and dying. Crushed in the middle. Ribs splintered and shiny guts in shades of pink and red and black spilled onto the hood of her family's car.

And on the hood of the Toyota was the body of her mother, empty, bloodied and broken except her face, which would look beautiful and serene in her open casket. Dawn stopped screaming, and in a crystal-clear moment of lucidity she wished her mother's nothingness for the deer, because surely it was better. And she watched its eyes until it stopped screaming, too, watched them as they faded, felt a peace as the light behind them extinguished and the pain subsided to something more bearable. In the short term, anyway. To the two broken collarbones she suffered, to Kenny's broken arm and the concussion that would cause him to repeat Kindergarten, to the swirling guilt of a father who turned *good* in those first few moments after the accident, to the mountainous regret he suffered when he discovered his dead wife, and finally, to the introduction of her own broken heart, newly motherless, that would never, ever heal.

CHAPTER 7 – REGROUP

The atmosphere in Dawn's apartment living room was nothing if not charged. The group was there in full force, eager and anxious to share with the ones who understood best.

But we aren't *all here,* Dawn thought as she scanned the group she'd begun just a few short years earlier. In that time, they'd rounded out, grown as individuals as well as a team. They'd become something akin to family, and for that she was overwhelmingly grateful, for her own had been flung far and wide.

Despite their father's incredible transformation after the accident, it seemed the siblings were left with memories that only ratcheted up in intensity when they were together. Cadence had become the centre-point that held them all together in an unexpected return home, but their father had kept them going, turning the wheel with dogged determination until he ran himself into the ground. There was something rewarding in his final demise, though. It was his heart that failed; doctors called it a "catastrophic event", in which the organ had fairly burst. And Dawn liked that, because they'd told him for years it would be the cirrhosis. So, in his death, his life seemed mirrored, first threatened by the damage he'd done with his own bad decisions, and then taken over all of a sudden by a change in focus – one which centered on the heart. And while her father's efforts did not heal the family's wounds completely, they did something even better: the change in him changed the very life paths of his children.

The fact that he'd worked himself to death was

something only Dawn had seemed to understand. She could feel the extent of his regret, after all... but her siblings only saw his suffering. They could not glean how healing it was for him to overextend himself for them. For *her*, an abused wife and mother who'd died before he'd had the chance to make any sort of amends. Hell, he hadn't even admitted his sins to himself before the accident. But after it, the weight of them threatened to crush him if he didn't change. Didn't make it right to some extent.

"Big Ed looks good," Mel said quietly as he sat in the new chair closest to her La-Z-Boy, and she snapped back to the present. Returned his smile and reached, just a little, to see if Mel's guilt was still overpowering him.

It was.

"I'm more worried about you," she said, clasping his hand in hers and instantly benefitting from the calm he unconsciously imparted. *If only he could affect himself in this way,* she thought for the hundredth time.

He shook his head. "I'm working on it, love. I just can't take the," he paused to look around at their friends, "the *knowledge* that I could have done more to protect her."

"We all could have!" She squeezed his hand. "Especially me: I brought her home, I tucked her into bed. I felt how unravelled she was, and just how tired. I felt that dark danger lurking, waiting. And what did I do?"

He lowered his eyes.

"I chose to be happy we got Jordan back. I chose to focus on Big Ed, and on recovery. And I left her." A surprise tear rolled down her cheek and she peered around the room, realizing her friends had fallen silent as she spoke.

"You didn't know, Dawn," Sheila said. "None of us realized the full extent of the danger."

The rest of the group nodded somberly.

"Doesn't mean any of us is walking around guilt-free," Ed piped up. The air changed, pressing in on them heavily.

"We can't focus on what's already happened," Jane said. Dawn saw that she and her sister were holding hands, and that Anna had Sheila's hand, too.

"We have to look ahead," Anna added.

"How do we do that when we all feel like we failed her?" Mel exclaimed, showing a rare outburst of emotion. Mel was the steady one. If *he* was off-kilter, how could any of them stand? Dawn reached for his hand, and he took Ed's, who accepted gratefully and then reached for Jane's free one. Sheila cried quietly, but her eyes shone with hope through her tears as she closed the circle by taking Dawn's free hand. They all watched Dawn, waiting.

Dawn hadn't felt much like leading anything in recent days, but she found herself rising to the need, now. She took a deep breath, then spoke. "What we gotta do now is stop thinking about how we failed Shya, and figure out how to bring her back." Dawn heard the strength in her own voice and took hold of it as she pushed forward. "She may have been taken, but we learned a lot about the demon that took her before that," she looked at each of them in turn, "and we learned about each other, too. About *ourselves.*" She squeezed the hands that held her own and the group exchanged looks, some even continuing to hold onto each other while others rested back in their seats. Sheila to Anna, who still held her sister's hand, and Mel to Dawn, no doubt enabling her calm exterior. *Thank God.*

Nobody said a word, but Dawn felt their responses. She looked at Ed, whose drive to help the woman he'd loved quietly for so long was compromised by his confusion over what he could do and the terrible consequences of it. Nonetheless, Dawn knew the determination that burned in him meant he would do it again, if it meant saving Shya… even if he had to sacrifice himself.

"Ed?"

He met her eyes. Dawn saw that Jane and Anna had been eyeing him, too.

"Mel's been doing everything he can to learn about your gift."

Mel nodded. "It's fascinating. Do you have any idea how *rare* it is for a *person* to be able to act as a portal?"

Ed shrugged. "Doesn't help much when I've got no idea what to do with it, or even how to use it without nearly getting myself killed."

"I've been trying to find a woman – she's known by a few names – 'Samvana,' 'Gate,' or… what was it, again?" He dug in his bag for one of his notebooks while the group waited. "Ah, here," he pointed to one of the many scrawls which appeared to have been made in great haste, but which Mel would tell anyone who asked that was actually a short-form he'd developed while studying. Dawn joked that not even he understood it all of the time. "'Bodhisatta' is the other word they use to describe her, where she's from." He looked up briefly to add, "Tibet."

The Seers sat quietly, various stages of puzzlement clear across their features.

Mel chuckled. "Sorry. Guess some context would help." He looked pointedly at Ed. "She's like you. But in Tibet, her gifts are viewed as almost God-like. Apparently, she's a teacher, living on Temple land, but very difficult to access."

"No surprise there," Dawn nodded.

"She's whispered about in religious groups – Buddhist, especially – and psychic communities. She's mostly thought of as a myth, an inspiration for people like us, or those just learning to use their own talents. Of course, religious figures are especially fascinated by the possibility she's real, that or they jump to label her a false prophet, or the work of the devil. But it's a rare person who truly believes she exists. Luckily, a friend of mine from the church is one of those few, says he knows an exorcist who sought her out for help with a possessed clergy member."

"You're saying whatever she's able to do was useful in an exorcism?" Ed made a face.

Mel nodded, leaning forward in the way he had when he was excited about something. Dawn smiled. It was good to see.

"It makes sense. A human portal between levels of existence? Of consciousness? One that can be controlled, at that? Can you imagine how incredible a tool that could be?"

Ed chuckled, and Sheila tittered in response. "Ed's a tool," she said quietly, and the women beside her pressed their lips together to keep from laughing while Dawn rolled her eyes.

"I can see we haven't matured much, despite our experiences," she muttered. But Ed was still laughing, so she allowed the smile that wanted to come, just a little.

Ed gently patted Mel's knee with an enormous hand. "Thanks for working so hard on this, my friend. I'm not going to count on finding this woman, but the thought of it gives me something to hope for."

"I'll keep trying to track the right people down. Even if we don't find her, I mean to confirm whether she existed at all, or whether someone else like you does."

Dawn nodded. "Good. And in the meantime, I think we need to do some exploration of our own."

Ed raised his eyebrows.

"None of us are going to go streaking right through you," Dawn smiled, though her heart ached as she said it. "But there must be some way for you to practice. To develop your gift." She looked to the women on the couch.

The twins were already nodding. "We can guide you, help you to interpret what you see, and to recognize when you're open. Hopefully you can learn to control it."

Sheila sat forward eagerly. "I can help, too. You know I do energy work – and while I can't explain it yet, I can say yours changes drastically when you're..." she lowered her eyes as she worked to find the word, "... *activated?*"

Ed was nodding, looking thoughtful. "When can we start?"

The women exchanged glances before Sheila said, "Tonight?"

Everyone looked at Dawn, who nodded. "We need to keep each other apprised of progress, and come together whenever some discovery is made, but you don't need my permission to practice on your own."

Sheila's face lit up. "Can we do it at your place? It's the perfect atmosphere and size." She looked to the twins, but they were still eyeing Dawn.

Their intuition was uncanny. "Before we get into who's doing what, I want to talk about some other ideas I have, and I want to encourage everyone to think about how your gifts can be best used." She looked at Mel. "Your ability to calm a person, or even a situation, will be as useful as always, as is your zest for research and knowledge." She turned to the women again after receiving a grateful smile from Mel. "And the three of you are essential for lending insight into what Shya is experiencing, but I'm hoping you can work on looking forward, on seeing anything about what is meant to happen."

The smile had slid from Sheila's face so her countenance matched that of the twins'. "Let's work on that together, too?"

"And separately," Jane interjected.

Anna nodded while Sheila frowned. "Sometimes solitude is needed to focus," she said, and then smiled at Sheila's continued befuddlement. "Even we need to work alone, now and then." She and Jane exchanged knowing glances.

Dawn laughed. "Well, see? We just learned something new, already."

The group laughed while the twins blushed at the attention on them. Dawn noted how pretty they were with a touch of pink to their cheeks. Wondered silently if there was any way to suggest a bit of rouge without insulting them, then dismissed the thought outright. Jane and Anna were interior designers as well as incredible psychics, and their unusual looks worked to their advantage; the most affluent of clients seemed to seek out the albino sisters as much to be able to brag about knowing them (they enjoyed quite a positive, if not unusual reputation), as to benefit from their award-winning style.

Sheila looked back at Dawn. "And of course, there's you."

Dawn blanched. Her friends knew she struggled to feel useful, even as they insisted her empathic gifts were critical to their insight as a group. And it was ironic, because she felt their sincerity when they encouraged her. Felt their admiration, their respect as plainly as she felt her own for each of them. But her gift had hurt her as much as helped others. It was hard to think of it as entirely positive.

When Dawn didn't reply, Sheila cleared her throat and went on, blushing even deeper than the sisters beside her. "Jane and Anna told me about what happened on the drive back. In addition to your ability to know others' emotions – Shya's and the demon's included – the fact that she sent a poem through you is amazing!"

Mel turned to her, frowning.

Dawn put her hands up. "What? We don't know for sure if that's what happened. I'd been asleep – dreaming, and..."

"Did *you* write the poem?" Jane asked pointedly.

Dawn shut her mouth with a strange popping sound.

"Why didn't you tell me?" Mel asked, and now he looked hurt in addition to being confused, and it swirled in him with the rest of his lingering guilt, and doubt, and Dawn felt sick for having contributed to it.

"I'm sorry! I just wanted to make sure first. I wasn't – I still don't know..."

"Dawn," Anna was leaning forward from the middle of the couch. Her long necklace fell out of her blouse, but Jane caught it blindly before it hit the glass top of the coffee table. Anna continued without pausing while the group internalized just another of the ways the twins could amaze, effortlessly. "Those words are Shya's. And if she can describe her situation – if she can keep coming through to you, that will be very helpful, indeed."

Dawn nodded, but frowned, still.

"What's wrong?" Ed leaned forward, too.

Dawn's cheeks burned. "If that's truly what's happened, I have no way of knowing if it'll happen again, or even *how* it happened the first time! Or why... I'm an empath. It's all I know." She gazed at her friends, appearing uncomfortably lost when they all looked to her for guidance.

"Maybe Shya's got more to do with it than you?" Ed suggested.

Dawn shrugged.

"Rory talked about her poetry as though it was therapeutic, and we've heard her say as much," Mel mused, his eyes distant. "Maybe to her, her poetry is representative of how she feels? Maybe that's why she chose to send it to you?"

Sheila cut in before Dawn could reply, leaving Dawn a little dizzy with the barrage of helpful suggestions. "The last poem," she said, her eyes wide, "we all agreed it was proof that the demon had hold of her even as it possessed Jordan, but what if it was something more? What if the demon wrote it entirely, through her, and now she's using the same trick to get to us?"

"Shit," Ed breathed. "What if we can't trust anything she has Dawn write, as mixed up as she seems to be with As..." he caught himself as Sheila, who'd reacted violently to the mere utterance of the demon's name before, tensed visibly. "Sorry – with the demon, as she is?"

Dawn shook her head. "I feel them, together and separate. I can discern them, at least I've been able to, up until now. They aren't as joined as even Shya believes, I don't think."

The group fell silent. Dawn's ears still rung with their words, though.

"Maybe we just need to keep tabs on that, make sure we take care to discern the two energies of anything that comes through, too," Sheila said quietly.

The guilt she'd been encumbered with since the discovery of Shya's absence surged in her, hot and new all over again. "I won't fail her again," she countered before she could think, and her voice was harsh.

Sheila looked stricken. "I didn't mean..."

"I'm sure Sheila only meant it as a precaution, as a group responsibility," Jane said, her tone metered and controlled.

Dawn became aware of Mel's hand on her shoulder and patted it. "I'm sorry, Sheila," she said, shaking her head. "I have to admit to being sensitive since I..."

Jane cut her off. “No.”

Dawn recoiled slightly. “Jane, I can’t say I’ve ever heard you speak so loudly.”

Almost eerily, it was Anna that answered. “I’m sorry, Dawn, but we won’t let you take the blame for what’s happened to Shya any more than you’ll let us take it. It’s happened. We are all suffering the consequences. Now let’s stop licking our own wounds and work on saving her.”

Dawn felt an unexpected smile bend her lips. “Right,” she nodded enthusiastically. “You’re right,” she looked at Ed, then Mel, “let’s leave tonight determined to spend some time practicing as we’ve talked about: Jane and Anna with Sheila, and with Ed, and Mel looking for anyone who can lend any insight into the woman who could help Ed.” She looked around the room, meeting each member’s eyes. “Does that make sense?”

They all nodded.

“Anything to add?”

“I think we should keep in close contact with each other and meet in a couple days,” Mel suggested, his eyes on Dawn, who nodded.

“Regardless if we’re making any breakthroughs, we need to meet soon. We need to keep moving forward. And there’s one more thing I want to do before we leave tonight.”

They all watched her expectantly.

“I want to set a date for us to return to the Québec side. The date when we’ll go and get her back.”

They all sat in silence, considering.

“Now, some of you have work to consider. I know that. Just because I’ve been lucky enough to live off an inheritance doesn’t mean I’m not sensitive to your needs. And we all got family wantin' things from us, too."

"This *is* my family," Sheila said, and to Dawn's amazement, every member of the group nodded in agreement.

"Well, ain't we lucky, then?" she looked around again, realizing it was true: they were all fairly alone in life, save the group. She inhaled and straightened in her chair, her mind going to her upcoming crime show like clockwork. "So, what shall we say? A week? A month? Surely not longer than that, knowing what we do about the beast that's got her." Bits of the dream she'd had flashed through her mind and she gasped, making everyone perk up again. "The poem – that last line about the gate – I saw it, too, like a rip in the sky. That thing is using her, somehow. It's planning something."

There was a heavy pause while they all considered the implications, and it was Ed who spoke up first. "A week isn't long enough for me, unless we want to invite disaster, or not use my ability at all. But you're right, no matter what the demon is planning, we can't wait any longer than we have to."

"Why don't we plan for the end of the month?" Mel asked, leaning forward again. "It's just over three weeks away, and we can always change it if we need to."

Sheila gave a wry laugh. "It'll be Halloween."

"Maybe that's to our advantage," Mel said. "It's a traditionally charged night, when even the most skeptical are open to the possibilities of ghosts and ghouls. Maybe the energetic boost will work in our favor."

"And maybe it'll work in *its* favor," Ed added, then held his hands up, palms out. "Sorry. You're right, Mel. Let's aim for Halloween." He looked at Dawn. "You gonna call Rory?"

Dawn nodded.

"I think we'd all appreciate an update on Shya," Ed added.

She nodded again. "Of course." She peered at Sheila and

the twins, next. "Let us know how tonight goes." Turning back to Ed, she continued to bullet point the events to follow. It was comforting for them all, she knew. "And maybe you and I should get together after you're done work tomorrow, and we can work some more on that incredible gift of yours. And maybe it'll allow Shya to come through again."

Big Ed's smile threatened to eat up his whole face. "How early can you be up? I'm still on sick leave, and have an idea for a practice area."

Dawn perked up. The reality of a solid time to begin was encouraging. "Come get me at nine." She smiled. "I need some *sleep*, y'all, and since I'm not allowed to feel guilty anymore, thank you very much," she grinned in Jane and Anna's direction while her friends laughed, "I have a feeling I'll be sleeping better tonight than I have in a while."

"Sounds good," Ed said through his own laughter, and the group parted amicably as always, while Dawn picked up her remote.

Mel, of course, stayed behind, but it was only to kiss her deeply and tell her he loved her before he went off to continue his research, as she knew he'd do. He'd been saying it since well before she'd admitted her growing feelings for him, having preferred to "stick to herself" as she'd described it to him, and it was true. She'd never wanted to have to justify herself or explain herself to anyone. At least with Mel, there was no need for any of that. But the guilt – the terrible guilt that came with knowing people's deepest pain and having very little power to affect it – that never went away, especially with those she loved. And indeed, she loved Mel. So, it was hard, but she'd gone ahead anyway, needing the deepening relationship more than she could explain.

So, she returned the words for the first time, her lips grazing his ear, and rode the soaring joy that rose up in him, let it take her completely as it took him, and for a moment, the guilt was forgotten entirely.

CHAPTER 8 – MANIPULATION

The autumn air was crisp and cool when Dawn arrived at Ed's suggested location. Angler Park was one of the more natural park spaces in the outer-Toronto suburbs, which meant less attention to aesthetics, and consequently, less crowding.

Perfect.

She wandered a bit as she waited; she was early. As predicted, she'd slept better than she had in weeks the night before, and she awoke chomping at the bit. Even calling Mel, and then Rory hadn't quelled her desire to get to *do* something. Mel had spent the majority of the night researching as she'd suspected he would, and was in desperate need of sleep before rising to make some phone calls, so she let him go. Rory hadn't any news for her, which wasn't surprising, seeing as how she'd called him the night before, but she asked that he hold the phone to Shya's ear so she could talk to her, and connected to her. It was a much more reliable way to uncover the true status of her being… and that time, it matched Rory's exhausted report.

"Let me know if they say anything at all about releasing her," Dawn said, out of habit.

"And you let me know how things go with Ed," he replied.

And as if on cue, she heard her name being called from some distance and peered behind her to find the man himself descending a set of stone steps toward her.

She'd walked further than she'd realized. "Hey," she called as she waved at him.

He was breathing hard when he reached her, but his excitement was just as obvious as his fatigue. He clasped her in one of his all-encompassing hugs, then set her back down, gently. "You look good!" he smiled.

"So do you, but you're out of breath. Don't overdo it, hon. You're still healing." She heard the motherly tone of her voice and bristled with self-annoyance. She rubbed his arm as if to temper her tendency to take care, something that had earned her countless admonitions growing up in a motherless home. But Ed only looked pleased to see her, and felt something else.

Excited?

"We made a bit of progress last night," he said, his eyes bright.

"Oh!" It was something she hadn't expected to hear. Though she had no doubt where the gifts of Sheila and the twins were concerned, none of them had dealt with an ability such as Ed's. "That's wonderful!" she smiled.

He nodded and started walking, one hand soft on her elbow and the other pointing to a clearing, where a cluster of purposefully placed tree stumps formed a circular sitting area. "I couldn't believe it either," he went on as they sat, an empty stump between them to afford Ed the space he so sorely needed, "but Jane and Anna..." He shook his head as he blew out a great puff of air.

"I know," Dawn nodded, "they're incredible."

He nodded. "We were just *talking,* you know? About the times I've been aware of seeing into a different level of reality, and then the times I've been used to cross over, you know?"

She nodded and motioned him onward.

"I didn't even realize they were figuring things out as I chatted with them!"

She smiled. "They're tricky, but I find it's usually for a good reason. We tell more when we're relaxed."

He shook his head again. "Even Sheila was surprised when they summed everything up; you know how they do that thing where they take turns talking? Seamlessly, as if they've rehearsed it?"

"What'd they *say*?" she laughed.

"They said it seems as though I can be used as a portal by those who are so inclined – like Shya – but that I can only be sure I'm 'open' as a portal when I can see into the realm I'm at the border of."

Dawn's face cleared. "Like the first time we did the séance to find Jordan?"

"Yes!" he nodded enthusiastically. "I was *searching* then. I didn't know enough to be afraid. So, I was able to cross over, myself, even if I couldn't interact like Shya could." Ed frowned.

"The twins have any insight on why?"

He shrugged. "Sheila thinks that in my role, I'm an observer. I can learn from what's happening because I'm witnessing it, but it's like I'm looking through a window rather than fully being there." He perked up. "Oh! Do you remember how Shya was being pulled toward the boy that first time? But I only felt a pull from *our* plain?"

She nodded.

"We think that even though I can help cross between places, it's not a natural state for me, and when I'm doing it *right,* it's like an out of body experience."

"So, you feel a pull back to where your body is," Dawn finished.

He sat back, hands on his knees. "Exactly!"

She remembered Ed's state after Shya had collided into him on that last day, cringed as the pain came back to her.

"What is it?"

"When Shya crashed into you that day..."

"She ran right through me, Dawn. We have to acknowledge that, as impossible as it sounds."

She nodded, though part of her resisted. *My logical side,* she reasoned internally with some humour. "And because you weren't open, you got hurt?"

"Yep." He touched his chest with his fingertips, but absently. "I'm still working that out, to be honest. I know I was terrified, because she'd sort of done a less... intrusive version of it the night before, remember?"

She did.

"And it was painful. I think she knew – or maybe the demon that was messing around inside her knew – that I could be used to transport her, but I wasn't focussed on controlling it in any way," he frowned again. "I don't know," he shook his head.

"Ed, you guys figured out a lot last night. Give it time; more will come."

He nodded, his eyes still distant.

"Is that all you did?"

He seemed to snap back to the present. "No. The twins wanted me to try and open up." He saw the look of surprise on Dawn's face and held his palms out. "Don't worry, we agreed there'd be no physical attempt before we even got to the house! They just wanted... what did they say?" He scratched his head, thinking, "Right. They wanted to see if I could help them see into that other place." He shrugged. "They can already see it in snippets, but it takes a massive amount of effort."

She leaned forward. "Did it work?"

He made a seesawing motion with a beefy hand. "They said they saw more, and that it was easier, but it was hard to depend on me for consistent vision."

"You need practice," Dawn finished for him, and he nodded.

"But interestingly, Sheila tried balancing my energy and then focusing it here," he touched his chest again, "and I was able to focus, even to see into that place purposefully, too." He ended the thought with a shudder. "I don't like seeing it at all."

"But could you feel her there?"

His eyes reflected puzzlement before clearing. "Yeah, but she's different."

"Of course," Dawn lowered her gaze.

"Anything happen with you since last night?"

She shook her head, that familiar guilt eking back in, but slowly.

"Maybe we can practice some more now, get another poem out of her?"

Adrenaline sparked in her stomach instantly.

Ed touched her shoulder. "Hey, no pressure, eh? We're *both* practicing, Dawn. No expectations except to learn something, you know?"

She forced a smile, but said nothing.

"What is it?"

She gazed into the trees, quiet for another moment. "It isn't just the idea of getting something from Shya. It's being there at all. It's that I feel *it,* too. I feel how... wound up together they are, and how it takes from her. How weak she is, how much she loses every second she's there." She shook her head, her features pulled into a grimace, then met his eyes. "Basically, I'm terrified."

Ed burst out laughing, and it was a relief for them both. But then he patted her knee, squeezing it a little at the end as his smile dropped a bit. "I am, too."

She patted his hand and they sat quietly for a moment as a jogger nodded in their direction. She imagined how they must look to others – so different in age and opposites in size, but obviously close, nonetheless. "Thank you," she said, patting his hand again. "But all I can do when I admit to my fear is to imagine Shya's."

"That's why we're doing this," Ed said. "The only reason I'm so eager is because I'm making progress. Maybe you will, too."

She straightened and took a deep breath. "How do we do this?"

"We just closed our eyes last night, and concentrated on finding her."

A recollection had her leaning forward again, interrupting him. "Did you see it this time? Any of you?"

He frowned, confused.

"Sorry – the rip in the sky. Like I saw in the car while I slept?"

His face cleared and he nodded. "We saw it, but we each saw it differently. Sheila saw it as the way back here; it was weird. She assumed it was me, you know?"

Dawn frowned.

"And the twins saw something else: a strange pathway from the tree to the sky. Ropes of light and dark, they said, but they didn't know how to interpret it. I only just realized it could've meant the same thing you and Sheila saw."

"And you?"

He looked toward the trees. "I more felt it there than anything. And to me it felt... *crowded.*"

Dawn recoiled slightly at the puzzlement and fear that accompanied his words. "That don't sound good," she said, and he chuckled.

"Didn't feel good either," he shook his head, laughing, "but like you said, things will get clearer as we go, right?"

She couldn't recall those words, exactly, but they felt like something she'd say, so she took another deep breath and nodded, straightening again as she readied herself to get down to business.

Ed straightened, too. "Ready?"

She nodded immediately so as not to lose her nerve.

"We didn't touch last night because we were being really cautious, you know?"

She frowned, displeased with further stalling.

"But today, I think we should touch – I don't want you to try and – use me, like Shya did!" he hurried to backtrack. "But it has to be safe to join hands, right? And maybe that would help us to focus on the task. On you contacting Shya."

"Pft. We been touching this whole time."

He nodded, reaching for both of her hands, which she gave, slowly. "But this time, I focus on seeing that other place, and *you* focus on seeing it, too, with a little clarity from me."

They clasped hands, both nodding as they met each other's eyes, and then closed them altogether.

"Let's go," Ed mumbled.

Dawn reached, like she always had, for connection, and

astonishingly, she felt a pull almost straight away, and then she was travelling, the warmth of Ed's hands fading as she moved at what felt like a dangerous speed in the nothing, and then there was a light. A destination. And she aimed for that, tensing as she determined to go, because she could already make out the water. Already saw the dark shore with its rocks made of bones, and the water cresting and falling beneath a wounded sky.

CHAPTER 9 – POSSESSION

It all rushed at her, roaring like a freight train as she sped toward it until she brought her arms up in a reflexive move and opened her mouth to scream – and then everything was still.

She exhaled, relieved, through her arms remained before her face and her eyes remained closed. Her feet were on the ground, that much she knew, but when she adjusted her weight, she could tell it was not the unsteady pilings of skulls and skeletons, but rather something smoother. Like sand. And she felt the air move on her neck, damp and stinging like only salt water could do. And then the smell hit her, faint at first but more intense with every breath and Dawn knew it to be the stench of rot. Of sickness. Death.

Her senses bordered on overwhelm, even as she maintained her self-imposed blindness, but then there was something else. A sound. A singing. She froze, not even breathing, straining to hear it, and it wafted on the putrid currents of air from a distance. The voice of a girl.

Dawn's flesh tensed as if to shrink away from the simple melody as it seemed to travel from somewhere ahead, mingling with the sounds of the waves and with something else… an odd, rhythmic splashing.

Unable to hide from it any longer, she lowered her arms. She gasped at the ocean spray that hit her face, then forced her eyes open.

She peered around herself, confused by what she saw…

and what she didn't. It was the shore that had first imprisoned Jordan, then Shya's mother, and now Shya herself, yes, but she couldn't spot the strange tower of a tree on the shoreline. But perhaps that was down to the quality of light, which waxed and waned unnaturally, for the sun streaked like a falling star across the sky, and the clouds rushed to chase and mask it in shades of blacks and blues and army greens. It was a live, mad painter's palette, and the world below it reflected its ever-changing state.

Dawn herself was on the narrow line of sand between the bones and the water, and now she squinted toward the horizon, from whence the nursery-rhyme-like tune still carried, and at first the only thing she saw was nothing but a speck against the mottled bruise of a sky.

She leaned, her hand habitually shielding her eyes, barely breathing for fear she'd lose it, for the speck was moving quickly, left, right, left, and seemed to grow closer and she tracked it. Unnaturally fast. And then it was closer, still, and a figure on its knees became apparent, rowing in fast motion, left and closer, right and closer, until Dawn could see it was a woman, and she was on a bed, paddling with an oddly-shaped oar that seemed to flop and flail as it was manipulated. And she moved with a ferocity that seemed to come from a force external to herself, for with each stretch forward her head lolled back and with each powerful pull of the paddle she was thrown, like a ragdoll, forward. But as the bed moved back and forth and ever closer, closer, Dawn saw something else: that the woman's head was always turned toward her, and no matter how violently it was tossed, its black eyes were on her, watching, watching.

A nauseating fear gripped her middle as something – a memory, tried to resurface. Something Shya had told them about a bed on the waves. About her mother's reinhabited corpse kept prisoner on her deathbed.

"No," she uttered, and there was laughter overlapping the girlish singing until the bed halted directly in front of Dawn, no more than thirty feet out on the water, and the sudden stop threw the woman, whose scant, dark hair was matted in chunks and wisped as she moved, and whose bones – some visible through holes in rotting flesh, cracked audibly on the metal footboard as she crashed into it.

And whose oddly-shaped paddle, which now floated on the surface toward Dawn, appeared to be the bloodied and hoofed hind-leg of a deer.

Her heart was suddenly thudding in her ears as visions of the gutted deer that had died beside her own mother assaulted her consciousness. And then the woman was jerked upright and her arms were reaching not toward Dawn, but for the paddle – for the leg, and it flew to her skeletal grip and it all started up again: the fast-forward paddling of a bed-for-a-boat while Shya's mother's body sang in a high, singsong voice and it was too much. Dawn found her ears with her palms and smashed them, she fell to the sand and cried out, screamed as she closed her eyes again, trying to regain any semblance of blindness, or anything to dampen what she could hear, see, feel, taste, *know* in this un-reality.

And then, it was quiet. It was so sudden her eyes opened before she could prepare for it, to deduce what had happened. And she screamed again, because the bed was on the shore, just scant feet away, and the woman was on all-fours, her eyes her own again, but *wrong* because they were rotted in her skull. And even though the flesh was scarcely clinging to her bones, Dawn recognized her tortured expression of helplessness. And then she was whipped back to her knees and some unseen force restrained her arms and pulled back her head. And she looked at Dawn and said, "I don't feel very well."

Dawn, a lifelong victim of the need to help the troubled, sick and dying, started toward her without a thought, but stopped just as quick, because the woman's eyes were black again, and she was smiling, and fear slithered in Dawn's gut like a burning snake. And then she started singing, again, but this time, Dawn heard every word.

One

Two

Three

Four

Asmodeus is at your door

The woman's head fell forward and she convulsed, then cried out, heaving, her face a mask of terror and her eyes her own again, until a stream of vomit burst from a mouth that tore, a jaw that hung on its hinges, dripping with the stuff when it was done. And then her head was jerked back again and those glittering eyes were on her as Dawn screamed, unable to move, unable to do anything but watch as the woman sang again, her jawbone loose and bouncing off her neck.

Four

Three

Two

One

The King of Demons is lots of fun!

And the eyes changed again so the woman was lucid and she shrieked before it happened: her jaw was shoved back on its hinges by the force that was her puppet master, and then dislocated entirely as it yawned open and the entire mess of vomit that had only just splashed out flew back in with such force that the woman's ruined body shook from it.

And then she was smiling and black-eyed and licking

her lips as her jaw snapped back into place once more and Dawn was screaming, pulling at her hair and fighting to leave, to go, even if it meant her death, she needed *out.*

And then she was awake, sitting back on the stump of a tree with Ed's hands limp in hers and falling right out of his grip and landing on the ground with another shriek but this one more real, louder, more *there* and then hands were on her, helping her up and it was a stranger, frowning down at her, asking her if she was alright.

And all she could do was run to Ed and look intently at his face, because he appeared to be sleeping, but also to be having the most terrible dream of his life, whimpering "No, no!" and shaking his head.

"Ed!" she cried, her hands on his shoulders, trying and failing to shake the mountain of a man.

"What's wrong? How did you fall?" the stranger asked from behind her, but none of that mattered.

"Wake *up!*" she screamed that time, and without thinking she was drawing back, then slapping his cheek, and feeling terribly guilty about it even as he was roused and then staring back at her and then taking her into his arms and crying, saying *"Oh, thank God, thank God you're OK!"* And *"Did you see her? Shya's mother?"*

CHAPTER 10 – COUNTDOWN

One

Two

Three

Four

Asmodeus is at your door

Four

Three

Two

One

The King of Demons is lots of fun!

CHAPTER 11 – CRUSH

Cadence was fascinated by the thing that made Dawn "different." At first, her curiosity had been a bit scary, for it was that reaction that clued Dawn in to the fact that she *was* different. But as she grew and her gift revealed expanding implications, Dawn was thankful for someone to confide in, and she told her older sister nearly everything.

Like that it was never *not* there. And Cadence had ideas about how Dawn could try and control it – maybe dampening it in situations where it became overwhelming to feel how everyone around her was feeling, and honing in on it when it was important. She practiced with Dawn, too, taking her to the mall and to the park and all kinds of situations, and watching her with shrewd eyes.

"How is it now, Dawnie?" she'd ask, and even more than the benefits she gained from all their work together, the genuine care she found in her sister's eyes was something that saved Dawn endless times over the course of her forty-something years. Even when things changed between Cadence and Dawn's father and Cadence's role changed yet again, Dawn couldn't fault her sister, for she'd always cared for Dawn. Always.

Her brothers cared for her too, of course, but their feelings or interest in Dawn's gift rarely varied beyond degrees of indifference and/or confusion. Kenny talked to her about it more than the older two, though, often having her describe the feelings of strangers to pass the time as they waited for the bus.

Cadence asked Dawn where it was the "loudest" (they often equated the intrusion of other's feelings to sound, or degrees of light, as if Dawn's unusual extra sense was easier explained by referring to those more readily explicable) while she was in school. Dawn had to puzzle over that one, for school on the whole was difficult to bear, given the sheer volume of souls whose feelings bombarded Dawn in a never-ending torrent. Throw in the effects of raging adolescent hormones and you had a recipe for inundation that overwhelmed her on regular basis. She couldn't imagine how she would have handled it without Cadence's help. But when she stopped to decide where the intrusion was the most difficult to handle, she settled on the classroom.

Sure, the constant barrage in the hallways as they teemed with her peers, always racing somewhere: home, to class, to the gym, to the lunchroom, to see if they could spot their current crush wherever they hung out at recess, was headache-inducing, but Dawn had found a way to dull the roar into white noise. She herded the emotions into streams as they hit her and she elevated herself to sail on the current rather than drown in the undertow. The lunchroom was alright, too, even fun, because she could relax. She could even trace the paths of people's interests if she managed to single out their feelings, and by God, did teenagers have powerful feelings, especially where dating was concerned. So, it followed that, while it was hard for her to be close to anyone, she tended to gravitate to the quieter kids who focused on their schoolwork. If not in the same way as Dawn, at least they related to feeling like a minority. An outsider. And they accepted her, where the others frowned, or stared, or straight-out asked what was *wrong* with her.

Coincidentally, Dawn worked to appear as though she, too, was most interested in getting good grades, and benefitted from the time she spent studying as a result of a desire to melt into the scenery.

But the classroom; the classroom was always hard, because she couldn't get away. She needed to focus, to raise her hand to make her charade believable, but the distraction of others' emotions and physical feelings alike was dependably intense. She told Cadence it was like squeezing thirty birds into a cage and then telling them not to sing, so the songs in them would build and rise and coalesce to the point of explosion before releasing them again, so they spilled out in a tide of relief, singing louder than they would have otherwise. Calling out, *we're free!*

Her own burgeoning hormones did nothing to ease the situation. It proved, to the contrary, to muddle everything exponentially, for it wasn't just a matter of knowing who Skylar Benson wanted to take to the spring dance, no, it was the yearning for Skylar Benson to want to take *her* to the dance and being crushed a thousand times a day when his eyes skimmed over her completely.

When the only times he *did* realize she was there was when she couldn't answer a question the teacher had aimed at her, and then he was confused, and a bit annoyed, because Dawn had her head in the clouds a lot, the teachers said. And the times when he'd catch her gaze, steady on him, and she'd feel his embarrassment. His hopes that nobody else would see that the strange girl with the often-vacant eyes and a look of suffering permanently etched into her features watching him.

And that was when she stopped telling Cadence everything, because how in the world could she help with that? Dawn *was* strange, and maybe sometimes it was cool, like Kenny said, or incredible, like Cadence claimed, but most days, especially in those years, she wished it were gone, if only to be like everyone else for a little while.

Or, barring that, just to *not* know how they all felt when they looked at her.

CHAPTER 12 – QUICKSAND

Dawn sat in silence. Her thumbs absently rubbed at the arms of her recliner. She was glad the group was meeting at the twins' that night; she needed time to think, time to figure, and couldn't imagine having to tidy up the place as well. Her friends never judged the state of her condo; she knew that, but she liked to make them welcome. Liked to offer them simple little snacks and hot coffee. She liked to take care.

But on that day, she was off. She equated how she was feeling to one of those dreams where you feel as though your legs are fighting through sucking puddles of mud or quicksand to get anywhere, even when you need to run. Even when something's chasing you. And in some ways, it was her dreams that were weighing her down – she'd been sleeping fitfully since she and Big Ed's foray to that other realm, night after night tossed on the waves between sleep and wakefulness until it was difficult to tell at all when she was truly conscious. So, her days begun to be interspersed with completely unintentional catnaps and she would dream then, too.

And all of the dreams were of the rocky, bony shoreline that was built by Jordan and the demon itself, but had morphed into Shya's personal Hell. And they all ran together until there was a pattern: the sickbed growing larger on the horizon until it was near enough to make out Shya's mother and her own, ongoing suffering, and then fading away again. The tree, sometimes reaching out toward that ever-moving vessel as if to catch it in its limbs and sometimes reaching to the bruised sky. The souls at the boundaries, hungry and wanting, their need like a thunderous rumble in Dawn's head. In her heart. In her own soul.

And the light. Wisps of brightness rising, sometimes from the branches of the tree or from the sea itself, to that swath of a tear in the sky.

Dawn was so sleep-deprived that she couldn't begin to piece it together. Instead, she faithfully recorded everything in a journal she kept on her nightstand, and though it was filling quickly, there'd been no poetic words from her friend, and that made her feel like she'd failed on the whole.

And there was something else. Something she hadn't fully admitted to herself, though by now she should have called an emergency meeting, she knew. But she was so tired. Even calling her friends was work. They'd been working without her, she knew, and she knew they were worried, too, but the only one she'd seen since that day in the park with Ed was Mel, who didn't ask permission. Rather, she found him beside her, his hand engulfing her own and the television on to true crime stories, just as Dawn liked. But she hadn't told Mel, either.

She was seeing things.

She'd never seen like Shya, or even Sheila and the twins. Her empathic talents allowed a certain insight, yes. A certain knowing. But though she felt ghosts all her life, she'd never seen them with her eyes. Until now.

And even now it was a strange sort of seeing, not like her friends had described at all. Instead of transparent figures or full-bodied manifestations, Dawn's experiences seemed tethered to the other place she'd been visiting, only instead of strands of light rising to the sky, she was seeing tendrils of shadow rising from beneath the earth. And it felt menacing. Hungry.

And she hadn't told the others because she wasn't entirely confident it was real.

In short, Dawn was feeling like perhaps she was going crazy.

She should have called them all together. She knew it with a powerful certainty that night, as she waited for Mel to buzz up and take her to Jane and Anna's. And she dreaded admitting her fumble, lest they lose faith in her as their leader. So, when something moved in the corner opposite, her first thought was that she was being punished. It was only when she roused herself to pay attention that she pushed that thought away.

It was behind the corner TV stand, mingling with the natural shadow there, but it moved like the sky at Shya's shoreline. Her stomach roiled in response.

"Who are you?" she voiced, but her mind was wandering again, flashing pictures of the other shadows she'd been seeing so she couldn't deny the truth: the vaporous darkness that floated up from manholes, the gauzy haze behind passers-by that clung to their physical selves like a visible odour, the new depths of mystery in every pool of shadow and mist of fog. How it oozed. How it seemed to weigh everything down, a new layer of gravity that made the heads and shoulders of neighbors droop like dying flowers.

And sometimes, it seemed as though others saw it, too. Or felt it, at least. Fellow taxi-hailers and bus-waiters tucked their chins into their collars and folded their arms across their chests, their eyes darting to the source of every noise and roaming the grey-white skies of oncoming winter as though the answers they sought were there.

People were scared.

And now, something lurked behind Dawn's quiet television. She made herself focus, straining forward in her chair and pressing the other thoughts away. “You don’t belong here,” she said quietly, for although she knew little else, that much was true about the shadows.

Now, she just needed to know whether she was only borrowing another of Shya’s gifts, like her poetry, or the others – her friends, at least - were seeing them, too. Suddenly filled with a sense of urgency, she stood, determined to meet Mel’s car on the street. It was time to climb out of the mud and free herself of her funk. It was time to do something.

CHAPTER 13 – A MEETING AT JANE & ANNA'S

It was a great relief to realize, as the group sat around the oval oak table in Jane and Anna's great room, that though she'd been quiet, the others had been quite the opposite. A relief, and a blow, too. It was rare she was so out of the loop.

Mel had filled her in on the way, seemingly delighted that Dawn had been more awake than she had in days. He was making progress in his search for the rumoured portal-woman, positively buzzing with excitement over what he'd found. And while she'd been flattened by her experience with Ed and the subsequent onslaught of nightmares, both waking and sleeping, he'd been propelled onward, redoubling his efforts to practice with Jane, Anna and Sheila.

"And how is it going?" Dawn asked, her thoughts racing. It was as though her usually practical mind was rushing to catch up after being stuffed into dormancy for too long.

Ed's eyes were bright as he shook his head. "Since we crossed over in the park, it's been easier and easier for me to see that other place." He reached across the table for her hands. She had to stand a bit to give them, but she did. "And the possibilities are starting to make themselves known."

Dawn frowned, but instead of continuing, Ed released her hands and looked to Jane and Anna, who headed the table as they always did, here.

"We started by providing a safe environment for Ed to open up," Jane said, "and then we experimented a bit."

Dawn sat back in her chair. "You crossed with him?"

Jane and Anna both shook their heads. Anna spoke, then. "No. After what happened with you, Ed was still reluctant."

"And who could blame him!" Sheila piped up, patting Ed's arm.

Anna nodded. "So instead, we... explored a bit."

"What does that mean?" Dawn's frown deepened.

"We had him look around," Jane leaned forward again. "He started looking for other levels – other realms, other stages of consciousness!"

"Of *existence*," Anna finished, grabbing her sister's hand in excitement.

"Sounds dangerous," Dawn heard herself say, and inwardly cringed. It was that motherly bent she seemed stuck with. At least the others didn't seem to mind.

"I won't deny it was scary," Sheila replied, "but we were careful. We didn't allow Ed to disconnect. We maintained contact with him, both physically and mentally, and interestingly, found we had to keep each other in check, lest we get caught up in our own little adventures."

Ed leaned forward again. "Even though we weren't trying to extend the *travelling* to anyone beyond me, all three of them found themselves taken with me, effortlessly."

"Like me?" Gratitude washed over Dawn like a healing balm when all four of them nodded. She peered sideways at Mel, tears swimming in her eyes, and he squeezed her hand.

"We think it's because of our own gifts that it's so easy to get sucked into the process," Jane went on, "but we're finding it doesn't mean we'll see the same things."

Dawn perked up again. "Right." She looked at Ed. "You *saw* Shya's mother on her sickbed, but were focused on the tree, while the sickbed, and what happened with Shya's mom was completely overwhelming for me."

He nodded. "Her mother's name is Clara, we think."

Dawn frowned, having only just realized they had only ever called the woman some form of "Shya's mother." "How do you know?"

The entire group seemed to withdraw a bit, and, guided by instinct, she chased her connection to them to learn what they were hiding by feeling when they wouldn't say the words. Guilt was what she found. "What?"

Sheila glanced at the twins, then opened her mouth to speak, but it was Mel that dove in. He clutched her hand in both of his own, imparting a stream of soothing calm as only he could. Dawn resisted the urge to pull away.

"We've been talking to Rory, and a bit to Shya's father, too," Mel said, his gaze level with hers, but it took a great effort.

And Dawn knew why. *She* was supposed to be point-guard. *She* was the one to keep in touch with everyone, to relay updates and keep things organized. But she'd been... preoccupied.

"Shya's at home, well, at her father's, anyway," Sheila explained. "She's still unconscious, but at least she's in her own bed. And Rory's still there. He's taken a sabbatical," she added, her eyes reflective of how they all felt.

She shook her head. "I've failed you all," she said, and the words were chased with a hiccough as she tried desperately not to cry. Of course, they all rushed to placate her, but she could feel the fear that mixed with their kindness. Part of what she'd said was true, and it had worried her friends.

"What you saw when we travelled was enough to knock anyone off-course," Ed said, matter-of-factly. The rest of them nodded in agreement.

Dawn took a deep breath and held it, contemplating a way to start. Knowing that if there was ever a time to tell them all, it was then.

"What is it?" Jane was frowning as she watched Dawn's expression. Her concern was echoed in her sister's features identically.

"That's not the only reason I been a bit… out of touch," she started. When they all continued to watch her expectantly, she went on, spilling everything – the dreams, the waking nightmares, and lastly, the things she'd been seeing in both states.

Mel squeezed her hand when she was done. Dawn turned to him, suddenly crying, despite holding back as she'd talked. "You knew something was wrong, but you never left. You supported me and didn't push." She touched his cheek as emotion welled in his eyes. "You are a sweet man, Mel, and I love you so much."

The atmosphere changed as they embraced. Sheila had her head on Ed's shoulder when Dawn sat back in her seat, and the twins were still intertwined at the hands.

"I apologize for not telling you all sooner. I've been so tired and confused…" she trailed off, but sensed their understanding immediately.

"It's not your fault, hon," Sheila said, sniffling. "But from now on, we need to keep better track of each other. *All* of us."

"I think we've been too comfortable with the assumption that you're the strong, clear-headed one," Ed laughed, then gasped. "I don't mean you're *not*!"

Dawn held a hand up. "No worries, Ed," she laughed. "I

get it, and I love you all for it, but Sheila's right; we can't wait so long to meet." She looked at Mel for strength. "In fact, I don't think any of us should be alone from this point forward."

The twins nodded eagerly, which was less than surprising, but Sheila was frowning. "I have work," she said.

Ed patted her hand. "I can come stay with you, if it's OK. I have work, too, but your place could be home-base when we're not working."

Sheila smiled and nodded.

Mel inhaled deeply. "That means I'm with you until this is over," he said, his eyes on Dawn but his calming aura pulled back. Dawn loved him for his sense of fairness, even as the core of her being balked at giving up her privacy so completely. "For some reason, you seem the most affected by Shya's state, and besides that being in our favor, I think it's also dangerous."

She couldn't argue.

"Alright?"

She nodded, then looked to the rest of the group. "Now, I gotta know: has anyone else been seeing things?" To her surprise, they all nodded, every one. "Really?"

More nods.

"And it's not just us," Ed said, quietly.

Now Dawn frowned. "What?"

The group exchanged looks. "There've been stories," Sheila started.

"Rumours," Anna added.

Ed looked at her somberly. "Nobody's saying anything with certainty yet, but it's widely known that things feel different, these days."

"What do you mean by 'widely known?'"

Anna looked sad. “We all assumed you’d be keeping up with the news. You and Mel are best for that. It’s usually you guys who update us.” Jane cast a chastising look toward her sister and Anna trailed off, somehow paling even further as she did.

Ed started again. “News reporters and weather statements are all going on about the gloomy weather… the sky is always dark. We haven’t seen the sun in days, and it shows no signs of letting up.”

“And social media is buzzing about a spike in depression, in ‘SAD’ – seasonal affectation disorder?’”

Dawn nodded. “But that stuff doesn’t usually start up until we’re well into winter.”

Ed nodded. “That’s not all. Suicide rates have gone off the charts all over the world.”

“Oh, my God,” Dawn murmured. She unconsciously moved closer to Mel.

“People are scared,” Ed said, then rested back in his seat, where Sheila was happy to lean against him, again.

Even we’re scared, Dawn thought.

They sat quietly for a moment, and then the twins were leaning forward, speaking together in that eerie way they had. “We want to ask you,” they looked at each other, laughing, and as if by some unspoken agreement, Jane continued, “about when you crossed over with Ed.”

Dawn nodded.

“About the hole in the sky. You talked about it in the car, when you dreamt about that place.”

She nodded again, but there was confusion eating at her. “I saw it that day, too, with Ed,” she recalled, her eyes distant, “but only when we first started.” She looked around at her friends. “After that, I only remember seeing Shya’s – seeing *Clara*. She was so sick,” Dawn shuddered as if to punctuate the statement.

“But the sky...”

Dawn shook her head, remembering how the clouds had moved – raced, really, a never-ending sea of storms to mirror the waves below. “I *did* see the sky, but it was different. It was moving fast, and dark, like a big storm was coming, but I don’t remember the hole.”

The twins exchanged a look.

“I didn’t see it at all,” Ed said.

Dawn looked to the three psychics.

“We think you’re being distracted from it,” Jane said, her voice nearly a whisper.

“Why?” Dawn frowned as she voiced the question they all needed answered.

“We think it’s the portal the demon is building... the gate the poem mentions.”

Dawn held her breath, remembering the words she’d brought back from that dream in the car.

“The one it’s using Shya’s...” Ed was leaning forward again, eyebrows raised.

Dawn sat up straight. “The one he’s building with the light he’s stealing from her,” she breathed, remembering the strands of light that rose toward the clouds. Remembering the opposing wisps of shadow. Here, on this plane. “Oh, God,” she whispered, “that’s where they’re getting through.”

They all fell silent and Dawn knew they hadn’t joined it up quite that way just yet. Felt their shock. Their fear.

“Oh, shit!” Sheila looked at the twins, then Ed. “She’s

right!"

Dawn looked at Mel. "Tell us where we are with getting some backup, Mel, because we just ran out of the luxury of time."

CHAPTER 14 – BODHISATTA

Mel straightened. "I've made progress in my search."

Dawn pinched him lightly when he failed to continue.

He jumped a little. "Sorry. I... this has been a strange few days."

Ed laughed. "Few weeks, more like."

Mel shook his head. "For me, chasing the rumour of this woman has been a journey of enlightenment, which is something, considering what we've all been dealing with." He focused on the patterns in the oak of the tabletop. "As easy as it's been to believe that other realms exist, that there *is* life after death and that we've seen evidence of it, even interacted with it... the world I've been exploring is something I could never have guessed at."

Dawn had to bite her cheeks to stop herself from making a sound of derision. She nearly sighed with relief when Ed took on the task, instead.

"Mel, you're a teacher and a scholar. A research scientist and expert in the occult and paranormal, not to mention your knowledge of religion. How can you..."

Mel held a finger up. "Until now, Christianity and other Western religions have been my focus, especially as they relate to the paranormal. Besides a surface knowledge of Buddhist tenets and history, I've been in the dark." His eyes took on a faraway look. "I've always wanted to travel to the Asiatic lands to experience the temples and teachings. The retreats and monasteries – all of it." He shrugged. "But I got busy, started my work, and time flew by."

Sheila leaned toward Mel from the other side of Ed. "There's time, Mel. You're young, still."

Mel laughed.

"Youngish!" Sheila added, looking to her counterparts for support, but the group only giggled. Mel *wasn't* an old man – he hadn't even reached his fiftieth year yet – but he behaved in some ways like he was. Dawn had teased him for it – his way of quietly considering before speaking, the depth of his knowledge and hunger to learn. And the wisdom he spoke with... it was nearly mesmerising. He'd worked in labs as a scientist, at universities as a lecturer and at conferences as a motivational speaker, and he was a well sought-after consultant in a collection of fields! Dawn had wondered if there ever was a time the man came off as anything but well-learned.

Mel patted the table in Sheila's direction. "Thank you, Sheila. And you're right, maybe I will make time to travel in the future." He smiled at Dawn, but there was something sad in his eyes. And then it was gone and he was back on track, before Dawn could explore his feelings. "In any case, signs point to this woman being in Tibet. Having been born there, actually."

"How did you find out?" Sheila asked.

"I found the exorcist that was rumoured to have met her."

The twins leaned forward. "It's true?" They exclaimed as one.

"He didn't admit to it so plainly," Mel said quietly, "but after speaking with him in person – which was quite a task to accomplish in and of itself, I assure you – I believe he did meet with her. I believe she helped him."

The twins sank back in their seats, their eyes wide and tremoring erratically.

"What?" Dawn eyed them.

They exchanged a glance, then looked at Mel. "We dreamt you went away," Anna said. "To a place with mountains and temples," she finished, voice barely audible.

Mel shook his head. "There's no time," he reasoned calmly. "Shya needs us now. Even if I went, this woman is nearly impossible to connect with."

"Shya does need us, but I'm afraid I won't do her as much good as I have the potential to do," Ed spoke up. Dawn watched him, aware of his need to do whatever it took to bring Shya back, but aware, too, that he felt sure he wasn't ready to use the gift that could accomplish the most.

She couldn't help it; she had to encourage him, even if it distracted the group from Mel for a moment. "You've been improving, Ed! You're learning more every time you open up to it. You don't need to be afraid."

He looked at her, his face blank. But behind it, there was anxiety. The fear of failing in the worst of ways.

"You just need to be careful."

The twins cleared their throats. "You *must* go," Jane said, looking at Mel.

Mel looked conflicted.

"I agree," Ed added, and punctuated it with a slap to the table, which made them all jump, loud as his impressive palm managed to be against the thick oak.

Mel looked at Dawn and the helplessness that dominated his feelings washing over her. She understood his angst. He shared her occasional self-doubt where their inherent usefulness was concerned.

"We'd miss you, but this woman might be the key to everything. What if she not only helps Ed, but decides to be involved in person?" Dawn tried to convey her understanding but worried she'd fail when his face contorted in confusion.

"If you all are going to head back to Québec soon, and that seems to be where this discussion was headed a few minutes ago, I want to be there. I need to be."

Dawn fought against an argument against his logic. He believed what he was saying, there was no question there. But she didn't understand why. Mel's gift was essential when emotions ran high, and they surely would the next time the group was in the same room with Shya... but wasn't finding the woman Mel sought more important?

Still, Mel said nothing.

"Will you consider it?" Jane asked, her face earnest.

Mel paused, inhaling, then said "Yes" on a long outbreath.

"Oh, good!" Sheila clapped a little in her excitement, and the atmosphere seemed to lower a few notches in intensity.

"In the meantime," Ed adjusted himself in the chair that creaked unhappily under his weight, "Mel's right. We need to make plans to face this thing, even if not to attempt to rescue Shya right away."

Dawn nodded her agreement. "If we're right and the demon's breached some sort of barrier between Hell and the plane of the living, we need to learn more."

"Yeah, like why now?" Ed folded and unfolded his hands. "Has Shya made it possible with her energy? If so, how? And I've been wondering about Clara, too. We know she's trapped in what appears to be varying forms of her... corpse. But..." he paused to look around the table, hesitant.

"But what?" Dawn urged him on.

"But, I mean, her *actual* body is in the ground and long decomposed, right?"

Nobody said anything. Dawn watched a mixture of emotions flicker over the faces of her friends.

"Of course," Mel finally said. "Just like Shya's body remains here, so does her mother's."

Ed nodded, but didn't appear entirely convinced.

"We're puzzling over the portal itself," Jane spoke up again. "It's strange – the version of Hell Shya's trapped in, is *its* border the same as the veil between the living and the dead?"

Ed immediately shook his head. "Not for me. For me, it's flimsy. That world, the shoreline, the tree... it was manufactured first by Jordan and the demon, and now by Shya, her mother and the demon. It's not permanent, you know?" His own questions were still furrowing his brow. "At least that's how it feels."

"Maybe because it's a world built on a possession rather than life or death..." Anna trailed off, her gaze meeting her sister's.

"I have some knowledge about portals," Sheila volunteered. She blushed when everyone peered expectantly at her. "It's something I've always done for clients – detected and closed them. But when we started suspecting Ed's gift being related, I started looking into it more." She looked around. "I've spoken to Ed about it, a little."

Ed nodded. "Sheila has a lot of experience, and some ideas, too. We need to take her seriously." He'd meant well, but withdrew as soon as the words were out, his cheeks going ruddy. He'd said the thing they'd all thought. Sheila appeared to be flighty, even ditzy, and was easily overwhelmed emotionally, but she was truly talented, and had a wide circle of contacts with whom she exchanged knowledge regularly.

Dawn cleared her throat as if to dislodge the awkwardness Ed was blushing over. “Of course. This is good, Sheila. Maybe you can teach us more.” She looked around the table. “But not tonight. Let’s meet once more this week – we’ll solidify plans and talk about how to go about dealing with this rip in the border, or sky, or whatever it is. Sound good?”

They nodded, but were quiet.

“I know it feels urgent, folks, but we need to rest. And we need to take care of the rest of our lives before going back.” They nodded stiffly, but still appeared forlorn. She scanned their emotions quickly, finding worry first and foremost, then a sense of helplessness. Of urgency held back by circumstance. Of fear.

They needed something solid.

She sat up straight, smiling. “Why don’t we tentatively think about this weekend as the goal?” There were murmurings of agreement, and the satisfaction of their relief. It was all she’d hoped for. She eyed Mel. “And maybe we need to know whether Mel is going to go looking for this woman or not.”

Mel averted his eyes and Dawn made a mental note to dig deeper into his reluctance. Then she smiled at her friends and declared the meeting adjourned.

CHAPTER 15 – SEEPING

Breached
Eons of effort
Finally coming to the fore

Helped
By gifted soul
In the tree upon the shore

Bright
Glowing embers
Borne of an ancient chore

Resistance
Pure endeavor
Inherited promise steeped in lore

Changed
Through possession
And a twist of something more

Dark
Malintent

An undead grudge leaves seeping sores

Pure
Antithesis
To the light tangled in gore

String
Ropes of Heaven
That power cannot be ignored

Inspired
A wicked seed
That now germinates in her

Light
Shot through with dark
Drawing shadow in droves and scores

Shredding
Through the veil
An abomination tore

Border
Falls to clashing
Product of opposites no more

One

Weapon of power
That has fashioned them a door

CHAPTER 16 – CONFESSION

Her hands shook as she found them filled – one with a pen and the other with the journal Mel had bought her, just in case Shya sent more words through her. It had been so thoughtful, but when he'd placed it in her hands the evening after the group had met at the twins', Dawn felt a hesitation, too. It wasn't that she didn't want to be prepared; it was that she didn't want to disappoint her friends if or when the book remained empty. Except for the first two poems Mel had carefully copied into the pages, that was.

But now, here it was: another set of verses streaming straight from dream to paper, with Dawn acting only as the middleman. And once she'd finished, she raised astonished eyes to Mel, saying, "It's *not* just her." It was an admission of something the group had been dancing around. An intimation first made in a room of the British Hotel in Aylmer when they first gathered on the Québec side.

It was that Shya wasn't just Shya anymore.

That night, Shya'd had to admit that the demon had been influencing her: first by knocking her flat with the migraine to end all migraines and then replacing the pain with a sense of well-being that was as powerful as it was inappropriate for the situation. Since then, she'd been inhabited by the beast that sought her, two times in a mad sprint toward Connor and Jordan's house, where Jordan fought for his life, and finally it had taken her wholly, tangling around her while she was distracted by its traps and leaving her body alive but empty.

And now, it seemed the two accomplished their goals together, Shya's being the need to reach out to her friends, and the demon's being the gate between the shoreline of Shya's own Hell and the physical plane.

It seemed impossible, yet there it was on paper, written by her hand but not of her own mind. Mel was scanning it intensely, a deep frown furrowing his brow. She watched him start again and again, shaking his head and muttering unintelligibly until she could stand it no more.

"What's going to happen?" she cried, her voice high.

Mel looked up at her, confused.

"It's done it – it's breached the border between the two levels. Everyone can see it, whether it's us seeing shapes and shadows or it's Joe Smith on high alert at the bus stop because the air feels different!"

Mel nodded, frowning, but said nothing.

"So, now what? What's it going to do?"

He looked down at the page again. He looked lost.

She put a hand on his forearm. "Does it want to scare us? Change us? Or does it want to rule us?"

"My God," Mel whispered.

"The group is right, Mel." Dawn recalled the group's singular reaction to what Mel had told them two nights earlier.

He raised his head. "I won't leave you. I won't fly to -" he made a wild sweeping motion with his arm, "to *Tibet* while you guys are getting ready to go back to Québec!"

Dawn held her breath, feeling the proximity to having the truth about his reluctance revealed. "I know it feels wrong to leave us," Dawn clutched at his arm, begging him to hear her, "you're our protector!"

His features softened in the dim light of almost-sunrise.

"You calm us. Smooth everything into something easier," Dawn went on, determined to make him know she understood, and his eyes said she was winning, "but if there's any chance you can find this... what did you say she was called in Tibet?"

"Bodhisatta."

"Right. You *have* to. You can calm *her,* too."

He grasped both of her hands suddenly. "I feel like I failed Shya. You know that, even though you know it's not rational. But I feel it anyway. I don't want to fail you, too. I - I was hoping we would go together."

That's it. That's his problem. Dawn shook her head immediately. "The rest of the group can go to Shya's side, hopefully to protect her, or to learn something, if nothing else! But you – *you* can read this woman's every emotion. You can convince her."

Everything in her resisted, but his all-consuming need to be by her side called for compassion. "In any other set of circumstances, you'd be right! I would know how to approach her, even how to convince her, with your help. But I can't – I have to stay, don't you see? I need to be this for Shya," she stabbed at the open notebook with hard fingertips. "I need to give her that."

He sat back, his face going blank. She breathed, taking in his outward countenance as well as the pall of disappointment that emanated from him. She held her tongue because there was something underneath it all. There was a grudging admittance that she was right.

Finally, he sighed deeply.

She smiled. "You see, right?"

He withdrew his touch, beaten, and rubbed at his eyes.

She was so focused on him that when her phone rung on the bedside table, they both jumped. She reached for it immediately, feeling Ed's energy and knowing something had happened.

"Ed?"

He was gasping for breath.

"Oh, shit. Are you OK, Ed?"

"Yeah," he panted.

"What's going on?"

There was a muffled commotion on the other end, which had Dawn tensing to drop the phone and bolt right then, needing to see him with her own eyes, to touch him to know what he was suffering, exactly, to have him so winded and afraid. But Sheila came on and Dawn held on, fists clenched.

"We saw something," Sheila said, her voice wavering as it tended to do with any emotion.

A dark figure flashed in Dawn's mind, and then the wisping tendrils of shadow she'd seen rising from manholes and oozing around corners. "Is Ed alright?" she asked, needing to know that, first.

There was a pause which felt like eternity, but then Sheila was saying "Yes, I think so, but his hand is on his chest," and Dawn could hear Ed protesting in the background.

"What's he saying?"

Another scuffle, and Ed was back on.

"I was dreaming; seeing that place again – where Shya is? And it was so easy, Dawn, like the boundary between the levels is weakening. Just like I was saying..."

"It's a damn good thing we're going back to Québec on the weekend," Dawn muttered.

"I don't think I can wait," Ed cut in. "I feel like I can help."

She frowned. "How?"

He made a sound of frustration. "I'm not sure. I need to talk to the twins. It's like – I feel like I can be a portal *and* help keep the boundary strong, too."

"Close the door rather than open it," Sheila's voice was clear enough for Dawn to hear, then shiver as the truth of her words clicked into place.

"Yeah," Ed said.

"But why was your hand on your chest?"

"I don't know. Whenever I see that place, it's like my chest remembers what it was like to have Shya use me to visit it."

Dawn pressed her lips together. He was being truthful, but there was something else, too. A physical thing that did *not* echo his words, a squeezing pressure in his chest. "I'm worried about you, Ed."

He was silent.

"What's she saying?" Sheila was asking.

"Your heart is under a lot of pressure, and not just from the fallout of having a person zip right through you," she chuckled weakly.

He didn't reciprocate. "I followed up with my doctor here last week, just to do what I promised the Québec doctors I'd do."

Her stomach clenched at the unease that colored his words. "And?"

"Well, it's nothing surprising. Nothing new, even! He just said my hypertension was a bit worse. Upped my medication a little."

"Oh." Dawn closed her eyes against the fear that tried to come.

"He told me to go on a diet, too," Ed laughed. "Even offered to get it covered by OHIP."

Dawn knew that the province's medical insurance would only cover such a thing if it was crucial to a patient's survival. "Ed..."

"It can't be the priority right now, Dawn," Ed cut her off quickly. "It just can't."

Dawn met Mel's eyes, which had been on her with curiosity and worry since she'd picked up the phone.

"I meet him again tomorrow, just to recheck my numbers and follow-up on the new dosage. Don't worry."

She sighed. Tears welled hot in her eyes and she closed them, pressing her fingertips to the bridge of her nose as if to hold back the deluge that threatened. *I don't think I've ever cried so much in my life as I have in the last month,* she thought, and suddenly Mel was easing the phone from her hands. She let him.

"Ed? Hi. Hi to Sheila, too. What did you see?"

She couldn't hear the words, not like she wanted to, but she could feel the fear. Feel the weight of the presence Ed had woken up to. Felt the urgency he'd felt as he'd called out for Sheila, and felt Sheila's panic when she spotted it, too, just before she flicked the light on it and chased the thing away. A beast, much more solid than the hints she'd seen, and larger, too. Watching the ones that could sense it. Sense the others.

Watching the ones that could threaten their mission, whatever that was.

"When are you leaving for Aylmer?" Mel was asking. Dawn perked up. And then he was saying, "Yeah. I wish. But Dawn hit the final nail into place for me tonight; I'm going to

Tibet."

The exclamation of surprise that came from the other end of the phone matched her own. She took Mel's hand and squeezed, smiling into his eyes.

"And we have news, too," Mel said after Ed had quieted. Mel lowered the phone, shaking his head. "I'm putting you on speaker, and you should do the same so Sheila can hear."

Dawn knew what he meant to tell them and reached for the notebook, her hand tremoring on cue.

"Dawn got another message," Mel said, "and it makes us feel that things are getting worse, quick."

Sheila made a low, distressed sound.

"Can you read it?" Ed asked, and Mel reached for the book.

But Dawn shook her head. If she didn't take ownership over what was happening to her, she'd always feel as though she was at its mercy. She cleared her throat, and read.

CHAPTER 17 – THE DISTANCING OF CADENCE

Strangely, it was only when she started pulling away from her older sister that Dawn really took hold of her gift and started using it with intention. In the first several years after high school, though, her intentions were somewhat unpredictable, but Dawn forgave herself for that. When you're living in a world always tinged by emotion – not only your own, but those of everyone around you – life is different. At least she imagined it was. In truth, she had no other basis of comparison.

And the evolution of her relationship with Cadence wasn't the happy, natural one she would have liked, that progression from childhood to adulthood where increasing independence means something new between the carer and the cared-for. Something that echoes their former relationship, one would think, but which reflects new roles, too. But it was different with Dawn and Cadence, and though it took a very long time for Dawn to be able to sort it all out in her own mind, the change appeared to be permanent, even after her father died and Cadence was just Cadence again.

Nobody else minded, or even noticed at first. Her brothers, all of them, were distracted by their own lives. But Dawn could not shut out the things her brothers never saw. After all, she could feel them. Even then, to an outsider, home life would have appeared to be fine. Pleasant, even. She and her brothers went to school and worked, Kenny even transferring a year before graduating to a mechanical college, such was his desire to work on heavy machinery. Jason and Freddie graduated one after another, found menial jobs and then moved out, having found another friend who was happy to share an apartment and go about a life similar to theirs: work, home, video games, lather, rinse, repeat.

And then Kenny moved, too, having found a job in the industrial park of Dartmouth, Nova Scotia. It was a hard loss for Dawn; Kenny was the brother she'd been closest to, the only one who seemed to care enough to sit down with her, to talk. Besides Cadence, of course. And as Dawn grew and started talking about going to university to take social sciences (she aspired to be a school counsellor, then), she saw Cadence change, too.

After their mother had died, Cadence had found a purpose: to take care of her half sister and brothers. To do her mother proud. It was all so easy, given the changed man Dawn's father was. Cadence had come back and slid right into a new sort of role – one that hadn't even existed when their mother was alive, for the atmosphere was one of wary anticipation, then. Of fear. Dawn's mother had tried, but her husband's anger had skewed everything, then. The nature of it had rendered all other things unimportant. Mealtimes, playtime, her mother's many jobs – any sort of routine or semblance of normalcy was second priority to the overarching presence of a man who hated everything, and was convinced everything and everyone hated him, too.

After the accident, though, all of that was gone. But that's not to say he did a one-eighty. Their father was not the opposite to what he was before; he was merely *changed.* It was true they were no longer ruled by his anger. In fact, it seemed his anger had simply fizzled out. Like a once-raging campfire in a sudden downpour, it was just – *gone.* But love did not flow in to the empty space it left, nor did kindness. To the contrary, where he had once raged, her father merely sat, complacent and accepting of his lot. His anger had died with his wife in that accident, instantly killed upon the impact of seeing her lifeless body on the hood of the car they'd crashed into, and instead of love and kindness, there was a well of guilt that readily filled the space where his anger once resided and ruled.

So, instead of determining to be the best father he could, which was something Dawn knew he hadn't even known to consider, he determined to *provide.* To be a passive presence at home and a powerhouse as a construction foreman, where he spent most of his waking hours, anyway. Because that was something else: his pain changed in the accident, too, and so he could go back to work. Whatever had been wrong with his back seemed to right itself with the jolt of the collision. He still had pain, of course he did, but only Dawn knew about it, because he never spoke of it again. And Dawn knew it was greatly diminished.

So, while her brothers and especially her sister exclaimed over how he'd changed, over how much of a better man he'd become, Dawn kept silent, knowing that guilt drove his actions. Knowing he'd never felt so good in his life. So calm. And knowing, finally, that his pain was manageable when several doctors had declared him to be severely afflicted until he was in the ground.

But she couldn't tell her siblings all of that, because not only would it make her ungrateful – even mean – but it would taint their outlook. They'd all lost their mother; but not all of them had to know the inner workings of the improvement of their father. For them, just the ability to be free in their own home was incredible – and they didn't see it as the result of a terribly high price, like Dawn did. They didn't see that if the accident hadn't happened, their father may never have changed.

And they would still have their mother.

Still, they had *peace*. How could Dawn take that from them?

And as they all trickled away until Dawn and Cadence were the only ones left, Dawn could see Cadence start to flounder. She'd given up her own life, after all, to care for them. It didn't matter that she hadn't given up much – a cheating boyfriend and the prospect of night school to make up her lost high school years. Oh, and the pregnancy that had been the reason she'd dropped out, the reason she'd moved in with said cheating boyfriend, the reason she'd nearly died after a terrible miscarriage and then of sepsis afterward, and came very close to having any chance at future children taken from her, but escaped it, narrowly. The great secret she'd kept from everyone. Everyone except, of course, from Dawn.

Dawn always knew, even when she didn't want to. *Especially* then, it seemed in those years when she hadn't learned to read people for her own purposes. For *good* purposes, mostly.

So, with all of that weighing her sister down, combined with the prospect of Dawn leaving, too, Cadence lost her confidence. Panicked, a little. Even when Dawn said encouraging things, like that Cadence could finally get her GED! That she could do as she *wanted* instead of as she was *needed*. That she could stop keeping house for a man who was never there, and was sleeping or silent when he was.

Despite Dawn's efforts, Cadence spun. It should have been freeing, but the prospect of taking her life back, along with the past she'd managed to leave behind for all those years, utterly terrified her.

But then there was someone who still needed to be cared for, though he never voiced it. Someone to cook for, to do laundry for, to clean for. In her sister's mind, Dawn's father became the last dark corner of refuge from a past too difficult to face.

It affected Dawn in ways that surprised her, despite everything. Watching Cadence throw herself into caring for a man who used to touch her in ways no man should touch a child made her nauseous. Everyone else seemed to have forgotten. Everyone else seemed eager to box the past away, to leave it in the shadows of the accident that had taken their mother and made their father into someone who was better, anyway. Someone who, in the absence of being wonderful, was no longer *bad.*

But again, Dawn knew it all.

She saw how Cadence's attentions made her father change again; made him look up from his own little world that had been limited to work and sleep and take notice of something, finally. And what he noticed was that his boys were gone, and that Dawn was leaving, too, and that Cadence was all he had left, just as he was all she had. And it scared Dawn, because a love started there, and the development of that would be something she couldn't reconcile with all that had happened before. Not knowing like she did. Not having felt it all, from all sides, the whole time, and having to deal with everyone's coping strategies as well as her own.

Of Freddie's stubborn tolerance of his father's fists so his younger siblings wouldn't have to feel them.

Of toddler Kenny's abject horror as he watched his mother be beaten, and the overwhelming sadness he felt every time she picked him up and he could see the remnants of his father's outbursts up close.

Of how it felt to watch him run a chubby finger along her cuts and bruises oh, so carefully and ask, "OK, Mommy?" then see her mother's eyes fill with tears.

There had been more... so much more, but that was bad

enough. That had sealed it for Dawn when she was just a tiny girl: her father was mean. Her father hurt them. Her father was *supposed* to love them, but he hurt them instead.

And when Cadence started loving him and Dawn could see the blinders she'd erected, just to make it possible, she lost faith in Cadence, too.

And for a while, she lost faith in relationships completely, because knowing everything she knew always, always seemed to fuck it all up.

CHAPTER 18 – LAST MINUTE ARRANGEMENTS

The tension in the air was very nearly palpable, especially considering the gifts of the souls who gathered for a final meeting in Dawn's living room. Ed was especially tense, his normally ruddy complexion a distressing shade of puce as he sat, lips pursed and knees bouncing with the nervous tapping of his heels.

"My flight is for tomorrow morning; Friday," Mel said as he surreptitiously placed a well-meaning hand on Ed's shoulder, but the piercing look he earned from Ed had him rushing to explain, if not remove his calming touch. "Let me help, Ed."

Ed looked around the room. "I shouldn't be here. I should be with Shya."

Dawn noted that Ed hadn't brushed Mel's touch away with a swell of emotion. *How can a man be so* good? She wondered as she gazed gratefully at Mel.

Sheila shook her head. "I know you're excited about the possibility of being able to *close* portals as well as acting as one, but we haven't tested it!"

"And if you go alone, you won't have the guidance you'll need to accomplish it," Jane leaned forward slightly, arrow-straight locks of her white tresses falling like a veil from her shoulder to the table.

Anna nodded her agreement. "I understand your sense of obligation, Ed, but they're right, and even more perplexing is the potential for further harm."

Ed, who'd been listening passively with his eyes on the bowl of pretzels Dawn had put out (which should have been demolished by that point, given their proximity to the giant of a man who eyed them almost menacingly now), looked up suddenly. "What?"

Anna recoiled just enough for Dawn to perceive a note of surprise – a rare emotion from either of the twins. Thankfully, Jane picked up where Anna left off as smoothly as if she'd been the one to speak her words.

"I *know* you remember what happened when your gift was used without testing it first," she said, her gaze level and sure.

Ed shook his head. "How can you all think that the risks mean more than..." he motioned wildly as he searched for the words, then exclaimed, "*than everything that's happening!*"

The entire group was silenced, and Dawn was unsurprised; Ed was a gentle soul, but impressive when he was out of sorts. She became aware of the eyes on her and took a breath, entirely unsure of what to say but also unwilling to fade into the background as she had the previous week. "I think they're – *we're* – saying that your intentions are shared by all of us, but your idea of consequences might be a bit skewed right now." Ed made a face, clearly frustrated. Mel, however, was gazing calmly but encouragingly in her direction. "After all, we watched as you *died,* Ed!"

Ed's face went blank in an instant. Dawn noted the nods of the women opposite her.

"You *died!*"

His eyes darkened, then hardened just as quickly, and he

slapped his chest with his palms. "I seem to be alright, now!" Defiance oozed from him, hot and determined. Dawn found herself pressed back by it as she understood the depth of the man's emotions. She put her hand to her chest absently, for there it was again: the undeniable pressure around her heart... but not *her* heart. She was feeling Ed's pain.

"And who saved you?" the twins countered after a beat, their voices doubly powerful, each gaining power from the strength of the other. Ed whipped his head toward them, clearly shocked at their outburst, but he said nothing.

Dawn's fingers tingled with the tension. She glanced at Mel, whose gaze went between Dawn and the twins. He stopped on her, though, with a slight nod. A wordless, "Are you OK?" if she'd ever seen one. And all she could do was nod in return. But a sense of failure began to rise in her again. She was a diminished leader of late and she knew it, and it seemed that her efforts to make up for it only rendered her more powerless, still.

"Shya," Sheila said, and all eyes turned to her, momentarily confused. Sheila's gaze darted between those of her friends as her cheeks pinked. "It was Shya that brought you back," she finished, finally, her eyes on Ed. And they were soft.

And Dawn felt something there, too.

Ed sat back, sighing. "I sort of forgot that part," he muttered, running a hand through his hair.

The group laughed quietly, then with the driving force of relief when Ed smiled and said, "*Shit.*"

Dawn straightened. "Good. You'll come with us."

He nodded. His shoulders lowered as he gave in, and Mel patted the one he'd been gripping, seemingly satisfied.

"We've gone over the new verses from Shya, as well as Mel's trip, and we've established that the rest of us will leave tomorrow morning. Is there anything else?"

"Does Rory know we're coming?"

Dawn frowned. "I left him a message, but haven't heard back." She fished around in the pocket of her cardigan, muttering. "Ah!" she peered at the screen with a squint.

"We need to get you to the Optometrist," Mel said, and the group giggled reservedly.

Dawn gave him a look, then sighed. "I know."

"You should check out the reading glasses they have at most pharmacies," Sheila offered. "They're really handy if you don't need a strong prescription, and they're cute, too."

"I have a few pairs I like to wear to work, sometimes," Anna commiserated, smiling in Sheila's direction.

Dawn couldn't help but smile, too, at the simple interaction that was as revealing as it was innocent. She had good people around her table. "You have a beautiful smile, Anna," she said without thinking, and Anna met her eyes, looking taken aback and then smiling again.

"Thank you."

Dawn was mulling over how touched the woman had been at a compliment aimed solely at her rather than at both she and her sister as if they were a single entity when her phone rang in her hand. "Oh!" She jumped, simultaneously dropping the phone and scaring the others, and was laughing by the time Mel had recovered the vibrating, singing thing and was handing it back to her. "Ah!" she exclaimed when she saw the name that appeared. "Speak of the..." she looked up, then cleared her throat. "It's Rory!"

The group fell into a low din of conversation as she answered, but in seconds they were silently watching her again, for she'd made another noise of shock. She put her fingers over the mic and whispered, "Something's happened," even as Rory cried into the phone at the other end.

And then she put him on speaker.

CHAPTER 19 – NEWS

"She was fine when we put her to bed," Rory started, his voice reflecting, for the first time since the group had known him, a note of helplessness. "Dad and I have fallen into the habit of sitting in the bedroom after we tube-feed her, and talking; we go over the news of the day, recount stories of work and friends... whatever comes to mind. The doctors say she might hear it," he trailed off and the group exchanged pained glances. They'd all either heard the doctors say the same or had updates from those who did. The exhaustion behind Rory's words easily explained his forgetting, but none of it spelled anything good. His fatigue, which indicated sleeplessness, the fear that laced his words. Whatever happened to affect the man so obviously daunted them all, despite the early stage of the story.

"After we talked a while, we did the routine of changing her," he continued, but a sob interrupted his story. "Which, by the way, she'd hate to know I was doing, so we'll all say Dad did it, or Mom – Mom comes to help out. You'll probably all meet her. Bethie and Conner come, too. Not Jordan, though. They say he's been asking to see her, but he doesn't know... anyway..." he paused and they knew he was drowning, and Sheila put her fingers to her lips, shakily.

"Rory?" Dawn's eyes were on Sheila still as she swallowed the lump that kept rising in her throat. "Is Shya alright?" She had to ask it. Rory was near-rambling and for all of their mental health, the need to get that out of the way won out over letting Rory meander through the story.

"Yes!" he exclaimed, and the group let out a collective breath of relief. "Well, as well as she's been anyway, but – I'm sorry, guys; I must have you all in a panic. I haven't slept. In any case, she's alive, and home again. Still in a coma, and the doctors say what happened is unusual, but a very positive sign that she's in there somewhere, and part of her wants out." He chuckled in a strange falsetto. "If only they knew, eh?"

Dawn shook her head. He'd skipped too far ahead, now, but she made an effort to hold her impatience at bay. What she felt from Rory was certainly as bad as the sound of his words. "Rory," she said, gently, "I know I skipped ahead before when I asked about Shya, because some of us were starting to panic," Sheila smiled at her through her tears and Dawn tipped her a knowing wink, "but can we go back a little, now?"

Silence from the other end, except for something that sounded like scratching. She frowned, but understood when one of the twins reflexively rubbed at her jaw. He was rubbing at stubbly skin. Unshaven. Without the benefit of sleep. And terrified. But, why?

"Tell us what happened, Rory, and then sleep with that sweet girl in your arms."

He laughed. "I'm currently the big spoon," he admitted, and there were smiles at Dawn's end.

But she heard the exhaustion in his voice, too. "Don't fall asleep on us, now!"

More stubble-rubbing and the other twin was absently mirroring him, however remotely, that time. "The doctors say she was sleepwalking," he said in a rush, his words breaking up at the end. Dawn knew he was crying again, or still. Knew he needed rest. But the shock of his words fought to win out over the instinct to let the poor man sleep. Thankfully, Ed had no such conflict.

"She got up? On her own?" he was leaning eagerly

toward the coffee table, where the phone sat.

"It sounds good, right?" Rory replied, crying shamelessly through his words. "But I'm having a hard time seeing it that way, considering how I found her." There was a muffled sound, then two male voices, but more distant.

"Rory?" Mel was leaning toward the phone, too.

"Uh – hi everyone. This is John?" He said it like it was a question, adding, "Shya's Dad?" which Dawn found touching. So unassuming.

"Is he alright?" Dawn asked, for the group, because she knew Rory was just overwhelmed. Just crying. Just wrapping himself around the body of his greatest love, inhaling the scent of her hair and wishing her back to him with such force that his chest felt it would burst if she did not.

"He's exhausted. And he was the one that found her: I only woke up when he called for me, and by then she'd collapsed. I didn't see her like he did."

"Hi, John," Jane spoke soothingly as she leaned forward, too. "This is Jane. Do you remember me?"

"One of the twins?"

It made Dawn tense, as sensitive as she was to the emotions of others, but as usual, the descriptor didn't phase Jane on any level she could perceive.

She smiled, in fact. "Yes, that's right."

"Hi, Jane. Is, uh, is everyone there?"

"We're all here, John," Sheila piped up.

"Good. Uh, hi, everyone."

"Can you tell us exactly what Rory found?"

"O'course. Right." He cleared his throat. His fatherly need to be calm touched Dawn, but she felt his exhaustion, too.

His bewilderment. His fear over losing the last piece of Shya's mother. Over losing the daughter he'd only just entreated to give him another chance. "It's funny," he tried to sound light, but his voice hitched involuntarily, "I've heard Rory tell the story a few times since last night, but I still can't wrap my head around it. And yet I can look up and see it on the wall, clear as day." The dampened sound of a door closing came next. "He's already asleep, I think," he said.

"John, are you being literal when you can say you see it on the wall?" Dawn had to ask.

"Uh, yes I am, actually. He, uh – Rory – he woke up suddenly. Said he was having a nightmare and woke up in a panic because he'd been dreaming he couldn't find Shya. That she'd disappeared right out of bed and, well, you can imagine how panicked he was when he woke up and she wasn't beside him!"

Dawn didn't have to imagine it. She felt it like a hot knife in the gut, just like Rory had. And she felt something else. A desperation. A massive undertaking of effort to surface. To get something through. Her fingers flew to her mouth. She was feeling what Shya felt. The group sent her questioning looks as Shya's father continued.

"And he heard a scratching sound, and a sort of garbled muttering underneath. He said he never would have guessed it came from Shya. Scared him to the point of feeling faint, but he was too determined to not let it overtake him, thank God." He paused, breathing loudly. Throwing sand on the eagerness of the flames that fanned his emotions. "Well, he got up instantly, saying her name, turning the light on, you know, and then he said he froze, because she was there, still in the room but standing at the wall."

The group was silent, barely breathing, frozen on the precipice of the crux of the news.

“Facing it, like. Facing the wall,” he stumbled over the words and Dawn felt the pinpricks of gooseflesh as The Seers all experienced it, multiplying the sensation of her own by five. “And – and the scratching Rory heard was from her. She was scratching letters through the wallpaper, right down to the drywall,” he tried pausing to breath again, but they all heard him let the tears come, finally. “Her fingernails – some are torn to the quick, but some came off entirely. I’m sorry to tell you that,” he muttered through tears, “but, of course she bled, bled into the letters she was writing, and Rory – well, to quote him, he was the most ‘freaked out,’ he’d ever been. And I saw it, too,” he went on before Dawn could say the comforting words she’d managed to gather through her horror. “It was like one of those poems she writes. Like she got up… came back to us just for a few minutes, or for however long it takes to scratch *words* into a *wall* with your *fingernails,*” he paused again, his voice having become strained with emotion.

Dawn surveyed her group, reaching like she did without a thought, now. It wasn’t an effort anymore; hadn’t been since she’d left her home to go to university and decided to take her strange gift into her own hands rather than feel at the mercy of it. Rather than letting Cadence help her shoulder it and manage it, she determined to use it. To master it.

“I’m sorry,” John mumbled.

“No,” Dawn said. She’d tried for soothing but heard the edge in her voice with regret. The emotions of her friends had nearly swamped her, though, and she’d be damned if she was going to let it hold her down. “No, John. Of course, you don’t need to apologize. We all love Shya, too. We all understand.”

The man cried at the other end, and Dawn feared they’d lose him like they had Rory. She worked to think of a question. An anecdote. *Anything* to put him back on track. “What did she write?” was what came out, and the way her group perked up and watched the phone was reward enough to know she’d gotten it right. At their end, anyway. Risking the overwhelm she'd so desperately fought against, she reached out to Shya's father in the ensuing silence. And it was confusion she felt. A sheer blank.

"Ah, I don't remember, exactly," he lamented, "but the first word was 'breached.' And then – oh! I took pictures to show the doctors. Just a sec..."

Dawn met the eyes of the twins as Shya's father fumbled around with the phone at the other end. They peered back at her with wide eyes. And then Mel was handing her journal to her and she was reaching for it as if through molasses, her hand appearing in slow motion to take the book as her eyes went to the verse Mel was pointing to. "Breached," she whispered. It was the first word of the poem Shya had sent to her the previous night.

John came back on. "Found it. Sorry, I'm still trying to figure out these phones, though I've been using them since they came out. Anyway, I was right about the first word. Breached. Then it goes..."

"Eons of effort," Dawn said, robotically, and the man gasped.

"How did you know?"

"Finally coming to the fore," she continued, mesmerized.

"Well, she didn't get that far. Is it something she'd read, or..."

"No," Jane answered, as Dawn simply couldn't.

Shya had been writing the words in her own blood as Dawn had received them.

Jane continued, "But – if you're alright with it, we're planning on coming tomorrow. We'll show you the whole poem. We think," she eyed Dawn until Mel touched her arm, rousing her to look up from the page and at Jane. She nodded, seeing that Jane was asking for permission for something, and giving it via a nod without a thought, "we think Shya's been communicating through Dawn."

"What?"

Sheila's fingers went to her lips again.

"We think it's a good thing, John. She's trying."

"But that's just it," John replied, his tears seemingly quelled, but replaced with a note of foreboding that was far more unsettling. "When Rory went to her and stopped her from ruining her fingers, she didn't show any sign of being lucid. Her eyes were open, but he said they were blank; that he couldn't find her there."

Dawn had to shake herself to comprehend, but even with all her focus, found herself as confused as her friends looked.

But John continued.

"But as soon as he went to her and stopped her, she went into hysterics... screaming, crying, and worst of all, digging at her wrists with her jagged fingernails!"

The group gasped collectively, their eyes seeking refuge in those of their companions, only to find their own terror mirrored back at them.

"And she made progress, too," John was crying again. "Tore up her left wrist to the point of damaging veins and nerve endings... her hand's all swollen."

"God," Dawn said, without meaning to.

"She's alright. Rory started yelling for me and he said that was it; she just dropped like a sack of potatoes, as if she left her body again, but she was bleeding bad. We had to take her to the hospital," he finished with something incomprehensible.

"I'm so sorry, John," Mel said, and put a palm on the table between himself and the phone. Dawn had seen him do it before, despite claiming he was unable to impart his gift remotely. She'd always suspected differently, and by the relief she felt in John, she was pleased to note his efforts a success.

"You say you're coming tomorrow?" John asked.

"Yes," Dawn replied. "We'll stay at the British again, but we'll let you know as soon as we're there."

"Please, if any of you wants to stay here, know that you're welcome. I have a pullout in the basement, and the couch is actually quite comfortable, and there's also Rory's room."

Dawn eyed her friends for their reactions, feeling surprisingly like it was a good idea. Deciding to save the decision for more discussion, she replied, "That's very kind, John. We'll see, OK?"

"Whatever's best, but if I'm honest, I'd feel better if there was someone else here. More protection, you know? I'm afraid Rory and I are rather more... frail, than when we started out."

"Of course."

"Why would she do that?" He circled back so quickly that Dawn was unprepared.

"I think we need to see her before we guess," Sheila said, and Dawn had never been more thankful for the woman's sense of hesitation. But John fell silent.

Mel leaned forward again, clearing his throat. "It's not uncommon to see a possessed soul so eager to end the situation," he said, delicately, "but given Shya's gifts, and the nature of her latest poems, I suspect that the demon is using her. And understandably, she doesn't appreciate it."

Dawn inhaled sharply. Mel had put it so eloquently, but she'd heard the truth in it: Shya would do anything to stop the

King of Demons from reaching whatever goals it had.

Anything.

CHAPTER 20 – PROMISE

Dawn faded from the group immediately after the phone call ended. She was thinking hard. Thinking of the shadows they'd been seeing, of Mel's upcoming trip. Of Shya rousing from her coma just to tear her wrists apart.

The group seemed to reflect her inner turmoil. She vaguely sensed that the twins were talking with Ed, low but with some urgency, and Ed seemed not to want to hear it, regardless. And Mel was holding Sheila's hand between his as they spoke, Sheila looking entirely spooked. But none of it coalesced in her brain, not enough to urge her to engage, anyway. And something else was happening; it wasn't entirely uncommon, but annoyed her anyway. Cadence and her brothers kept popping into her thoughts. Since she'd become estranged from them all, they'd show up like that, especially during times of stress or chaos. As if to exacerbate the situation.

Now Sheila was leaning in to contribute to the more heated discussion between Ed and the twins, and Mel was moving to squat by Dawn's recliner, his eyes hard on hers.

"What's up?"

"I think I need to stay at Shya's house," she mumbled. She hadn't even been able to consider the alternative since John had mentioned it.

Mel nodded. "I agree."

She nodded toward the rest of the group. "What's going on?"

He sighed. “The twins say Ed needs to come to Tibet with me.”

Dawn frowned. “Why didn’t they mention that before?”

“They say they didn’t have to; they say it’s fated and that it would happen anyway.”

“And Sheila agrees?”

Mel nodded. “She says she’s seen it: myself and Ed on some mountain, doing ‘magic.’” He tried to laugh, but Dawn knew that he was spooked, too. And there was something else – something unsaid, behind his eyes. Something he was hiding that she didn’t know how to dig up. Not yet.

Dawn regarded the rest of the group. “If she’s trying to end her life, we need to get her out, *now.*”

“I can’t believe it,” Mel lowered his eyes and she felt a sympathetic squeezing in her chest as he held back tears.

“If there really is a breach between the realms and given what we - and others! – have been seeing, it seems there is, then the potential for this to get worse quick is heightened.”

Mel nodded, his eyes still distant.

“And that girl, strong as she is… *trapped* as she is… she’s still trying to make things right.” Dawn bit the insides of her cheeks as her own tears tried to come.

“We always knew she was special,” he said, touching her cheek as if to smooth a path for the tears that threatened. And one did fall.

“I don’t know how to do this,” she said, so quietly she barely heard it herself, but Jane held a hand up to quiet the little group at the other end of the coffee table and they all looked toward her. Dawn put a hand to her mouth as if to push the words back in.

“We have an idea,” Anna said, after Jane had gotten

everyone's attention.

Of course, they do.

"Thank God," Dawn said, and chuckled. And then they were all laughing, a bit hesitantly, and Sheila was touching Ed's arm, reaching over the table, smiling into his eyes.

Ed still looked incensed. When they'd all quieted again, he met Dawn's eyes. "Aren't you missing your show?"

Dawn instinctively looked at her watch, making Mel chuckle beside her.

"It's not even the right day for it," Sheila giggled, and Dawn let her hand drop, laughing.

"Got excited there for a second," she admitted, and everyone laughed.

When silence stole over them again, Ed rubbed at his face, then looked to the twins again. "There's nothing in me that wants to go with Mel tomorrow. How do I know it's the right thing?"

The twins only looked back at him, their faces unreadable.

"I feel it's right, too," Mel said, and Dawn looked to him, surprised. Her hand found his arm and he patted it absently. His eyes were still on Ed. "You need to learn from this woman. There's only so much I can bring back."

"You could bring *her!*" Ed exclaimed, but he'd lost the gusto he'd been fighting with before.

Mel shook his head. "But time's not on our side. If I find her and convince her to come back with me – which I doubt – there'll be little time for you to learn. If you come, and even if we can't convince her to get involved, you can still gain something from her."

Everyone watched Ed, whose anxiety was etched into

every feature.

"It makes sense," Sheila said it softly, her hand still on the man's massive bicep. And Ed looked into her face, seemingly mulling over her words, then nodded, just a little. But his acceptance was there.

Mel squeezed Dawn's hand.

Ed looked to her. "I think you should stay at the house with her."

Dawn nodded, knowing he meant Shya. "I just said that to Mel."

The big man's eyes were swimming.

Dawn's chest filled with compassion. "I promise to take care of her, Ed." Her breath hitched, because she was thinking about the last time she'd taken care of the woman, brushing her teeth as she teetered on her feet with exhaustion. Leading her to bed and tucking her in, knowing she was spent. Terrified at how vulnerable she felt. Leaving to go back to the saved boy and the rest of the group with a sick stomach and an ache in her heart, because she felt Shya being pulled and knew her own proximity wouldn't save her. Convincing herself to trust that Rory or Shya's father would see it if something happened, and that they'd call and they'd come to stave off the demon.

But she'd slipped away so quietly. Nobody knew, not until she wouldn't wake in the morning.

This time, she wouldn't fail. She leaned forward, toward Ed but still clutching the hand of the man who'd leave her the next morning, and said, "I won't let her die."

CHAPTER 21 – ENDINGS AND BEGINNINGS

Going to university in New Brunswick was like embarking on an entirely new life for Dawn. It had been all too easy to pull away from family: her brothers were ensconced in their own lives – new careers, new families, and Cadence seemed willfully overwhelmed with taking care of Dawn's father.

There was something satisfying about starting out on her own and putting everything else behind her. She found that ceasing to make an effort with her father, in particular, meant that the inherent guilt that came along with thoughts of her mother had vanished. As though she was unable to get past the fact of her mother's death until she went back to shunning her father. And indeed, striking out on her own seemed to usher in a new ability to connect with the ghost of her mother for the first time since the woman had been so violently ejected from her mortal shell.

She spent little time ruminating on the fact that sadness was the overarching emotion she sensed from her mother's spirit.

Dawn was *excited* about her clean slate, and determined not to look back.

As such, she delved into her classes as though possessed. She started study groups and found herself making new friends, and *easily*, at that! Rather than struggling to cope with the barrage of emotion from those around her, Dawn found herself paying attention. Sorting it out. And finally, using it to connect. Her circle of friends was wide, if not particularly intimate. Even with her new success with her peers, Dawn grew increasingly disenchanted with that old idea of feeling like she belonged.

And so, in her third year of university and having proven herself more than capable on the school and social life fronts, she developed a new fever for learning – but this time, the setting was not a classroom or a circle of friends. She begun to spend chunks of time at the library, reading everything she could get her hands on about the occult. About being empathic. Or psychic, or intuitive. Even about Wicca, and practices of majick. She schooled herself on the unusual and strange, and for the first time in her life, began to feel as though there was a place for her.

She just hadn't found it, yet.

But her eyes had been opened. And as she dreamt of ways to find others like her, she began to feel lighter, as though her own burden had been relieved in a pre-emptive expectation of being shared with those who *knew.*

Her friends noticed. They commented on her increased enthusiasm for studying with teasing upset, noting her absences at Friday night pub crawls and Saturday morning hangover breakfasts at the local diner. But it truly was only teasing. Her friends' loyalty was not easily shaken, and that was due to another unexpected turn of events that developed during Dawn's third year of her new life.

She'd been pairing them up.

She would never cease to be amazed at what had taken her so long to discover: that her undeniable advantage at knowing people could make her instincts with love relationships into much sought-out counsel. It was when friends of friends began to approach her with increased regularity, even offering to pay for her services, that the idea of turning the gift into a profitable business struck her.

And profitable it was. Soon, she was widely known on campus as *the* dating service to frequent. And Dawn was having fun. She'd given her business the moniker "Duos" and looked forward to the excitement of matchmaking each day. One conversation with a hopeful single was all she'd need to develop a custom pair of goggles she would wear, just for them. She imagined them for each person, creating them with color, shape, and size to match the wants and needs of love-seekers. Finding a match was often as simple as donning the imaginary glasses and touring the campus, on alert for the soul whose nooks and crannies fit into the notches of her paying clients, and vice-versa. A unique sort of puzzle building, all her own.

It was easy.

The irony of it – the successful use of her gift in the field of love and connection as she simultaneously built blinders between herself and her own family members – was a factor she quite successfully ignored. She was busy, after all. Busy, and popular, and confident. Life was good.

It was during her fourth and final year that things took a turn. Cadence had been making bolder efforts to reach out, even showing up on campus to find Dawn, but Dawn steadfastly refused to see her. Even the slightest peek at her half-sister's emotions solidified Dawn's suspicions: her father was sick. And Dawn had already made up her mind not to care. It was only when her brothers took up the challenge of trying to get through to her that Dawn was momentarily thrown for a loop.

It had been one thing for her siblings to choose to be blind to the inappropriate relationship between their father and half-sister, but taking over where Cadence had failed in getting Dawn's attention was a newly-fresh insult.

There *was* a little voice... of course there was. A little voice that asked why she carried on in her ignorance. Why it mattered. Even asked if maybe she was wrong. Had been from the start, because it was easier to think badly of her father than it was to forgive him of all he'd done.

But that little voice was quiet, especially in comparison to her new success, and the money that had been building dependably as a result of her burgeoning business. And she showed no signs of slowing! She'd already hired a contractor, who was fitting up a small office for her downtown to operate from once she graduated.

It was true that, when her friends and clients inquired after her own love relationships, Dawn shrank in the light of their curiosity. But she didn't think about it much. She was so busy, after all. Too busy for a love of her own when others were so needful.

A final message from Kenny on her voicemail nearly broke her resolve. He spoke of their father in tones of foreboding, asked Dawn to consider her brothers during this time if nobody else. Begged her, in a surprising, final push of effort, to reach out with her gift and feel her father's situation. Feel Cadence's, too, to see that their love was companionable, and nothing more. Never had been.

If it hadn't been for the final declaration of the message, she could easily have chalked it all up to desperate, last-ditch efforts to get her to jump on board with a family of delusional folk, whose sense of right and wrong had been twisted first by an abusive father, and then by the tragic death of their mother.

She almost never thought of that last statement, now. Years later, after her business grew and boomed and in a sudden fit of exasperation (perhaps due to her own inability to build love relationships of her own), sold to a *very* high bidder, she held on to her assertion that her father was mean, that Cadence was wrong, and that her brothers were too weak to stand against it.

Her portion of the inheritance her father built up for his children still sat, a cheque in a safe deposit box, in case her business money ever ran out. A lawyer got in touch once per year to beg her to cash it. Just to take it, so he could be done with it.

The final thing her younger brother had imparted in the voice message that had remained engraved in the recesses of her mind, despite her determination to ignore it, was that their father had been living with Cadence and her new husband for the final year of his life.

Cadence. And her *husband.* Dawn shook her head as she read her father's obituary then pushed the paper into a drawer.

Her continued ignorance was made easy by another development of her fourth year at university, though Big Ed would be terribly upset to learn it. In Dawn's continued efforts to find others like herself, she'd had little success. It was only by chance she met Ed, who contacted her as a potential client for Duos. And Ed knew an older gentleman – a professor – who was searching, too. And suddenly, Dawn had the beginnings of a new family in two new and gifted friends.

A new family to grab hold of as she let the other slip away.

CHAPTER 22 – WANDERINGS

A flashing light on her phone, which had been winking, blue and insistent, since sometime during the group's meeting, perplexed her. Not many others except for the group knew her number, or deigned to use it if they did.

Like her little brother. She and Kenny had had a brief acquaintance on social media when it had been new and seemingly innocuous, and she'd given him her number, surprising both of them. Just in case. But she made it clear that it would have to be an incredibly precipitous "just in case" for her to want to hear it, and he acknowledged a disappointed sort of understanding that she had no interest in the family she left behind.

And sometime shortly thereafter, Dawn noticed that Kenny had seemed to block her without a word, and she didn't let herself feel that injury. Didn't mourn the consequences of a stubborn decision that seemed far too final to change, given all that had happened.

Given all she'd refused to be a part of or even analyse in an overdue, back to the drawing board sort of revisit.

Regardless, she wasn't tempted to check the source of that blinking light on her phone, given the fact that she'd just spoken to everyone she was immediately concerned with, Rory and Shya's father included. And Mel had come home with her, sure he'd left his toiletry bag in her bathroom, only to remember he'd already retrieved it and packed it on his last visit.

He was harried and distracted, which was to be expected, but Dawn didn't like how distant he already felt. How easy it was for him not to see the turmoil that roiled inside her as she pondered the next day's events.

The old Dawn, the Dawn who was their leader and strong foundation before the rude interruption of the demon Asmodeus, would be in a flurry of activity now. She knew that, even as she sat in her recliner, hands clutching one another tightly in an effort to still not just her body, but her mind. She'd be helping Ed make arrangements, making sure he'd refilled his heart medications before he left, and researching the remote area in Tibet that he and Mel would venture to, their hearts hoping for an almost unheard-of audience with a woman who could traverse the boundaries of life and death, and live to tell the tale.

To a very select few. Understandably.

She'd be reassuring Mel, going over his packing list and making a game plan for the entire group. She'd be strategizing!

She'd revel in how wonderful it felt to have some measure, regardless of its significance, of control.

But none of that seemed to rouse the Dawn of such a short time and such monumental events ago. Mel rushed around her, muttering to himself, his energy sizzling with anticipation and fear. Mel was off, too.

They all were.

And it didn't end with her close-knit little group of gifted souls. Apparently, the whole world was feeling it. Seeing it, each soul in its own way. And Dawn, given her extraordinary gift, found that her extensive efforts to develop a counter-gift, one which allowed her to throw up a wall to block the incoming emotions that had plagued her in the worst of times, was flagging.

She felt them: the shadows that moved of their own accord, the monsters that bared their teeth in the light of day rather than just in the safety of night. The bold ones that crept from their rightful realm into this one, hungry and menacing, because they *could.*

Because, through the determination of an ancient and clever demon and the equally old and powerful gift of an extraordinary human, there was a door.

An ache twisted in Dawn's chest. It was a simultaneous squeeze of guilt and sorrow, so much like that force that squeezed at Big Ed's heart, woven through as it was with a desperate missing of their friend. And the increasingly urgent need to save her.

And now, Dawn had a new knowing that was impossible to deny; that saving Shya meant saving all of them. And that she wasn't the only one who knew that saving her might not work. And that in the absence of that, there *was* another way to shut the portal. The door that only existed because Shya did.

Dawn heard herself gasp as another realization struck her. If Shya died, it would be akin to the death of a king without an heir. Her family's gift flourished in but one living soul at a time, passed from mother to daughter – *only* daughter, as history had shown, and fate had ensured - upon the mother's death. Shya was the last living daughter in that royal line.

What would it do to the balance of the realms to lose that gift? Or to have it exist on the side of death rather than in a living soul?

Dawn didn't know, and that was what bothered her most. She knew in some recesses of her heart that she had been wrong in this lifetime. So wrong that the costs were too hard to face. But as the shadows deepened, teeming with a darkness independent of the waxing and waning of the sunlight, she felt all the uncertainties she'd neatly filed away into a mental drawer marked "Past", clamouring to burst forth at her.

"Your phone's blinking," Mel pointed as he passed her chair again, going toward the bedroom with laundry spilling over his arms. Dawn recognized her own clothes in that pile, grey joggers sandwiched between Mel's jeans and t-shirts. The clothes he relaxed in. With her. And then he was gone, muttering again, and she was glancing at her phone again.

"You should pack, too!" he called from the bedroom, and on some level, she knew he was right, but her eyes remained glued to the blinking light, which, now that she was looking, pulsed with a sort of anxious, but needful determination. And it was the determination of the caller she felt. And the person felt foreign and familiar all at once.

Family.

She pressed her lips together.

A shadow snaked out from behind the TV stand, peripherally. She darted her eyes to it, wondering in some detached way whether they appeared more easily when the energies around them were afraid. Because Dawn was afraid of the source of that blinking, now.

"Mel," she called, her eyes on the oozing shadow, which halted, then retreated, when she did.

He appeared beside her, padding quietly but quickly in his sock feet on her carpet. "Huh?"

She pointed.

He stared. He placed a calming hand on her shoulder and she pondered, not for the first (or last) time whether one could become addicted to the type of drug that was Mel's soothing touch.

"You see?" she asked, her eyes fixed on the indistinct lump of shadow that showed above the stand.

“Not like you do, I don’t think” he murmured, his voice quiet. “But I know it’s there.” He squatted, then gently pressed her cheek so she would meet his eyes. “I won’t go if you need me here.”

She placed a hand on his unusually stubbly cheek, tempted to ask him to stay, and not just for her. The chaos behind his eyes scared her. For him.

But the purpose of his – and Ed’s! – departure trumped her fear. “No,” she whispered. “As much as I need you to stay, we *all* need you to go.” She leaned forward, wanting the salvation of his eyes and feeling troubled at its absence. “It’s just distance. It doesn’t mean as much, now that we know what’s at stake.”

He nodded, his eyes darkening further. “All the levels. Everything.”

Now she nodded.

“You should check your message,” he nodded toward her phone and she closed her eyes. “Who is it?”

She shrugged. “Some family member.”

His eyes cleared as she opened her own. “That’s – well, it’s been a long time, hasn’t it?” Mel knew some, but not all, of the history with her family.

“This one’s new.”

He frowned.

She reached for the phone, fortifying herself with his presence and determining to face it now, for what if she couldn’t when he was gone? She frowned at the unknown number.

“What?”

She looked at him again. “Do you know what a difference you’ve made in my life?”

Tears sprung to his eyes. Dawn knew their relationship had been the product of his quiet persistence. He'd told her more than once that he was positive they wouldn't be together at all had he not acted so stubbornly like it was supposed to happen. The fact that he wore her down over time, and with the not-unsubstantial assistance of his gift, which he claimed Dawn seemed to benefit from more than anyone in his life ever had, was something he acknowledged as necessary, even if it wasn't a comfortable knowledge. "Well," he sputtered, feeling simultaneously like he was teetering on the precipice of losing her and like this was his opportunity to strengthen what he'd worked so hard to fill, "you've changed my life, too," he finished, finally, and she smiled sadly.

"Thank you," she whispered, then pressed her forehead against his.

She could tell he was trying not to sob, hearing him swallow hard. The effort had him trembling.

"Do you know I love you?"

He couldn't prevent the sharp intake of breath, nor the grateful sound that followed it. A wordless emission of relief and joy.

She laughed, then kissed him. "I do love you, Mel, and at the end of all this, I'm going to ask you to marry me, and we're gonna grow old together."

His face was awash with joy and overwhelm, and suddenly he was laughing as the tears finally fell.

"Don't cry," she said, wiping his tears even as she pressed her forehead against his, still.

"Sorry," he managed, then hiccoughed.

"What do you think you'll say?" she asked. Feeling more vulnerable than she had in so many years.

He smiled, and surprised her. "I guess you'll have to keep

that promise to find out."

She pulled back, searching his face and gasping, then laughed heartily. She could feel his effort at remaining calm. The man who imparted calm with an effortless consistency, regardless of how he himself was feeling. She felt him want to stay, want to make her propose to him now. She felt him want to skip all the sadness and the fear and just get on with their life. Together. "You're gonna say yes," she laughed.

He laughed, too. Averted his eyes, then stood and headed back toward the bedroom. "We'll see!" he called over his shoulder.

She smiled. Then she looked for the shadow behind the TV, and it was there. Almost quivering, if a shadow could quiver. But she kept smiling.

She still was when he kissed her goodbye. When he met her eyes and promised to see her soon, and call her every day before then. Every hour, if she let him. Then said, "I love you," before leaving her to prepare for her own trip.

But first, she listened to the voicemail that still blinked at her.

CHAPTER 23 – DEJA…?

The five-hour drive from home to Aylmer, Quebec, was a strange one. Dawn had insisted on driving, hoping the distractions of the route would ease her apprehension. It was during the last drive home that she'd been given the message of Shya's first poem in a dream. The last drive, when they all hoped answers would come before they returned to get Shya back. When they assumed they'd be a full compliment, Mel and Ed facing any dangers of the supernatural sort with them, rather than be flying to Tibet while the four women of the group drove toward their sleeping friend and ultimately, the demon that had stolen her from them.

But the drive did nothing to hamper her anxiety. When Sheila touched her arm lightly from the passenger seat, a quick glance at the concern on her face was all it took to make Dawn realize she'd not only tuned her friends out as they strategized around her, but she was bent forward, almost touching the steering wheel with her chest. She made a concentrated effort to relax back into her seat and lessen the death grip she had on the steering wheel.

"OK?" Sheila asked softly, her high-pitched whisper nearly drowned out by the sound of the tires on the road.

Dawn found she had to mindfully unclench her jaw before answering, and in that moment of hesitation, the twins grew quiet in the back seat and focussed on Dawn.

"What you two talking about back there?" she eyed them in the rear-view mirror, deftly dodging Sheila's question.

"We were talking about the levels of existence," Jane

leaned forward slightly, her hand going to the back of Sheila's seat, "or the ones we can say we've seen or understand in some way."

Anna nodded, her pale eyes shuddering when Dawn met them again in the mirror.

It had become a habit to watch both women when either of them spoke; it was like each completed the other in an enmeshment of spirit Dawn hadn't felt in any other sort of relationship before. And that was saying something.

"And?" Dawn made a motion for Jane to continue, but met Anna's eyes again.

"And we can't figure out where Shya's shoreline fits in," Anna finished. Jane nodded and sat back in her seat again.

"Maybe it's Hell, or *Shya's* Hell..." Dawn frowned at her own suggestion.

"But it was Jordan's, first," Sheila said, and she also frowned. "But does that mean every soul that is damned has a separate afterlife? There's no one plane that is 'Hell?'"

"We can't think in such a linear fashion," Jane shook her head. "We've gone over this."

Anna touched her sister's leg before leaning forward, herself. "We know it's impossible to even fathom the answers to those sorts of questions."

Sheila visibly withdrew, her gaze focused on her hands as they clasped each other in her lap.

"What we're trying to figure out is whether Shya's prison is something she actively needs to take part in, in order for it to exist," Anna continued, squeezing Sheila's shoulder and earning a tiny smile from her friend.

"And whether the fact that it may not be entirely under the control of the demon means the boundaries between that place and *this,*" she gestured toward the windows and the scenery beyond, "are different, too."

Dawn gasped. "It would almost *have* to be, in order for a living person to exist there so... *solidly.*"

"Like a bubble between the lands of the living and dead." Anna sat back now, nodding.

"But maybe that boundary is still effective, you know? At keeping us and *them* separated, unless someone from *this* side," Sheila paused, her face scrunching up as she attempted to piece her thoughts together.

Dawn finished for her. "Maybe the breach only exists because both Shya and the King of Demons are both concentrated on it?"

Sheila looked at her, nodding, but still confused.

"It makes sense with everything we know," Jane murmured.

"Everything Shya's been trying to tell us," Anna added.

Dawn tried to swallow the panic that was mounting in her. She watched the trees whiz past on either side of them and noted the sign for Belleville as they went by it.

"What is it, Dawn?" Jane was leaning forward again.

Dawn found herself leaning into the steering wheel again, even as Sheila nodded in her peripheral vision.

"You've been tense," she said, quietly.

Dawn laughed wryly and Sheila shrunk back again.

"Of course I'm tense, girl," she smiled in Sheila's direction, eyes on the highway.

The answering silence threatened to blow the top off the volcano she'd been simmering within, so she gave herself a shake, then answered with the truth. "This drive makes me nervous."

"Because of last time," the twins stated in that eerie synchronicity they shared. Dawn thought it wouldn't be so unnerving if they ever reacted to the occurrences with any sort of surprise, or even delight. Instead, the occurrence was rarely acknowledged, and that instance was no different; both women leaned forward, eyes resolutely on hers in the mirror.

Dawn could do nothing but nod.

"Well, you won't be dreaming as long as you're driving," Sheila tittered breathily, obviously making an effort to lighten the atmosphere.

"But maybe you should," Jane voiced.

Dawn laughed for real, this time. "You think I should *try* for one of them dreams?"

Sheila peered back at the twins. "She's *driving!*"

Dawn tried to recall another time when either of the twins rolled their eyes as they both did, in perfect unison, now. She couldn't. She laughed again, and Sheila playfully swatted her.

"If the dreams don't hurt, maybe trying to connect with Shya is the thing you should be doing," Anna voiced, then smiled at Sheila, her gaze softening on her friend. The three women were close, even outside of The Seers group.

Sheila sighed, seemingly released from the teasing, and eyed Dawn. "Do they hurt?"

Dawn shrugged. "They *suck*."

Sheila laughed. The twins had retreated into one of their impenetrable powwows.

Dawn glanced sideways at Sheila again. "I think that's the hardest part for me: not knowing what to do. I don't mind the dreams, if they help. I don't mind the words she sends through me. I just want to *help* her and despite all that, I feel helpless to know what to do!"

The twins fell into silence again.

"We all feel that way, Dawnie," Sheila said.

Dawn clenched her jaw. Sheila had never used the nickname; Dawn hadn't told anyone about it. It was her mother's nickname for her. And sometimes Cadence's, and that was OK, because she kind of mothered Dawn, too.

"OK, Dawnie?" Sheila said, then, and Dawn recoiled as a flashback hit: her mother in the passenger seat, leaning back with a smile to talk to Dawn, just before the..."

"Dawn!" the twins cried out in unison as Dawn turned to confront Sheila, but saw her mother's face looking back at her, instead, with a smile and then a shocked turn toward the windshield, where Dawn finally saw a deer rearing up, not twenty feet away.

Dawn's entire body reacted, hardening at every joint until she was standing on the break, hugging the wheel into her belly as she tilted right and away from the creature with its rolling eyes and flaring nostrils, and onto the shoulder of gravel, then grass, skidding, skidding until they were stopped and surrounded by dust.

Dawn dropped into her seat and whipped her head around to find the deer, which she spotted as it bounced into the trees at the median, it's white tail quivering as if to wave goodbye.

A cement truck thundered by, its horn blasting her back to herself as visions from the accident tried to engulf her. Her little brother unconscious on the floor, his arm crushed beneath him and poking out from behind him at an odd angle. The shouts of her older brothers – shouts of fear and surprise, crashing over her in waves. Her father, panicking, running.

Pleading, denying, bargaining with God. Changing.

And her mother, or just her shell, her face perfect and more peaceful than Dawn had ever seen it in life, dead on the hood of a blue Toyota, and the deer that was crushed between the two cars, its eyes crazed and then fading as it screamed in pain, watching Dawn as it went through the process of dying.

She screamed, recoiling from the sudden presence of the speeding cement truck and its horn, and Sheila caught her. Looked down into her eyes, saying "What happened?"

Dawn scanned her friend's face, just to reassure herself Sheila had returned and no trace of her mother's face lingered there. Then, finding her friend to appear entirely herself, let go and sobbed, squeezing her eyes shut and letting herself rest in the warmth of Sheila's arms, just for a moment. Then she turned her head to meet the eyes of Jane or Anna. Either one. And said, "You're driving."

CHAPTER 24 – LOST

Dawn stared blankly into her lap as the tears fell. Her face burned; her shame had overcome her as she spoke, but she hadn't confronted the reasons behind it. She just opened up, telling the story of the accident first – she couldn't *not* tell them, after what had just happened! – and then there were questions, of course. Where were the members of her family now? What sort of relationship did she have with her brothers? Her father? Her half-sister?

Why hadn't she told anyone the whole story? Ever?

She *hadn't* told them everything. In fact, she hadn't told *Mel* everything, and he knew the most.

A pale hand reached for her dark one and she let herself be comforted. It was Anna who sat in the driver's seat now, and who grasped her hand lightly. Nobody spoke. The group had pulled off at an exit and currently sat just off the highway, surrounded by tall pine and birch trees that had seemed to burst up to engulf them as soon as they made the detour.

"I have a question," Sheila broke the silence from her new seat in the back, and Dawn raised her eyes to find she and Jane clasping hands, too. "Why did you get so scared when you looked at me?"

Dawn let her head fall again, squeezing her eyes against the memory of her mother's face peering back at her. Kindly. Softly... and then whipping around to see the deer, her visage a haze of shock and fear. "I saw my mother," she managed. The defeated sound of her own voice renewed the heat in her cheeks.

Anna squeezed her hand gently. "A warning."

Dawn inhaled sharply, meeting her friend's eyes before nodding, then burying her face in her hands, a fresh deluge of tears breaking the dam of her resolve, again, to bury her past forever.

"I think I felt her," Sheila breathed.

"Me too," Jane spoke up.

"And I said something, but didn't remember deciding to say it. I didn't even hear it. I felt relaxed. Tired." Sheila reached forward to touch Dawn's shoulder. "She felt lovely, Dawn. Even when I saw the deer and felt afraid, it was an old fear, like a memory, and I knew everything would be alright."

Dawn shook her head, overcome.

"I wish you'd told us," Anna said. "We could have shared it with you, helped you process."

Dawn raised her eyebrows, sniffling, and looked at her friend. "Process? This was thirty – more than thirty! – years ago! It changed my life. Changed my family's *world.* I don't want to process it, anymore. It's in the past."

"My God," Anna shook her head, her face contorted in a rare show of emotion. Dawn thought it was pity that shone in her eyes. She pulled her hands back.

"I don't need to process it," she muttered, her eyes going to the trees.

"Was that the first time you've seen her since it happened?"

Dawn tried not to let the question land; tried to shove it back out. But she grew dizzy and realized she was holding her breath with the effort, the held air having turned to stone in her chest and pounding against her sternum, wanting out. She released, the air whooshing from her on the wave of a sob.

"Uh-huh," she squeaked when she'd gotten her breath. Because it *had* been the first time she'd even thought to connect with her mother, even just to acknowledge the energy she felt around her every day since that fateful event that had meant everything.

"Then you haven't processed," Jane said, low and steady, and Dawn knew she was right.

"Jesus," she cried, shaking her head and closing her eyes. Her tears wetted her hands, which wrestled each other in her lap, now, twisting and pulling in a show of angst that would not be contained.

"What else?" Anna asked.

Dawn peered up at her. "What?"

"There's something else. A girl. Another… empath?"

The previous night's events rushed back at her. The message she'd finally deigned to hear. There had been previous messages, but she only heard some. She could only assume the others went away after some period of time having sat, unacknowledged. It had been Kenny, as she'd expected, as he was truly the only family that still reached out, but the message wasn't about him, or even Cadence.

"I have a niece," she found herself blurting, shocking herself, and then her hand flew to her mouth to stem the flood that tried to follow. There was so much more. She had a niece. Her name was Charm. And Charm's father was *not* her own father, as Dawn had convinced herself would be the case, should Cadence ever have a child. But that wasn't all. Dawn had suspected. She'd known, from what she'd gleaned through years of unanswered pleas, from the undeniable connection she still had to her family, despite her wish to sever herself from the past.

She'd suspected there was a child.

A child like her.

Her friends were speaking in a flurry, their words coalescing and then dropping away as they bounced against the hard shell of her shock; something she hadn't been aware of erecting. She was aware, however, that though her friend's words were distant, the very acknowledgement of her family – of the lifelong denial she'd maintained so well – had indeed opened the floodgates, and she was newly unable to deny the emotions of her family.

"Where is she?"

Jane's voice was muffled, as if she spoke through water. Dawn felt her half-sister, her desperation. Her fear, because her daughter was missing. And she felt Kenny's frustration, his anger, his acceptance of her abandonment on top of their mother's. Acceptance; not understanding. It had happened, but it hurt.

She felt years' worth of sadness from them all, all at once. And she feared it would drown her.

"Dawn?"

She couldn't even tell which direction to swim for the surface. And it was getting so dark.

"Dawn!"

Something was wrong. She was falling, and the suffering of her family was sucking her down.

"She's – what's happening?"

And then there was something else; another pull, and it was better than the flood that had stolen her breath, so she swam toward it.

It felt safe. It felt familiar. And suddenly, she was there. On a bus. The pressure of her backpack between her back and the seat, allowing only a perilous balance on the edge of the padded bench. But she wouldn't take it off, because if she had a seizure, anything could happen. Her pills, her journal, her clothes, her photos, her camera! All of it would be there for the taking.

"Dawn!" a voice screeched and she was yanked from the scene, out of the girl, who turned to watch her go, her eyes fixed on Dawn in determination and curiosity. Her eyes that were so much like her mother's. Her skin lighter, certainly, than Dawn's and even than that of Cadence, whose father had been white. And then she lifted her fingers, just for a second, and fluttered her fingers.

A wave.

And she was there in the car, eyes twitching from face to worried face: Jane, Anna and Sheila. Gasping. "What?"

"Oh, God!" Jane exclaimed. "She's awake!" Dawn saw that Jane was holding her phone to her ear. "Yes." She lowered the phone and looked at her sister. "They want to know if we can drive her to a hospital, or if we still need the ambulance."

Anna peered down at her, eyes inquisitive.

"Of course, she needs the ambulance!" Sheila cried.

Dawn shook her head emphatically, but couldn't seem to voice her denial.

"What? You don't want an ambulance?" Anna asked, though Sheila was tugging on her shirtsleeve, her eyes ricocheting between the sisters incredulously.

"No," Dawn found herself saying, and was pleased. "No," she said again.

Jane pulled away and spoke into the phone in hushed tones. Coming back to herself fully, she met Anna's eyes and found understanding, so turned to Sheila. "I'm fine. I just – something happened that's never happened before." She pressed herself up, then swayed, simultaneously dizzy and surprised to find herself in the grass, her friends on the ground around her. She peered around herself, dazed.

"You saw her?" Anna asked.

Dawn was watching Jane, who was still speaking into the phone, but was pacing beside the car, whose passenger-side door hung open. Suddenly realizing the dizziness had faded, and that the air smelled sweet and fresh, Dawn met Anna's eyes, then nodded, "I *was* her, I think."

Anna furrowed her brow.

"What?" Dawn couldn't imagine how this astonishing event could be a bad thing. In fact, all her previous apprehension seemed to have been lifted, as if meeting her niece, even in the manner she had, had smoothed everything out. She pictured her niece at one end of Dawn's lifeline and herself at the other, and between them, they pulled, solving all of the wrinkles and pitfalls in one quick tug. But when they put it down again, she could see there were still flaws. It was OK, though, because it was *better.* And because Charm was there.

"I was worried," Anna said.

"Why?" Dawn asked, innocent.

"We thought you were having a stroke, or a heart attack!" Sheila exclaimed.

"We brought you out here, so you could lay down, because you were twitching. We thought you'd hurt yourself in the car. Like you were having a..."

"Seizure," Dawn breathed, at once aware that her niece had more issues than her gifts had determined.

CHAPTER 25 – WARNING SHOT

Success

1

2

Exaltation

3

4

Infiltrate

5

6

Dark Trespassers

6

6

Chaos

1

2

Melancholia

3

4

Despair

5

6

Decay

6

6

Timeless effort

1

2

Deflected

3

4

But for leaks

5

6

Temporary

6

6

Then, victory

1

2

Through possession

3

4

Of the bright one

5

6

Through her fears

6

6

Now her army

1

2

Surges forward

3

4

To confront us

5

6

Laughable

6

6

Come, weak ones

1

2

Learn your own fears

3

4

Let us teach you

5

6

Drag you in

6

6

Doors work both ways

1

2

The King's shadow

3

4

Seeks to stop you

5

6

Don't tempt him.

CHAPTER 26 – IMPOSTER

She burst violently into wakefulness, gasping. Her seatbelt reacted and held her back, immediately sending her into another panic attack, endless flashes of the accident that killed her mother assaulting her mind.

Anna's hand found her arm from the driver's seat. "Alright, sweetheart," her ever-calm voice eased Dawn from the precipice she'd landed on, held her steady.

Dawn turned to see the pale woman, whose eyes remained on the road, then around to meet the eyes of Jane, then Sheila. Sheila leaned forward, concern overtaking her features so entirely that Dawn wondered if the woman's face would ever clear again. Dawn smiled, a little. "Seems you always look worried these days, girl."

Sheila's eyes did clear, then, and she laughed, relief flooding her face as she relaxed back in the seat. Jane, meanwhile, was watching Dawn calmly, and she held out the tools Dawn would surely have asked for in the immediate moments to follow, as the words flooded back: Dawn's notebook, with the previous poems she'd received from Shya, or from the Shya of that other place, as enmeshed as she was with the devil's servant, and a pen. Dawn took them without hesitation, and was writing before she'd settled, facing forward in her seat, again.

Once spent, she puzzled over the words in silence, aware that her friends waited impatiently, but unable to volunteer the results, just yet.

"What is it?" Jane inquired, finally. Sheila sat forward again.

Dawn shook her head, then turned to look at the women. "It's different. I don't think it's real." She made a sound of frustration, unhappy with her own explanation.

The women were silent. Dawn looked at them again. "It doesn't feel like Shya at all," she said on an outbreath, then relaxed a bit. *That* was right.

Jane held a hand out for the notebook, which Dawn reluctantly gave. Then, the woman read. And at the end, all three agreed: the new poem *was* strange.

"What does this mean?" Sheila often spoke her questions as they came to her, and it was most times a relief, because she spoke what those around her were thinking, when they simply couldn't. "It – it doesn't even sound like the demon; it *references* the demon, even talks about Shya's possession, I think!" She looked to Jane. "Right?"

Jane's face remained passive, save her eyes, which jittered slightly in their sockets as she met the identical gaze of her twin in the rear-view mirror.

"It wasn't Shya. I agree," Anna said, making Dawn jump, then pull her focus back to the front to look at her. "And it focuses on their seeping into our plane."

"The shadows?"

"The darkness."

Sheila and Jane had responded simultaneously, with a question and a statement, respectively, but Jane's contribution seemed to satisfy Sheila's need for confirmation.

Anna put a hand up and continued, "But I don't think they could come through without Shya."

Now Dawn frowned. "Come through with the poem, or to our level of existence?"

"Both," the twins chorused, inciting gooseflesh to tighten and crawl along her arms.

"Dawn," Sheila strained to meet her friend's eyes, though she sat directly behind her. Dawn twisted, grateful someone else was carrying the conversation, for she was bereft of words for the moment. "I think you have to call your brother, Kenny. Or your sister."

Dawn knew her responding expression was likely reflective of her reaction – that Sheila was losing it - but seemed unable to stop it.

Sheila laughed. "I know. Random; sorry. But I have this feeling," she said, her fingers rubbing at her sternum.

Dawn had seen that look. Sheila's gut was uncannily on point, regardless of how out of left field it seemed to flow from.

"If your niece really is like you, maybe she could help interpret; help *receive* these messages, even, without a cloud of fear for Shya hanging over her." Sheila's fingers flew to her lips as soon as the words were out.

Despite the obvious regret on Sheila's face, though, Dawn gave her friend yet another disapproving look. "This ain't exactly an easy job, Sheila, and frankly I'm feeling rather less than confident about it, even without your doubt!"

Jane shook her head emphatically as she put a hand on Sheila's arm. Sheila's face, in its constant transparency, had revealed the hurt Dawn's words had caused, but Jane seemed bent on stemming her response. But it was to defend her. "She's right, Dawn. It's your perspective that interprets what she's saying as an attack."

Dawn opened her mouth to respond, but Jane merely shook her head.

"She's right, Dawn," Anna said.

Dawn flopped back into her seat, feeling rather childish. She didn't *want* them to be right. She hated that they were. But she nodded, because she knew Sheila had been bang on with one observation: she needed to contact her family, tell them she'd seen her niece, even remotely, and that she was headed for Dawn. How Charm was accomplishing that was a mystery to Dawn, given that Dawn was currently travelling, herself, but she knew it as well as she knew she'd been wrong to abandon her family for so many years.

She'd see her niece in person, and soon.

CHAPTER 27 – A STRANGE REUNION

Nothing felt right.

Dawn had slipped outside into the chill night air, using the excuse of calling her brother, but in truth it was to escape. Their group was a diminutive version of itself compared to the last time they'd gathered there, given Mel and Ed's absence, and they'd all been able to see Shya – her sleeping form, anyway – and touch her forehead, her face, her curling mass of dark hair, which continued to be the most animated part of her. They all spoke quiet words to her, too, some tearful despite the collective effort to bring positivity to their friend, only. It should have been a relief, all of it, but the air in the house was stifling, as though squeezed in a fist that meant to stymie them all… and their efforts.

And by all appearances, that intent had been successful where John and Rory were concerned. At least Rory still railed and complained as he paced, making suggestions and offering up theories about Shya's situation. *Everyone's* situation. Shya's father was different. Silent.

Defeated.

And Dawn couldn't look at Shya's bandaged wrists and swollen, bruised hands and forearms. She didn't need evidence of the woman's self-assault; her energy was saturated with that same dark, imposing energy that the house was. The oppression that said *"Stop. Don't try. Just let it be."* And Shya wanted to obey. She wanted to take it to the extreme, to stop for real.

Dawn had searched her friend's consciousness – what she was able to find – and grew all the more wary. Before, there was some relief, there. She'd assumed it was because Shya was with her mother, but now she questioned everything she'd assumed before. She felt no motherly presence at all. Felt no sense of triumph over saving little Jordan. There was a complete disconnect between Shya and anything that had felt like a saving grace at the start. Now, there was just despair.

She fiddled with the touchscreen on her phone, her eyes on the road. She half expected Charm to come into view, backpack flung over her shoulder and doggedly conquering the last part of her journey, but even if the girl had known to come here, Dawn couldn't fathom her knowing which house to visit. *She's probably in Toronto,* Dawn reasoned, picturing her pretty niece exploring the city in all of it's bright-lights splendor before she went to knock on Dawn's door.

Her heart thudded, and she realized the thought made her anxious. Charm had appeared to be thirteen, fourteen, maybe. Too young, in any case, to be in the city alone.

Giving herself a shake, she sucked in a breath and did the thing that seemed least difficult in the moment; she dialled Kenny. The irony twisted her mouth into a smirk. The one thing she'd sworn never to do, lest she tear apart the world she'd labored so hard to create, was now the preferred course of action.

It rang once.

"Dawn? Jesus," her little brother was off and running before she could even say hello. "We're pulling our hair out, here."

"We?" she asked. The first thing she'd said to any member of her family in years.

"Cadence is here. I mean, we're both at her house, holding down the fort just in case she comes back, but I don't think she will, sis. Not until she's found you. She's desperate."

Dawn had to unclench her teeth before she responded, noting her entire body had grown tight and cold. "Give her the phone."

"What?"

"I need to talk to her."

Kenny ignored the request. "Can you connect to her, Dawn? Even if you've never met her?"

She wanted to say it to Cadence, whose energy was nearly palpable, even at a distance. She wanted to soothe the woman who'd cared for her when their mother couldn't, who'd been her confidante and mentor. Who she'd shut out of her life in an extended fit of overwhelm and mistaken perception of betrayal.

She wanted to get this over with.

"She's coming to you. We know that. She's always known about you but now, things are changing for her. Getting harder for her, like they did for you at this age. She's gotten it into her head that learning from you is the only way for her to… to be OK!"

Dawn was listening to the slight Southern US twang they'd all picked up from their parents. Remembering some of her origin story. Putting reason to the way she herself spoke, besides being headstrong and priding herself on speaking her mind. And she was peering down the road, in the direction of Jordan's house, because someone was coming toward her. She reached out to feel their energy, but didn't recognize it. She breathed a sigh of relief.

"Dawn? Are you even there?" Her brother's voice had grown louder, and had a distinct edge to it.

Her eyes still on the approaching figure, whose silhouette was dark against the backdrop of a streetlight. "I'm here," she muttered. Maybe the energy *was* familiar.

"Don't do this, Dawn. You've called, now be here! Please!"

"I'm sorry," she responded, feeling Kenny's desperation. "I've seen her… in a vision. She was on a bus. She's OK."

She heard nothing, and then a muffled sob. Kenny was crying. She heard him cover the mouthpiece, then he was saying something, presumably to Cadence. "Kenny?" She stepped back from the road. The approaching figure was a woman, hands buried deep in the pockets of an oversized cardigan. She raised a hand as she neared, and Dawn gasped.

It was Bethie.

"Kenny? I don't have long. I need to speak to Cadence," she spoke in measured tone, deliberate and clear. She raised a hand to return Bethie's wave, then started toward her as the woman put some speed in her steps.

It was while the woman embraced her that Cadence's voice came over the phone, and Dawn found her eyes forced shut. The combination of Bethie's changed energy (which explained why Dawn couldn't identify her at first) and the sound of her once beloved sister's voice was too much for a moment.

"Dawn? Dawnie? Oh, God, thank you for returning the call. I know things have been…"

"No," Dawn cut in. Tears soaked her cheeks and Bethie's arms tightened, intuiting Dawn's need. She squeezed right back, patting Bethie's back with gratitude. "No. I'm – I'm so sorry," she cried.

"Aw," was all Cadence seemed able to say, and for a few moments, the three women let the situation, regardless of its clarity (especially for Bethie) pause, giving each other some time to just be.

Dawn pulled away slightly, smiling through her tears at a woman whose energy wasn't the only thing that had changed. Her once gaunt face had filled out. Dawn regarded her, head to foot, overcome with joy. She looked healthy. She *felt* happy. Things were good in her world, which meant they continued to be good for Jordan, and for Connor, too

"You look wonderful!" Dawn whispered, and Bethie wiped a tear of her own away.

She pointed to the phone, eyebrows raised, then to herself and then the house.

Dawn nodded.

"You do, too," Cadence cried at the other end, and Dawn laughed while Bethie jogged off to the house, giving her a wave before going in. Dawn recalled Rory saying Bethie had been a frequent presence since Shya… went away. Her chest filled with warmth.

She didn't correct her sister. "Cadence, Charm is alright, but do you know where she would've gone to find me? Because I'm not at home."

"She'll find you." Cadence didn't sound surprised.

"How?" Dawn scrunched up her face. If her niece was like her, GPS tracking wasn't part of the package.

"She's incredible, Dawn. *So* gifted. She's always felt you, knows your energy. She does know your address, but I have every confidence she'll redirect when she doesn't find you there."

Dawn shook her head. "She's tracking my location by… feeling me?"

"Yes."

Dawn rubbed at her forehead, amazed and confused at

once.

"But, Dawn, she's sick. She has epilepsy; absence seizures, mostly, and she takes medication to keep it under control, but she's had breakthrough seizures, too. Grand Mal."

Dawn suddenly felt like sitting down. She did, right there on the grass of Shya's childhood front yard. The cold dew of the grass dampened her pants right away, and it was an uncomfortable - and welcome - distraction.

"Dawn?"

"I'm here."

"She's been having more lately; absence, not Grand Mal. Her doctors are having a hard time adjusting her medication since she hit puberty. Apparently, that's common, but what they don't know is how it all affects Charm. Her gifts."

"And how is that?"

"Her seizures make her vulnerable, and lately, she's having visions. She comes out of her fits with stories of dreams. Nightmares. But that's not what they are. I know it."

Dawn squeezed her eyes shut again. "What is she seeing?"

"A door," Cadence replied. "A door ripped into the sky with lightning. Streams of it."

"Shit," Dawn muttered.

"Do you know what it is? Does it have something to do with all this stuff in the news? The weird weather? The suicides?"

Dawn nodded, then remembered she was on the phone and said, "Maybe."

Cadence made a noise of frustration. "Where are you?"

"I'm in Quebec. Aylmer."

"Why?"

"My friend... she needs help. She's trapped."

"It's all connected, isn't it?"

"Sounds like it." Dawn peered around herself, breathing deeply.

"I knew it."

"Should I go home?"

"No. Charm *will* find you. We've never given her your number, though she's begged for it, but if it's alright with you, we will, should she call."

"Of course."

"Thank you."

"Why didn't you before?"

Cadence fell quiet.

"You don't have to answer that. I *am* sorry, Cadence."

"I am, too. I was scared back then. Grasping at straws, afraid I'd be nothing without someone to take care of. If it helps, I want you to know that forgiving your father was the best thing I ever did for myself."

Dawn was shocked into silence. Cadence had forgiven him. For herself.

"I hope you're able to heal in that way, too."

Dawn shook her head. "Still taking care of me," she said quietly. Thinking, *even when her own child is missing.*

"I think I always will."

"I'll call if anything happens. Anything at all."

"Me, too."

"I guess it was Mom, huh?"

Cadence didn't answer.

"Who passed it down. This 'gift.'"

"Oh. Well, we've talked about that a lot. Apparently, her great-grandfather in Mississippi was a..."

"Please don't say 'witch doctor,'" Dawn managed a laugh.

"No!" Cadence laughed, too. "But he *was* a doctor. A very good one. People went to him for everything."

"Maybe a witch doctor, after all?"

"Or maybe just felt, or *saw* people so strongly that he knew just what they needed."

Dawn felt a puzzle piece click into place in a nearly-surreal moment of discovery. She couldn't help but wonder what life would have been like, had she discovered this earlier. With her family. "Oh, God," Dawn was crying again.

"Don't cry. We have time, don't we? We'll talk."

Love surged forth from whatever place she'd stored it for so many years. "I love you, Cadence."

She laughed. "I love you too, Dawnie. We all do. Um... but people are mad, too."

"I get it."

They sat in silence for several seconds.

"Dawn?"

"Hm?"

"Will she be alright?"

Dawn's stomach dropped. "I want to say 'yes', but it would be better if she was far away from what's going on, here, especially with her seizures. Nobody so vulnerable should be here. We're dealing with something dark. And, worse, it's clever." She bit her tongue before she told her the demon had already taken one bright soul, and would certainly like a backup.

"Oh," Cadence breathed, and then she was muttering to Kenny, bringing him up to speed.

"I'll do everything I can to get her back to you and away from here, if I have to get on a plane with her, myself."

"We're only in Stratford."

Dawn grimaced. So close to her. And yet only as close as Dawn had allowed. They may as well have been across the world.

CHAPTER 28 – BIPOLAR

Rory, Bethie and Dawn were still gathered around Shya's bed long after the remainder of the group had left for the British Hotel. Dawn took comfort in that the hotel was only a short distance away; even at a walk it would take twenty minutes, tops, to reach her friends, should it be required.

John had retired to bed early, seemingly relieved to have a stand-in in Dawn, where keeping vigil over Shya was concerned. Dawn had watched him as he left the room, feet dragging. His entire countenance appeared weighed-down, and it was easy to know why.

Despite the heaviness of the situation, though, the three who remained seated around Shya's unconscious form had managed a comfortable reunion. Bethie had updated Dawn on Jordan and Connor, to whom she was engaged to be married the following summer. Shya, of course, would be maid of honor.

Bethie was determined it would be so, and nobody seemed willing to suggest any different.

Rory had begun to work again after a brief sabbatical, and regaled them of the more interesting clients he'd been dealing with – all remained nameless, of course. Rory was nothing if not professional. But even as he joked and entertained, Dawn could not deny the dullness of the man's eyes. He was gorgeous, still, but a certain spark was missing from his easy charm. Touching his spirit confirmed it: Rory was sad. And keeping up appearances of normalcy had become a chore whose importance was dwindling of late.

Dawn tried, too. She opened up to the two, and to Shya, too, for she *was* with them in a fashion. Dawn's inward assertion that the woman could still surface, could still connect, only grew as she spent time next to her still form. Maybe it was the shock of the changes with her family, or just the effects of Shya's possession on the people here in Aylmer that kept her company, but Dawn found herself to be sharing more easily. Letting people in.

Maybe, too, it was Mel's absence. He and Ed should be updating the group sometime early in the morning, but just on their flight and arrival in Tibet. What came next was still a mystery. It had been one day since she'd been in Mel's presence, but she felt his distance keenly. It was as if her connection to him – his spirit – had fallen quiet when he left bodily, and she didn't like it. She could connect to Ed with just a thought. He was still a little pissed, still desperate to help Shya, still wholly uncertain that he'd done the right thing by getting on the plane. But Mel – Mel felt *closed off.*

He *had* been a little strange lately. Self-doubt and helplessness had seemed to change him in some fundamental way, and his stubborn determination to take responsibility for Shya's situation never flagged.

So, she needed that phone call. She needed to talk to Ed, to make him understand and have him watch Mel for her. It would give Ed a welcome distraction, too.

"Dawn?"

She roused herself, flicking her gaze to Bethie, who was smiling at her. "Sorry; what?"

"I was just saying I need to get back. I asked if you and the rest of the group have a plan."

Dawn sat up straight, nodding. "We're going to do some exploring; see if we can gather more information, especially on how things have changed since we've seen Shya… where she is now, I mean."

Rory's face was dark.

"Ror?" Dawn reached for his hand and he stared at it as though wondering what it was, then reached back, putting his face in the other hand. It happened so fast: his pain surged into her, radiating up her arm like a shock and then settling in her chest and squeezing at her heart. "Oh," she cried, then pulled her chair closer to him so they could embrace. They leaned heavily into each other, crying openly.

After several moments, during which Bethie had stood and put her arms around both of them, Rory sniffled loudly and swiped at his cheeks. Dawn pulled away, sniffling, too. She met Bethie's eyes, also red and shining in the dim light from the bedside lamp, and let out a little laugh.

Rory peered at them as if they were crazy. His expression was one of such confusion that Dawn laughed some more. He looked at her, wide-eyed. "I try not to cry in here," he said, his face a blank, then let out a surprised guffaw. And that was it; they were all laughing through tears, grabbing each other for support.

"I haven't done this in so long!" Bethie wailed as they started to wind down, sending them all into peels of laughter all over again.

Dawn was breathless when she finally sat back in her chair. The room was considerably lighter. "I think I needed that," she said, her voice high.

Rory was looking at Shya again, a small smile still at his lips. He truly was a beautiful man. Dawn took his hand again, and followed his gaze. Shya looked the same, in seeming defiance of the changes in her company. It was more sobering than Dawn had anticipated, and shortly she was wiping a fresh tear from her cheek. She let herself cry in silence, though, squeezing Rory's hand.

"She's so beautiful," Bethie said, tears running fresh for her, too.

Rory put his face in his hands, leaving Dawn's cooling in his absence. Unable to acclimate, she found herself standing and going to Bethie on the other side of the bed, and hugging her sideways. She put a hand on Rory's shoulder. She remembered to block his despair first, though. She was full to overflowing with sadness already.

Some time later, after they'd all gone quiet, Bethie whispered. "Can I be here when you guys go in tomorrow?"

Dawn was momentarily flummoxed by the terminology, but quickly realized what she meant and nodded. "The more love she's surrounded with, the better."

Bethie gave Dawn a final squeeze, then moved to hug Rory. "Just let us know when?"

Dawn shot Bethie a stern look. "'Us?' You're not bringing Jordan in here. He can't be exposed!"

She shook her head. "Of course not. Even Connor stays away, for fear he'll bring something back," she tried to chuckle, but it ended in a soft sob.

"Oh, Bethie. I'm sorry," Dawn took a step toward the woman, but she waved the apology away.

"It's alright, Dawn, I know you're just being careful," she managed a smile. She tapped Rory's shoulder and he turned halfway. "Maybe you and John should get out while we… sit with her, tomorrow," she said. "Get some much-needed time away."

Rory shrugged almost imperceptibly and went back to staring at Shya.

Dawn caught her eyes and nodded. A silent bid of support.

Bethie waved her fingers, then stopped short mid-turn. “Oh! Your niece! If she’s here, will she take part?”

Dawn frowned. The two situations – that of her blood relatives and the other of The Seers, those who’d become the family of her heart - refused to coalesce in her mind. She shook her head. “No way.”

Bethie nodded. “She can stay with us if you want to keep her from all of this. Might be good for her to be so close, but not involved, you know?”

Dawn swallowed a lump in her throat, remembering Sheila and the twins’ assertions that Charm could be of help. *Only from a distance,* Dawn inwardly decided in that moment.

She wouldn’t lose two family members to this beast.

CHAPTER 29 – NIGHT TERRORS

Dawn woke suddenly.

The basement was pitch dark, which was fine with her. She slept better that way. But for a moment she was disoriented, bits of the dream she'd been having still clinging to her as she surfaced. She had to smile though. *A normal dream,* she thought, with gratitude.

Her phone's indicator flashed blue, explaining what had woken her. But just then, there was another sound, too, from upstairs. A dull thud, a shuffle, then muffled footsteps, as though padded. Dawn thought of the slippers she'd seen on Rory's side of he and Shya's bed. *He must be going to the washroom,* she thought, but as she reached for her phone, her stomach somersaulting in anticipation over a text from Mel, another thought occurred to her; she hadn't even thought to look for Shya's bloodied scratchings in the bedroom. She frowned. Surely she would've noticed them, had they been there, though. Had the men repainted in such a short time?

She flipped to her texts, shaking her head. *John said she'd scratched right through the wallpaper. No way did they re-paper the walls.* Her stomach dropped. She thought of the last poem she'd written in the notebook Mel had bought her. Of the imposters. And then of Shya's bandaged wrists. It *had* happened, but where was the evidence. Her mind raced as she opened a text from Mel. But then she stopped thinking entirely.

Mel: Hey babe. Safely landed and bedding down for some shuteye.

We're both well and will head to the monastery tomorrow...or later today, I guess. Be in touch after that.

She stared at the words, which were fine by themselves. But no matter how she reached, she felt no emotion attached to them.

He's tired.

The padded steps had started up again on the upper level.

She reread the words. Considered calling... but no; they'd be tired. A text popped up from Ed, making her jump.

Big Ed: I'm sure Mel's already let you know, but we made it. Please let me know how things are going there. Any changes?

A drawer opened in the kitchen, followed by the sounds of rummaging. Rather loud sounds. She frowned toward the stairs, wondering if she should call out for Rory. She started replying to Ed, determined to inspire a sense of calm in the man, then hopefully find out what was up with Mel.

Dawn: Not much has changed. It's sad here, my friend. I'm thinking you and Mel are on the lighter side of things right now, if one exists. How are you? And what about Mel? How has he been?

She stared at her reply without sending it, knowing it was odd to ask Ed how Mel was, when she could simply reply to...

More drawers were being opened upstairs. The rifling was getting frantic. She put her phone down and stood, reaching out for the energy that was in the kitchen. Afraid, suddenly, that it wasn't Rory. And perhaps for the first time in a very long while, the gooseflesh that broke out on her arms was due to that pure, unadulterated fear you experience as a child when you are alone and realize you might be in trouble.

"Rory?" She called out the name, half to reassure herself that the energy she felt was not as strange as she might have presumed. Hoping John would answer, tell her with a laugh that he couldn't find the band-aids or find a pen. And the other half called his name to wake him, because the energy *was* strange.

But if she was afraid before she'd called out, the reply chilled her to the bone. A woman's voice echoed back to her, "Rory?"

And then again, but more drawn out, with a high-pitched giggle at the end, *"Where are you, Rory?"*

"Shit," Dawn whispered. She wanted to call out again, but she was frozen. Listening.

The rifling, which had paused, started up again, and for some reason, she breathed out a sigh of relief.

Because you were afraid it was coming down, her inner voice taunted. She shook her head. *It?*

There was another sound, now. A high-pitched muttering to accompany the sounds of the drawers being ransacked. But it was only when things started hitting the floor that Dawn's joints seemed to unlock and she was bolting for the stairs.

"Rory!" That time she screamed it.

She heard the drawer-rifler run from the kitchen as she rounded the stairs at the landing. By the time she reached the kitchen, the only evidence someone had been there was the state of the floor, and the drawers and cupboards that hung open, having had their contents spilled out haphazardly.

The light to the bathroom flicked on, and Dawn immediately started down the hallway, only to instantly halt, a hand flying to her mouth to stifle the scream that rose there upon discovering another figure at the other end. It was a man; not Rory, he was too stocky. *John!*

Shya's father raised a finger to his lips, then pointed

to the bathroom, where sounds similar to those that had accompanied the disaster that was now the kitchen had started up again.

The pause, along with a commiserate presence, allowed Dawn to realize fully that the person they stalked was Shya. Her breath hitched when the muttering started again. And at the close proximity, she could hear the words, though Shya's voice was barely recognizable.

"Where, where?" She was saying. And, "Oh, please, I have to hurry."

John took a couple steps forward, and Dawn met his eyes as they became visible in the light of the bathroom. They regarded each other, both helpless, both desperate.

Both realizing Rory was nowhere to be seen.

"Yes!" surged a triumphant cry from the bathroom as the rifling stopped, but the voice was stranger, still, twinned somehow with a deeper resonance.

Dawn recognized it.

"Blood, blood, blood," she began to chant, Shya's voice twisting with that gravelly, deep one, and John burst forth, screaming, "*No!*"

Dawn was on his heels when they found her, sitting in the corner, against the tub and the wall, smiling gleefully at the straight-razor she'd pressed against her bandaged wrists.

She whipped her head up to growl at them, like a lioness warning hyenas away from her cub, and her eyes were dark and hollow, her lips cracked and bleeding as they stretched around bared teeth.

"Shya!" Dawn cried, and the woman's features went slack as she peered blankly at Dawn. John lunged for the razor, which was given up without a fight, and Shya went limp in the blink of an eye. Dawn knelt beside her, crying and gasping, feeling the woman's ice-cold neck for a pulse, then taking her head into her lap, cradling her, murmuring over the rough, red patch on her cheek where her feeding tube was usually taped.

"Oh, God," John muttered, his voice barely there. Dawn peered up at him; he was squatted over the women, now, hands spread open and covered with blood.

Shya had given the blade up easily, but John had grabbed for it expecting a fight, and now it lay embedded across a palm, oozing blood on both sides of the blade. He looked at her. All the colour on his hands was contrasted by the little that was left in his cheeks. "Sit down," she ordered, the hand that was not cradling Shya's head pressing down on his forearm, gently.

He obeyed robotically, his eyes on his gushing hand.

"Shit," Dawn said again. Her heart sped up as she considered her options. No matter which way she figured it, it came down to this: she needed help. Suddenly remembering Rory, she yelled his name again.

John looked at her as though shocked. "Where is he?"

Dawn shook her head.

And then there was a muffled cry from the bedroom.

The woman in her arms begun to laugh.

Dawn peered down into the face of her friend, suddenly stiff, fighting the urge to push the woman away and run, just run from the beast that smiled up at her through her dark eyes. Somehow, Shya's face was slack, and yet smiling, her mouth pulled up at the corners, stretching cheeks that slept on. And the eyes, deep and black and endless, no whites to be seen, like Jordan's had been.

"What did you do?" she asked it. Too loud, because it was repulsive to look into its eyes from so intimate a distance.

The smile vanished, and again the cheeks stayed slack.

The mouth moved as if independent from the muscles of her face when it replied, calling "Rory?" in Dawn's voice, so perfect it was nauseating, and not just for her. John leaned over and vomited unceremoniously as he cradled his injured hand to his chest. Blood ran down his white t-shirt. Dawn did put Shya down, then, and backed away. The demon in her watched her go, making grotesque shapes with its mouth as though it had perceived how it mortified her. She tore her gaze away and looked at John, who was back against the tub, breathing fast, and looking like he'd faint any moment. She stopped, thinking twice, and went back to the man. She squatted, avoiding the puddle of stomach contents deftly, and reaching for his badly bleeding hand. He offered it after a moment of consideration, then closed his eyes, as if anticipating something unpleasant and bearing no strength to stop it.

She did it quick. She opened his palm and pulled on the blade, which surprised her by refusing to disengage, and pulled again, hard, feeling it slip free with the thought, *Oh, God it hit bone; it was stuck in his bones.*

She glanced at Shya, whose face was her own again, and back to sleeping. She looked so fragile, so pale. She reached for a towel and wrapped the blade in it with haste, then grabbed another and wound it tightly around John's wounded hand. He grimaced and groaned, but did not open his eyes, and when he failed to respond to her urgings to put pressure on the wound, she knew he'd passed out.

She pressed the towelled hand beneath the man's thigh with some effort. Sweat beaded on her lip and tasted salty as she used one hand to lift his leg and the other to push the towelled hand beneath the weight of it.

A low, rumbling chuckle erupted from Shya, and Dawn stood again, backing out of the room. Shya's face showed no signs of consciousness, even as the laughter grew louder and then doubled, then tripled, and changed. Dawn's features stretched as she was consumed with fear. It was her own laughter coming from Shya's throat. Hers, and Rory's, and Bethie's.

She ran. The basement was first, though she'd tell The Seers later that she hadn't consciously planned it that way. She'd been thinking of Rory, but she'd been hearing him, too. He was alive... she knew that, so she ran to the basement to get her phone and dial 911.

She was spitting out the address as she ran back upstairs and down the hall, only glancing into the bathroom where John and Shya slept on in silence, for the laughter had quieted and now Rory's distress was louder.

"An ambulance is on the way," the male voice at the other end assured her. "Can you tell me what's happened?"

Dawn actually laughed.

"Ma'am?"

"Sorry," she breathed. She was standing at the end of Shya and Rory's bed, looking between him and the wall. "I – it's complicated. There are three people. One has a very deep cut across his palm and is bleeding heavily. He's passed out."

"And the other two?"

Dawn went to Rory and pulled the gag from his mouth. Still, he didn't speak. He just shook his head *no.*

She frowned down at him as she struggled to untie him with her free hand. He shook his head again.

"The other two are alright, I think," she said quietly.

She pressed the phone between her cheek and shoulder and attacked the knots with renewed fervor. Rory *was* OK. He was just... compromised. And Shya – well Shya couldn't be helped by paramedics, cops or firefighters.

"Ma'am? There's an officer at the door. Can you let him

in?"

Rory was helping her with the second knot, his first hand having been freed. Dawn noted the cloth that had been used. It appeared to match the sheets. She absently pulled the covers back and confirmed it: Shya had torn strips from the sheets to both tie and gag Rory before going in search of a blade.

"Jesus."

"Ma'am?"

Rory was free and running. He spun, pointing at Dawn and then to the door, and then he disappeared into the bathroom.

"I'm here," she said. "I'm going to the door, now."

"Alright. You can hang up, now. I wish you the best."

She moved as if through molasses, peering sideways into the bathroom, where Rory was gathering the limp Shya into his arms and John seemed to be waking, his eyes blinking slowly. She looked back as she reached the stairs. Rory was disappearing into the bedroom and closing the door, no doubt to lay Shya in the bed so she wouldn't be implicated, or even considered.

She wondered if he'd put the tube back in. Or if he'd pretend to have slept through it all.

But most of all, she wondered how he'd explain the words scratched into the wallpaper with bloodied fingernails, or if he'd have time to retape the matching sheet of wallpaper back over it again before anyone could see.

CHAPTER 30 – IMMINENT ARRIVAL

"Aunt Dawn? Is that really you?"

She'd only just discovered the existence of her niece, but somehow her voice felt familiar. "It is. Charm, I'm very happy to be talking to you."

The girl sighed. "You *are* sweet. I knew you would be. Mom's always said I had to wait for you to reach out, but I couldn't wait anymore! I knew you wouldn't be angry. I knew you'd help me… you *will* help me, won't you, Auntie Dawn? I'm so confused." The girl finally took a breath, but it was a shaky one and followed by inevitable tears.

Despite her sense of overwhelm, Dawn found herself tearing up in response. Could she be so connected to her niece already? She took a breath, eyes closed. Focused on the cold, rough concrete of Shya's family's front step beneath her bottom, which was quickly going numb. Still, she'd rather be outside than in, where the exhausted Rory sat resolutely beside Shya's bed, staring ineffectually at his laptop as he tried to catch up on some files. "Charm, I *am* glad to talk to you, and I promise I'll do what I can to help you get hold of your gifts; God knows your mother did that for me when I was young."

"She told me," the girl interrupted, her voice high.

"Where are you right now, sweetheart?"

The girl sniffled loudly into the phone. "I'm at your condo."

Dawn's jaw dropped. "What?"

She giggled. "Not inside! I mean, I found your extra key in that magnetic box you hid behind the hallway radiator?"

"Uh-huh," was all Dawn could get out.

"But I wanted to talk to you before going in, you know? I'm not a *criminal*!" She laughed again, then sniffled through tears that hadn't quite petered out.

"Charm..."

"Is it OK if I go in? I couldn't get a hotel room, even if I paid cash, isn't that ridiculous? Oh, just a sec."

Dawn perceived some altered breathing from the other end. She imagined Charm unlocking her front door. "Um, Charm, before you go in..."

"Huh? Oh, no, don't worry, I wasn't going in. Just a little seizure. I'm taking my medication, but all this excitement..."

"You just had a seizure?" Dawn's voice had escalated significantly.

"It's alright! It was just a little one. I call them 'blips,' but the correct term is 'absence seizure,'" she finished, deepening her voice and making an effort to sound professional, just for the last couple of words.

"You need to call your mother!" Dawn protested, entirely certain she wouldn't get a word in edgewise if she didn't demand it.

"Aw, come on," Charm started.

"No." Dawn made an effort to lower her voice, but she inwardly rejoiced at how firm the word had come out. "Your family is terrified you'll be hurt, or get lost. You *have* to call them."

She sighed. "I know. I just wanted to get here, first, so I could tell them I found you."

"But I'm not there!" Dawn's voice was uncharacteristically high. She inwardly noted that her decision not to have children was looking pretty much validated at that moment.

"I know, but *they* don't know that, do they?"

She's smart and *sneaky!*

"Actually, they do. I've been talking to them."

"What?" the girl's disappointment couldn't have been more obvious.

"Of course, they contacted me! They're freaking out!" Dawn frowned. She'd need to reign it in a bit if she was going to get anywhere with her niece. She closed her eyes again, wishing she could just be home, just for the half-hour it would take to get Charm onto a bus back home. *She'd never go,* her inner voice pointed out, and she clenched her jaw. It was true.

"But you haven't spoken to anyone in *years!*" Every sentence uttered by the girl seemed buoyed by a generous sense of drama.

"How old are you?" Dawn asked.

Momentarily derailed, Charm replied, "What?" and then, "Thirteen. Almost fourteen, though."

Dawn rolled her eyes, then rubbed at her forehead. She was a baby. "Charm, please let me say something, OK?"

"Can I go inside first? I gotta pee, and if I don't get into your bathroom, there'll forever be an unpleasant reminder of my visit in the form of a nasty-smelling stain outside your front door."

Dawn covered her mouth to stifle a laugh. "Go," she managed between her fingers, then angled her cell away from her mouth so she could let out the trapped air of her mirth in a quiet "*puh!*" sound.

"Oh, thank you. Just a sec; I'm going to put the phone under my arm, but I won't hang up. If I do, though, I'll just call you back. Thank *God* you still use this number. I was so afraid I'd get here and not be able to even get in touch with you. I knew you wouldn't be here; I could feel that, you know?"

"Charm!"

"Huh?" There was the sound of a door opening, and then shutting again moments later.

"Uh – lock the door," she blurted, though the fleeting thought was far from what she needed to say to the girl.

"There, done! Don't worry; I know how to take care of myself. I took home alone classes and babysitting, too, and also an emergency action course given at the local grocery store; weird, huh?"

Dawn was beginning to wonder if Charm's promise to put the phone away for a moment would ever be fulfilled.

"Be right back," Charm muttered, and then there was rustling, followed by the unmistakeable sounds of the girl releasing her bladder. "Aaaah, oh, man, that's better," the girl's somewhat distant voice exclaimed, and Dawn was smothering her laughter again. Sounds of hand-washing were next.

"Charm!" she said again. A car was advancing toward the house, and she recognized it as the rental. She stood. "I only have a minute, Charm."

"Oh! Sorry. Anyway, I know you're in Gatineau, but I'm not sure *where*, exactly."

It took a few seconds of silence for Dawn to realize it was her turn to talk, and she jumped on it, afraid it would be taken back just as suddenly as it had been given. "Don't come here!"

"What?"

Silence again.

"No! I mean, I want to meet you. I'm really looking forward to it, actually! But things here are... dangerous."

The girl's voice took on a darker tone. "I know. I can feel it. But you don't need to worry, like I sai -"

"This is no joke, Charm. And your family is going nuts. You need to go home! I promise I'll come to see you when this... business, is taken care of, here. But you shouldn't be around it;

you're too vulnerable."

The girl's breathing was the only answer.

Unwilling to waste the opportunity, Dawn continued. "Charm, I've apologized to your mother and uncle for all the time I've been so…"

"Gone?" Charm supplied.

The twins and Sheila were getting out of the car. Dawn paced in the opposite direction. "Yes. And I *am* sorry. To you, too. I mean to make up for it. But right now..."

"It's not a good time?"

Dawn nodded, inhaling the cool air deeply. "Right." She turned to see the twins disappearing into the house. Sheila, however, was sitting herself down on the step, where Dawn's numb lower cheeks had been seconds earlier. She met her eyes and pointed at the phone, mouthing, "*Charm.*"

Sheila nodded, but stayed put.

"Well, frankly, Aunt Dawn, I don't care."

Dawn frowned at the phone. "What?"

"I don't want to be rude to you, but I figure you sort of owe it to me to forgive me if I can't help it."

Dawn remained speechless.

"I'm only thirteen, but you need to understand that I've needed you *my whole life*, and you haven't been there."

"But..."

"No. You *haven't* been there for me, so now, when things are harder than they've ever been, you're going to meet me in person. You're going to sit down and listen to me. And then, you're going to help me."

"Ch -"

"*No!*"

Dawn's mouth snapped shut. Her young niece was doing

the thing no one in their family ever had: she was calling Dawn on her bullshit. She was forcing her to take responsibility. And goddamn it if it didn't feel *good.* Tears filled her eyes and she remembered Sheila. She shook her head at her friend's concerned expression.

"This time, you aren't running, and I don't care what you've got going on there. In fact, I think I can help. I've been seeing things… dreaming of a dark-haired woman. Really pretty."

"Shya," Dawn whispered, then covered her mouth again. She'd been determined not to divulge anything to her niece.

"I'm coming. And I *will* find you, even if you refuse to help me. And, Dawn?"

"Huh?" Dawn swallowed the ball of shame her niece had served up, and felt well-chastised.

"*I* decide when we're done."

"Shit," Dawn muttered before covering her mouth again.

Charm laughed. It was a relief to hear.

She let out a long breath of defeat. "OK, kiddo. You're right. And I don't know how to convince you otherwise."

"You can't."

"But there are conditions. I'm the adult, here, and I have a responsibility to your mother, too."

There was a pause, then a reluctant, "OK?"

"You won't stay where I'm staying. The – everything is happening here, and it's enough to turn *my* hair white. You'll stay just up the street, with some close friends."

"Fine," Charm replied, and her voice was lighter, perhaps with the recognition that she'd won.

Dawn went on, "And you'll call your mother."

Charm sighed.

"That's it, girl. That's the last one. I'm not asking much."

"And you'll give me the address?"

Dawn inhaled through her nostrils. She went to the step and sat beside Sheila, needing the support, and hoping for a little warmth, too. Winter wouldn't wait much longer, that was clear in how day was transitioning to night with a dependable shock of chill in the air. Sheila, however, was cold, as she always seemed to be. "God, why you gotta be so willowy," Dawn whispered over the phone. Sheila smiled and put her thin arm around Dawn, hugging her tight. She raised the phone again and said, "I'll give you the address for the friends up the street. That's all I can do, Charm. And I'll come see you as soon as you arrive."

The silence was a relief. Dawn leaned into her friend, simultaneously grateful for her presence and dreading retelling the story of the previous night's events, which was exactly what her group was expecting.

"OK," came the reply, finally, from the rather resolute-sounding teen on the other end. "Can I eat this bread?"

Dawn shook her head, thrown again. "What bread?"

"The stuff on the counter." There was some rustling. "Got any peanut butter?"

Dawn couldn't help it; she laughed. "Try the cupboard above the sink, to the right."

"Ah! Thanks. What else you got?"

Dawn smiled. "You can eat whatever you find... oh! Just not the Tupperware with pasta in it, top shelf of the fridge."

"You want it?"

"No! I just... don't know how old it is and have been reluctant to deal with it." She said it fast, her cheeks burning a little with the admission.

Charm giggled. "OK. Can I sleep in your bed?"

"Guest room to the right of the bathroom."

"Ah, I saw that one. OK, cool. See you tomorrow, Auntie."

"I'll text you the address."

"Cool."

Charm hung up. Dawn held the phone in front of her herself, staring at it with a puzzlement that Sheila couldn't help but laugh at.

"First conversation with the niece?"

Dawn nodded and lowered her phone, shivering. "Let's go in." She started to rise.

Sheila touched her arm, and Dawn sat, eyeing her. "I *know* you ain't warm, girl!" Sheila smiled, but it was shaky, and Dawn suddenly wondered why the woman hadn't gone in in the first place. "What's wrong?"

She shook her head. "Nothing! Well, not nothing. I – I heard from Ed. I think he met the Bodhisatta today... or he will soon. He was cryptic," she frowned.

Dawn nodded. "I know; apparently they've been sworn to silence, or the whole thing is off."

Sheila nodded her head.

"Is that all?" Dawn was shivering and bordering on impatient.

"Ed's worried about Mel," Sheila spat, then pressed her lips together as if to halt the words that had already spilled out.

Dawn repositioned herself to face the woman. "Why? I mean, I've been a little worried, too, but I don't know what's going on. He hasn't even called me; just sent a text last night."

"Ed said he was really quiet on the whole trip there. And that he's been having private meetings with the monks that he says have nothing to do with why they went there, but he won't tell him what they *are* about."

Dawn scrunched up her face.

"I know," Sheila nodded, taking Dawn's hands in her

frigid ones. "Ed thought it would be best not to tell you, in case you got too worried to focus, you know?"

Dawn squeezed her hands. "Thank you for doing it anyway."

The dark-blonde-haired woman nodded, looking unsure. "I didn't tell Ed anything about last night. I wanted to know all the details first." Guilt was written all over her face.

"That's for the best, hon. You made the right choice, there."

Sheila nodded, but still looked unsure.

"Let's go in," Dawn said, standing and pulling the woman up with her.

"What's happening with Charm?"

"I'll meet her tomorrow, if all goes to plan," Dawn sighed heavily. "She's agreed to stay with Connor and Bethie, so at least there's that." They entered the house.

Sheila hugged her sideways in the narrow entryway. "You're not alone, Dawn. We're all here to help." She pulled away to meet Dawn's eyes. "I would love to go with you to meet her, tomorrow."

Dawn, warmed by the sentiment and the offer, turned to the woman and embraced her fully. "Thank you," she said. But she couldn't deny, even inwardly, as she had been so skilled at doing in regards to her own family, that she feared the guilt would be too much if she took anyone's full attention from the task at hand.

Shya wouldn't suffer as a result of Dawn's actions… or inaction, come to think of it.

She'd do anything to make sure of it.

CHAPTER 31 – SWEPT AWAY

The group sitting vigil around Shya's unconscious form was a somber one, indeed. They'd rehashed the night's happenings, the twins and Sheila staring with confusion and shock toward Shya's now unmoving figure.

Dawn looked to the twins. "Why is this happening, and why only at night?"

"Does the demon sleep?" Rory leaned forward, clasping his hands between his knees. Sheila reached over and rubbed Rory's stubbly jaw, making him jump and rear back to look her way, as though he'd forgotten she was there.

"You need sleep," Sheila said, in that honest, unassuming way that only she could.

Rory stared at her for a few uncomfortable seconds before collapsing toward her, crying again in the continuance of a seemingly unending stream of despair.

The twins were both standing and bending over the two in a flash. Dawn seemed rooted to her chair, watching her loved ones with growing anxiety. Even the twins were crying, their façade of calm control momentarily diminished. Dawn wondered over their pale, pale eyes and how they shimmered through their tears. Bereft, she turned to look at Shya, whose face was impossibly serene, considering the state of her visitors.

"We have to do this," she muttered. She looked at her friends, who were separating as if in a daze, their eyes on Dawn in confusion. "Don't you see what's happening?"

Her friends peered at each other, faces blank.

"It's changing us! Making us feel hopeless!"

Jane seemed to wake up. She shook Anna's shoulder until they were gazing into each other's eyes; mirror images of awakening souls.

In Sheila, Dawn perceived only a burgeoning sense of fear, surging forth with the realization that they were being manipulated by dark forces. She whipped her head to look at Shya, then the twins, then Dawn, to whom she exclaimed, "Oh, my God." Then she turned to Rory, who was still slumped and crying, now into his hands. She shook his shoulder, saying his name. "We need to see Shya!" She placed herself directly in front of him, her hands on both shoulders. "We need to show it we won't be stopped."

Rory had roused enough to give Sheila another look of puzzlement.

"It's drowning you!" Sheila bent to force eye contact. "Don't get sucked down, or you could end up trapped where *she* is!"

Dawn inhaled sharply. She hadn't realized that conclusion; she'd only considered the fact that they'd be discouraged into inaction, not that they'd be trapped, as well.

Rory's eyes seemed to flash, some spark of recognition emerging at the truth of Sheila's words. He turned to Dawn. "What do we do?"

Dawn was thrown for yet another loop; Rory was assuming he'd be part of the circle as they tried to contact Shya.

A great wave of relief rolled over her when Anna stepped in, but it was quickly stymied by surprise as the woman spoke. She leaned forward, saying, "Why shouldn't he be involved? He can ground us, like Mel did," she asserted, her strange eyes dancing between their faces, shuddering rather more than Dawn was used to. She resisted the slight grimace that fought to emerge. The twins had explained that their condition was barely noticeable to them, so nobody witnessing it should worry for their comfort. But on the rare occasion that their eyes were especially animated, Dawn herself was uncomfortable, and struggled to know just where to focus. But now, Dawn was distracted by Anna's comment about Mel in past tense, as though his absence could not only be replaced by any average person, but that his participation in the group's activities was something relegated to the past. Anna met her eyes again briefly, and Dawn registered something new; the twins knew something about what was going on with Mel.

"Dawn?" Jane reached across Shya's legs to touch her hand. "Do you agree?"

Dawn struggled to recall the conversation.

"I *should* be part of it," Rory cut in, then cleared his throat, as though even his voice was emerging from the funk he'd been so ensconced within. Dawn studied him.

"You need a break," she said quietly.

He shook his head. "Does *she* get a break?" He gestured a bit wildly toward the sleeping woman that was his love.

Dawn struggled again. The man was a mess. He'd been tied up and gagged by the very woman he referred to, rendered useless, as he'd exclaimed to the woman as they went through the events for those lucky enough to have been asleep at the time. And Dawn knew he hadn't slept since. Besides which, she'd committed to assisting Bethie in getting the man out of the house, even if only with a look.

Sheila leaned toward her now, from the opposite side of Rory. "The only way he's going to relax is if he can *do* something to help."

She was right. Dawn looked at Jane, the only one who hadn't spoken for either option. She nodded immediately.

"OK," Dawn said. She looked at her watch again, the undercurrent of Charm's impending arrival a constant distraction. Then she met their eyes again, each of them. "We stick together. We *only* communicate with Shya, and it's going to be hard to know what's her and what's not." Her eyebrows rose as she asked wordlessly for their understanding. Each of them nodded. She reached for Jane's hand, and watched as the action went around their little circle, Jane to Anna, Anna to Sheila, Sheila to Rory, and Rory closing the circle by Taking Dawn's remaining hand.

He met her eyes at the same time. "What should I do?"

"You should think of yourself as a guardian, keeping watch." Dawn held his gaze as she spoke. "Try not to break contact," she nodded to their hands, which she wouldn't even have mentioned, had it just been The Seers. It was more important for newcomers and inexperienced participants for them to retain a physical connection.

Rory nodded as he pressed his lips together.

Dawn looked at Sheila. "You gonna raise a shield, girl?"

A flash of joy crossed the woman's face. It was the first time Dawn had brought it up. Sheila would have, had she not, but Dawn saw the appreciation in her friend's face and realized how good it felt to consider everyone. A hot well of tears sprung to her eyes, made of regret. And a rogue thought that found it's way through, even as they prepared to begin: *What if I've been selfish in my relationship with Mel, too? Like with my family? What if he's taking the opportunity to run?*

Anna cleared her throat and Dawn shook herself back to the present, heat pooling in her cheeks. She inhaled deeply. "Let's go," she said, her voice newly steady, and the three women closed their eyes while Rory watched, alert and ready for trouble, though if asked, he'd have to admit he hadn't a clue what he'd do if trouble did hit.

CHAPTER 32 – A ROUGH LANDING

They were on the rocky shoreline.

Dawn gasped to realize it; she hadn't meant to go there, even alone, but as she peered around herself to regroup, she saw that Jane, Anna and Sheila were there, too, with various expressions of shock on their faces as they registered their surroundings.

"Should we go back?" Sheila's wide eyes met hers.

Dawn wasn't sure *how* they'd accomplish it, but she nodded. This could lead to nothing good. But the assertion was already too late, for the twins were pointing toward the water. It was instinct for Dawn to follow their gazes, not a decision, and Sheila followed suit.

It wasn't something new to Dawn. Nonetheless, the rough waves, the odd, perpetual twilit state of the light, as though that moment between sunset and pitch-black night was on pause, lending everything its own eerie glow. It was reminiscent of that strange atmosphere during a solar eclipse, when a thin vein of fear hums below the excitement of the event. The soul's recognition of something new. Something that is entirely different, and therefore may be a threat.

But it was the figure that had drawn the twins' attention. Silhouetted against the form of the monstrous tree rooted just at the water's edge, was the unmistakeable form of their friend. It was Shya, dark in the forever-waning light, and she was walking away from them and toward the tree.

Sheila began to run immediately.

Dawn estimated the dark form of their friend to be a hundred feet away at most, but it was hard to be sure; in addition to the sucking shadow of the tree, Shya was weaving side to side and lurching, her outline not quite solid. She seemed to pulsate, almost, as if she grew to be closer and then faded further away from one moment to the next.

The twins ran after Sheila.

Sheila was screaming for Shya. The urgency in her cries struck a note of panic in Dawn, and suddenly, she was moving forward, too, though she couldn't have said whether it was to warn her friends, or to save the one they all ran toward, their feet slipping and ankles turning on the rocks.

Dawn fixed her eyes on the shape of Shya as she ran. Her lungs burned as they fought to draw in enough air. Her entire physical self, in fact, felt heavy and far too hot. She gasped for air, dragged her feet as though through something thick and syrupy. Her friends continued to advance, though, appearing as though they operated in an entirely different set of surroundings than Dawn as they shrunk, moving further away. But Dawn stopped, hands on her knees and wheezing, stars bursting in front of her eyes. And when they cleared, she peered down to her feet to find the cause of her flagging speed and saw the oozing shadows they'd all witnessed on the living plane, wisping from corners and hiding behind the television. The dark energy flowed like molasses and floated like smoke, through and around the rocks and curling around her shins.

She felt herself grimace, tears streaming down her cheeks. And she was sinking, her feet immovable now in the sucking shadows, the dark twists of demons wrapping up to her knees and rising.

She straightened, panic gripping her heart, and saw her friends, who were slowing as they reached the vast and crooked tree, and past them, Shya, who stood, now, beside its monstrous trunk. Slowly, she gazed up, toward the injured sky, and then pointed, reaching up with an arm that twisted and grew like the branches that reached beside her. Up, up toward the brilliant tear on the sky, where it flashed and burned at the edges and pulsed and whirled at the vacuum of its center.

And there were demons, like those at her feet, demons rising like a plague rising through the unnatural sunset, lit by the strands of light that rose through the clouds and were anchored to the tree.

Dawn was frozen. Frozen in fear and in conflicting urges to run both away and to her friends, to scream and to sink down and cry. Frozen to the spot by the quicksand scourge at her feet. But then her friends had halted, too, and they all were watching Shya, who seemed to levitate as her twisted branch of an arm dropped and she slumped, seemingly held up only by the thick strands of root entangled around her legs. They lifted her, she could see that now, elongating between the tree and the girl, if that was truly what she was, for Dawn suspected differently, now, as the body flopped as a doll's would, her long hair draping down in a curtain and then dropping to the rocks, transformed into black smudges and globs.

She saw Sheila drop to her knees, hands flying to her mouth where they muffled a scream. She saw the twins grasp each other as more of that body seemed to melt and drop away, dripping black wax, wooden limbs, screams and falling tears, fading fast into the ground and growing the roots that remained suspended in the air, holding nothing now, but wriggling and flapping about as they grew. Creaking vines, twirling tendrils, cracks of bark now, too, as the tree towered and climbed, black and menacing.

"Jane!" Dawn cried, her voice cracking and painful in her throat, but there. "Jane!"

Jane turned, bless her heart, and Dawn sobbed in relief, and was nearly dragged down by it when she let go and the blackness climbed higher, to her waist, hot and ever so heavy. With great effort, she motioned for Jane to come to her, and even at the distance, even in the maddeningly low light, she saw the face of her friend clear. And Jane snapped into action, hands on her sister's arms, voice calling her name, then

Sheila's, then they turned, pulling Sheila, who still cried Shya's name, still turned back, still reached for the tree.

But they were coming.

And Dawn felt a pull. She looked backward and it was there: the room at Shya's house, and Rory, reaching. Rory calling her name, lit in a halo of light from behind him that made Dawn frown absently. She turned back and they were closer, but the tree was bigger, too, and a chorus was rising from its roots as it grew. A cacophony of whispering, a roar of dark energy in unison. A quest for the sky, and as the twins and Sheila neared, they rose, too, dark masses of evil, to the crack in the boundary.

And then Jane's hand was gripping hers and Dawn yanked, hoping Anna and Sheila were attached, and they fell through the door that they'd made, somehow, landing back inside their bodies, and then crashing down to land upon the unforgiving floor.

Dawn looked up at the women, and then at Rory, desperate to get it out before it faded: "How did that happen? How'd we make a portal?"

Rory shook his head as he reached for her and pulled her up. "She made it," he cried, nodding toward Shya, then he went to pull the other women up, as well.

Dawn looked at her friend, and it was there, at her fingertips, sizzling golden threads of light, the same as that line of energy that was anchored to the tree and stretched all the way to the rip across the sky in Shya's own Hell.

CHAPTER 33 – MEDIUM

Dawn rushed to Shya's side, grabbing up her hand, which still glowed, and received what felt like a static shock. She held tight, eyes on Shya's face.

"I saw, Sweetheart," she whispered, bending close. The room, which had been full of the sounds of her friends as they exclaimed and regrouped, quieted. "I saw the shadows dragging us down, and how they rose up to the portal – the one he's using your energy to make."

The twins each put a hand on one of Dawn's shoulders, and she was thankful for the warmth. Sheila was sitting on the opposite side of the bed, her tear-streaked face dazed. Rory watched her from the end of the bed, standing, appearing lost, entirely.

"I know what you're trying to show us, sweet girl. Oh, I understand, but I don't agree." Dawn jumped with a gasp, making the others follow suit, but she could not recoil, for her hand was being grasped in a desperation that was vise-like.

"Is she squeezing your hand?" Rory's voice was full of desperation, laced with envy.

Dawn didn't answer, because Shya not only gripped her hand; she whispered in her mind, as well.

The voices in the room scrambled and then hushed, but she couldn't have made them out if she'd tried; Shya's voice, parched and tortured, was all her mind could comprehend. Her eyes even closed, to lend focus to her words. Then, suddenly, she was reaching with her free hand, a blind, mute soul with a message to write, and one of her friends placed a pen in her fist, then lowered it purposefully to cool, smooth paper.

She wrote.

Eyes closed, breathing shallow, she let her hand be controlled without complaint or fear, because it was Shya who'd taken over. Shya, soft and sad. Shya, determined and terrified, reaching out so hard it hurt, gripping Dawn so furiously it took her breath away.

But she would have given it to Shya in that moment, if it would bring her back. She would have given up her breath and the beating of her own heart to bring her back, but Shya didn't want it.

Shya saw one option, only.

When she was released, Dawn let out a whoosh of breath and fell atop the chest of her sleeping friend as though to follow her back within herself. Her face stung with tears. She squeezed Shya's hand, over and over, muttering, "Come back."

She perceived hands on her back, but shrank from them, wanting Shya back. Her eyes were still squeezed shut.

"I'm going to take this, Dawn, alright?" one of the twins spoke in her ear and the notebook slid out from between she and Shya, where it had been pinned.

"She takes her, almost," she heard Sheila whisper.

It made her pause, take stock of her surroundings, open her eyes, a bit sheepishly. Thinking, *she's right. Shya holds me so tight and takes me over so completely, I nearly lose myself.* She sat up, peering into the face of her sleeping friend from a new perspective.

"You OK?" Rory asked.

Dawn looked around, nodding. She saw the twins, bent over the notebook behind him.

"What did you see?" Rory pressed. He pulled a chair over for himself and gestured toward the one behind Dawn, for her.

She sat, still stunned.

Sheila leaned forward. "I saw Clare," she said, eyes swimming. "I saw her face in the base of the tree, frozen, with an expression of," she paused, moving her hands as she searched for an appropriate word, then blurted, "terror!"

"I didn't see that," one of the twins piped up. Anna went around the bed to sit beside the shaken Sheila. "I saw Shya, but as though she was made of roots and branches, and then when she rose up and started coming apart, I saw *her* face in the tree. But it wasn't frozen. She was screaming."

Dawn twisted around to look at Jane. "What about you?"

Jane shook her head. "I saw massive strands of light flowing from the base of the tree to the sky, where they lit up the tear and the shadows that flowed through." She met her sister's eyes. "And I saw Shya, too, walking away from us. After *she* pointed to the sky, I sort of got lost in it."

Dawn straightened. "We all saw things a little differently. I saw everything you've said, except for Clare, of course. I was too far away for that, though. But the difference is that I was being held back by those shadows; they were wrapping my legs up and sucking my feet down like mud or quicksand."

They were silent for several beats. Dawn could feel her own pulse in those moments. She jumped when Rory spoke again.

"Your phone was making noise," he said, his voice flat.

Dawn frowned. "Huh?"

"You left it in the kitchen," he gestured over his shoulder.

Dawn studied his features. "What did *you* see?"

The other women, who'd been whispering and looking again at the notebook, looked up, suddenly silent.

"Nothing like what you guys saw," Rory said on an outbreath, rubbing his stubbly cheeks. "But I felt something.

She was humming," he gestured toward Shya in the bed, then took up her hand, seemingly remembering something. "Not like singing, but like a current. Like electricity."

They all nodded.

"What do we do?" Rory asked, but it was rhetorical. His face crumbled and he retrieved his hand to cover it. Dawn replaced Rory's touch with her own, feeling somewhat maternal, as though Shya needed care and their touch would convey their love and comfort.

"We close the portal," Jane piped up. Her voice was calm and clear.

Dawn nodded. They had to close the portal before Shya forced it closed by cutting off its source entirely. But, *how?*

"Go check your phone," Anna said, her eyes unusually steady on Dawn's. "We need help."

Dawn inhaled sharply. She didn't know whether Anna meant Charm or Ed… or Mel, for that matter, but she didn't need to know. She just needed to see who'd reached out, and then reach right back. She stood, but caught herself, reaching for the notebook.

"This can wait," Sheila hugged the notebook to her chest.

Dawn shook her outstretched hand, though a bolt of adrenaline coursed through her at the look of dismay in her friend's eyes.

"Don't you know what you wrote?" Jane asked. But her expression revealed that she already knew the answer.

Dawn wiggled her fingers, eyes on Sheila, and deigning not to answer a question that was more an attempt at distraction than anything.

And after glancing briefly at the twins, and then toward Rory, who might have been sleeping, his face had been buried in his hands so long, Sheila handed it over.

CHAPTER 34 – WEAK LINKS

You, with the broken heart
Love unrequited makes its mark
Your heavy chest where boundaries part
She tore right through just to depart
And now, your task to find a start
To save the bludgeoner of heart
Is doomed to fail and not so smart
A fitting end when torn apart

You, one soul split in two
Impossible to see just you
Half and half, dependent, too
Your strength, your path, and your death, too
Will tear away a half of you
My twin is gone, oh no, boo hoo
The second falls, for what to do
But follow where the first leads to

You, timid one in all but words
You, making sure your voice is heard

Brave when it comes to prophet heard
But failure's all that's self-assured
When faced with horrors skewed and blurred
A fading friend, a portal spurred
Dark shadows rising, demon birds
Your shrieking efforts fall, absurd

And you, the strong one, quiet now
The one knowing and practical
The teacher is not teaching, now
For to your knees you've fallen, cowed
When faced with chaos calm can't plow
Frightened one, shaken toe to brow
No gentle touch will save the sow
Fade, beaten one, relent, and bow

And you, hello, the one who feels
Whose perception speeds on relentless wheels
Tortured by suffering otherwise concealed
There's no escape, no solution revealed
You, compassionate one who hears the squeals
The pleading wails, soul's flayed skin peeled
From her spirit, so bright it blinds and reels
And the coming one, another bonus, what a steal!

And you, bright one, you, glowing love
Who's kindly torn the sky above

Opened the door with forced glove

'Twixt heaven and the Hell your shell is still part of

Sleep, bright one, my silent messenger, my dove

Dwell not your thoughts on those that flutter restlessly above

For now you've joined us, instigated balancing thereof

Of dark and light, of love and hate, of misery your world's been as yet far too void of.

CHAPTER 35 – REVELATIONS

The front step was as cold and hard as the last time she'd sat upon it, but she didn't care. Her trembling legs needed a rest. *Too much, too fast,* she pondered, closing her eyes and inhaling deeply through her nose. The insides of her nostrils felt dry and cold as the harsh air bit. It provided a welcome distraction for a couple of seconds, and then she was staring at her phone as she scrolled robotically.

She had two calls: one from Ed and one from Bethie, and a multitude of texts, all from Charm, who, judging by the onslaught of attempts to reach Dawn, must have arrived at the house up the street.

She dialled Ed before thinking, lest she become overwrought with all that daunted her and freeze, able only to ruminate on it all.

"Dawn?" Ed answered halfway through the first ring.

She exhaled, rubbing her forehead. "Hi, big guy. How are you?"

"Weird. I'm weird. Things are happening over here, none of which I am at liberty to share at this moment, but what I really want to know is how you guys are over there? Because I'm thinking it's all connected."

Dawn frowned. "How can we figure that out if you can't say anything?"

"*You* can say something."

"But then *I* won't know anything new!"

Ed sighed. “No, but I would, and what I’m doing here is trying to get some tactics to bring home, you know?”

His frustration was very nearly palpable, despite the physical distance between them.

“I’m sorry,” she sighed. “Yes, things are happening here; last night, Shya had another... episode.”

Ed gasped.

“Don’t worry; Shya’s fine. Everyone’s fine except John, but he will be fine. He just has an injury to his hand, quite deep. You wouldn’t believe the number of stitches...”

“What else?”

She frowned. “Today we tried to communicate with Shya.”

“And?”

“And it was rough.” She rubbed at her forehead again. “What’s going on with Mel?”

Ed paused.

“He’s not talking to me, Ed, and I’m worried.”

“To be honest, Dawn, I’m not sure how he is. We spend our days apart, only seeing each other at night, when we’re both exhausted.”

“Bullshit, Ed.”

He made a sound, which Dawn imagined was meant to sound upset at being disbelieved. But then, he sighed. “Stupid for any of us to try and keep anything from each other, I guess.”

“Uh – huh.”

He let out another whoosh of breath. “I mean it when I say I’m not sure what’s up with him, but I’ll tell you that I’m a little worried, too. He’s not himself.”

She nodded, sucking in a breath through her nostrils again.

"I only have another minute. What happened today when you tried to contact Shya?"

She supposed his honesty deserved the same from her. "We found ourselves on Shya's shore," she said.

"Not just seeing it?"

"No; we were pretty much immersed."

"Who?"

"The twins, Sheila, and myself. And we thought we saw her… I don't know what's her and what's our demon, but it looked like her… at first, anyway. She – it was like she was warning us; she was pointing up to the portal. And there were dark energies going through, Ed. Masses of them."

"Then what?"

"Isn't that enough?" Her voice rose to something far more shrill than she'd intended.

He sighed. "Let me be specific; it'll help, I think."

She waited silently, inwardly pushing the emotion down; hers, Ed's, and so many others.

"Did you get another poem?"

Dawn sat up straighter. "How did you know that?"

"I was with – we were connecting at the same time, and I got one, too. Only, I don't think it was from her. Maybe *through* her…" he trailed off.

"Sounds like what we got, too. Basically, a rhyming tirade attacking our individual shortcomings or fears?"

He chuckled. "Starting with me?"

She closed her eyes. She'd only read it once. "Yes."

"I can't believe it. This thing is strong."

"Does this mean she's not communicating solely with me?"

"No, I don't think so. But this one wasn't all her, Dawn."

"What else?" She glanced toward the main road, where her niece no doubt awaited her arrival. And if she didn't show up soon, Dawn suspected Charm would come to find her. She stood, eyes going to the second-floor windows, where she knew Sheila kept watch over Shya, and Rory prepared to head to the hospital to check on John. The twins had departed quickly after they'd dissected the poem as a group, saying they would be back before dinner to take a turn sitting with Shya. Dawn had perceived their discomfort over their section of the poem – not surprising, considering it referred to the death of one or both of them, but then each and every verse had hit where they'd truly feel it: Ed's heart, his chest, which suffered so much the last time he'd served as a portal. And his love for Shya, so different than how the woman felt for him.

They'd all been poked, each having their fears acknowledged by a dark spirit whose specialty was that very thing: using people's fear to hurt them. And Asmodeus was exceptionally skilled at it.

"Is there someone new?" Ed's voice brought her back to herself."

She gave herself a shake, then looked once more toward the upstairs windows before starting to walk. She could wait no longer, though she felt entirely unprepared to meet her niece *and* ensure Charm got no closer to the action. As if the very action of seeing her in person would provide a bridge between the girl and the demon. "What?"

"Someone new. The demon thinks this new person is just like Shya. It wants her. There was a reference in the poem, too – in your section."

"Charm," she whispered.

"What?"

"My niece. I have a niece, and she's gifted. She's here, actually. Not *here*, at the house, here, but at Connor's."

"Why? My God, she needs to stay away!"

"I had no choice, Ed! She was already coming, whether anyone approved or not!"

"She needs to go back home."

Dawn shook her head as tears spilled out, flagrantly ignoring her own assertion not to let her emotions boil over. "I agree!" she replied, hearing the desperation in her own voice as her breath hitched.

"I'm sorry, Dawn. I didn't mean to sound like I was attacking you."

She walked faster. Focused on how cold her tears turned as they exposed themselves to the chill air, leaving trails that stiffened down her cheeks like veins of ice.

"But I saw – it means to get her. Add her to the collection."

Dawn remembered Sheila's exclamation that she'd seen Clara, Shya's mother, in the tree. They hadn't even had time to talk about what that might mean. "But Charm is like *me*," Dawn said, mostly to herself.

"I don't think so," Ed replied. "But then, you're there and I'm not."

"Ed?" A feminine voice sounded from Ed's end. It was slightly muffled, but the mere sound of it made the hairs on the back of Dawn's neck stand on end. Made her want to know her with a pull she'd never experienced before.

The Bodhisatta?

"I have to go."

"OK. I'm going to see Charm now. I'll try and get her to go home *again*. But can you please tell Mel to call me?"

There was a maddening pause from the other end, and then Ed said, "I'll ask him."

Dawn was lowering her phone before she could hear

Ed sign off, eyes on the figure coming toward her as she reached the main street and turned toward Connor's house. She knew it was Charm before she could make out her features, knew, somehow, her walk, and the way she swung her jacket playfully, hands buried in her pockets. And then the figure was halting, twenty feet from Dawn, and Dawn stopped, too. Both stared for pendulous moments, both aware of each other in a physical sense for the first time, but realizing that they'd been connected much longer than that. Dawn's fingertips went to her lips, which were trembling, and at the same time, the teen just ahead of her, who was at least as tall as the vertically challenged Dawn, squealed, before running full-tilt to her aunt and they embraced, Dawn closing her eyes against the intensity of the emotional flood that crashed down on her.

Charm pressed against her, giggling and crying simultaneously. She smelled like home.

CHAPTER 36 – MERGE

Bethie was waving from the step, and calling out, "She swore she'd stay on the main road! I was watching!"

Dawn pressed gently against the girl, her hands on her shoulders, to look into her eyes. They were so familiar. They were Cadence. They were her brothers. Her mother. They were her. "My God," she whispered, and the girl smiled brilliantly, and *that* was different. "You must have your father's smile," she murmured, and her fingers went to her niece's chin of their own accord, and ran up the line of her jaw to her ear, where she pushed a heavy mass of dark hair, in bad need of styling, to the side. She had to touch her. She had to make sure she was real. The girl's skin was lovely and clear, darker than that of Cadence but lighter than Dawn's.

The girl laughed throatily. "What are you doing?"

"I'm studying you," Dawn said. She noted the absence of chaos in that moment as she looked at her niece, whom she loved without a doubt, immediately and in a way that gripped her heart in such a way that Dawn knew it would never let go.

Her eyes were light, almost amber. Kenny's were light like that. Their mother had always said it ran in the family "down South". She realized she was clasping Charm's hands and they were larger than her own. She pulled her arms out at her sides, admiring the girl's long, plaid wool jacket. Then she gazed into her face again. She tried to find the regret she'd been terrified would come when she first met her niece, but it was nowhere. There was only joy. *Maybe her gifts* are *different than mine,* she wondered, for surely it was a gifted influence that shielded her from a guilt that by all accounts, *should* be present.

"You're beautiful," Dawn smiled, her cheeks aching, cold as they were, and tight where her tears had left their trails only moments earlier.

"So are you," Charm, too, was grinning ear-to-ear.

Dawn remembered her conversation with Ed and made a grand effort to arrange her features into something believably stern. "You can't walk that way," she stated, gesturing over her shoulder with her head. "I don't want you anywhere near there."

The smile faltered, but only momentarily. "I know," she said, but Dawn saw doubt in her incredible eyes.

Dawn motioned toward Bethie, who was still on the step, arms folded over her chest. "Let's go in."

Charm nodded, looping her arm around Dawn's as though they'd known each other forever. "Your friends are really nice," she said, and with that, the floodgates fell open and Charm was saying so much about so many things that Dawn found herself overwhelmed again, but not unpleasantly so, this time.

It stopped when they reached the steps, and a boy pressed the screen open, beaming toward Dawn before flying down the steps and into her arms.

Dawn was crying again, because this healthy, full-cheeked, exuberant boy with light in his eyes was Jordan. It had to be; it *felt* like him, but in no way matched the image she'd had in her head of the boy since they'd last seen each other. The child's arms squeezed in what felt like an intentional show of strength, and Dawn looked up at Bethie, whose eyes were swimming at the sight. "Is this Jordan?" Dawn whispered theatrically.

Bethie nodded, but seemed unable to speak.

The boy pulled away a bit. "Did you feel how strong I am?" His smile shone up at her, and Dawn saw it, then. Little hints of how he'd suffered only a few short months ago. But she kept her smile genuine and steady as she observed the dark bases of his teeth and the nearly-completely faded scratches on his face. She looked up again at Bethie to steady herself as the lump in her throat pressed up, threatening to squeeze tears into her eyes again.

Bethie reached toward them. "Come on; we have warm tea and hot chocolate."

"Yay!" the nine-year-old cried as he barrelled up the steps and indoors, and it was a relief to see, because it was exactly what a boy his age *should* do, despite the evidences of his recent trials.

"He's so cool," Charm said as they mounted the steps. "I don't know everything about what happened, but your friends," Dawn assumed she meant Bethie and Connor, "won't say anything. It's Jordan who talks about it."

Dawn looked sideways at her. "Does he?"

Charm nodded. "He talks about it like it was any other event; like an illness that happened to him, and now he's all better."

Dawn pressed her lips together. "I think that's good."

Charm laughed. "It is!" She went in ahead of Dawn, almost skipping.

Connor took her up into his arms when she entered the kitchen, having taken an extra-long moment at the door after taking her boots and jacket off. She was reaching down inside herself, monitoring her feelings, wondering how she'd shaken the absolute chaos of her perspective just by changing houses. Just by looking into the eyes of her niece for the first time. It had been like going home, to a place she hadn't been aware she'd been searching for. *Is it her?* She considered what little she knew of Charm's gifts and settled on the truth: she didn't know enough about Charm at all to begin to assess her gifts. She'd *assumed* the girl would be like her, but that had been an ignorant – if not subconscious – decision.

She shrieked as Connor picked her up and squeezed her. He chuckled as he placed her gently on her feet again, and looked down into her face. Her breath caught. Jordan hadn't been the only one changing since his ordeal. Connor was nearly painfully handsome, with his fair coloring and sincere smile that twinkled in his eyes.

"Wow; what's happened to you?" Dawn swatted an undeniably muscled arm.

Connor glanced toward his son, then at Bethie, who was smiling over her shoulder as she prepared hot drinks at the counter. "I got happy," the man said, finally.

"Well, it looks damn good on you," she beamed up at him, enjoying a brief moment of satisfaction in the fact that she'd had something to do with the family's positive transformation.

"He's gone back to work," Bethie smiled as she placed a heavily-laden tray on the table.

Charm had been standing just behind Dawn, her hand warm on her shoulder, but now she leaned forward and snatched up a chocolate-covered cookie. Having observed the bold move, Jordan snaked a skinny arm between the adults, clumsily grabbing a few for himself, then took off, squealing as Bethie chased him, crumbs flying. Charm looked wide-eyed at Connor, who waved any regret away.

"Sorry!" Charm said anyway, then kissed Dawn on the cheek before heading in the direction Bethie and Jordan had gone in.

"He loves her already," Connor smiled as they sat at the little kitchen table.

"She's only been here half a day, right?" Dawn's brow knitted together in confusion, but she was eyeing the teapot. She was finding it difficult to feel anything but uplifted.

Connor motioned toward the pot. "Go ahead."

She poured tea for the three adults and was stuck on

considering whether Charm would want some when Bethie breezed in alone.

"They're playing video games," she laughed as she motioned over her shoulder, then sat, reaching for her tea. "It feels like she's always been here," she shook her head in Dawn's direction, then added milk to her cup.

Dawn gazed toward the sounds of laughter floating to them from the hallway. "She seems so…"

Bethie shook her head again. "I know. She's incredible, Dawn!"

"I need her to stick close while she's here," Dawn motioned to the walls around them, wanting to get it out before she relaxed.

Both Connor and Bethie nodded enthusiastically.

"I've got work, but Bethie'll be home," Connor squeezed Bethie's hand as he spoke. Dawn observed how his eyes softened when he looked at her.

Bethie seemed to melt toward Connor before turning to Dawn, saying, "We thought it best that I put off going back to work. Take care of Jordan one on one until the new year."

"He seems… amazing!" Dawn smiled.

Connor leaned back in his chair, still holding on to Bethie's hand. "He is. Except for the nightmares."

Bethie patted his hand. "The therapist says it's completely normal, hon."

Connor nodded, but pressed his lips together.

Bethie looked at Dawn again. "Therapy's been really good for him. She says it's a good sign that he's dreaming about it. He's working through it on some level, even though he's feeling better than ever during waking hours."

Dawn nodded. "Makes sense."

"How is Shya?"

Dawn met Connor's eyes, but no words came. She was reluctant to darken the atmosphere that was so healing.

"Anything new?" Bethie patted Dawn's hand, now.

Dawn shrugged. "I don't know. It's bent on warning us away, it seems. And I'm worried that," she stopped abruptly, her eyes flicking to the hallway again, in the direction of the children.

"What?" Connor leaned forward. "It's alright to talk about it, Dawn. We're pulling for her, even if Jordan and I don't come to lend our support in person." Bethie patted his hand.

"You're doing right," Dawn assured him. "It's not a good place to be, right now."

"What were you saying about being worried?" Bethie gestured toward the chocolate cookies and Dawn reached for one absently.

"She had another episode last night," she said quietly. Reluctantly. The warm pads of her fingertips melted into the thin layer of chocolate covering her cookie, but she couldn't seem to bring it to her mouth. "What I started to say was that I worry our efforts to rescue her won't work as long as she's determined to solve this another way."

Bethie nodded, a faraway look transforming her features.

"You can't help someone who doesn't want to be helped," Connor murmured.

Dawn nodded, then popped the cookie into her mouth in an effort to shove her emotions back. It was a lump in her mouth, tasting like cardboard. "Thank you for letting Charm stay," she said around her cookie with some effort.

"She's wonderful. Jordan loves her," Connor smiled.

"So, what's next?" Bethie asked.

"For Charm?"

Bethie shook her head. "For Shya. For the group."

Dawn sighed heavily. "It's all connected, now. Charm is in danger, here. I need to convince her to return home."

Bethie looked doubtful. "She's pretty strong-willed. She says she's staying until she gets the help she needs."

Dawn made a sound of frustration.

They sipped their tea in the ensuing silence.

Dawn leaned forward. "As for Shya, I hate to admit it, but we need reinforcements. We need Ed. And Mel," she added the last without conviction, but hadn't the time to reflect on why.

"Have you been in contact with them?" Bethie wondered.

Dawn nodded. "I spoke to Ed just before coming over." She purposefully avoided addressing the lack of contact with Mel. "The demon's too strong, and smart," she continued, "and it's not just us being affected; the whole world is feeling the consequences of the portal it's used Shya to create."

Connor's eyes widened. "Have you seen all this stuff about how major news media aren't covering it?"

Dawn frowned.

"It's assumed they've got gag orders," Bethie nodded.

"But it's all I hear," Dawn said, incredulous.

"But you're hearing through social media, right?"

"Or the radio," Connor added. "They can't be gagged."

"But it's being treated like a conspiracy theory by anyone with any authority," Bethie shook her head. "To me, that's more frightening than the changes themselves."

"Well," Connor started, "you also have the very rare vantage point of knowing *why* things have changed." He peered out the window, his eyes on the sky, which had been noticeably less clear for weeks. Less blue than purple and grey. Less bright on the whole.

"Religious groups are declaring it as the beginning of the

apocalypse," Bethie noted, her voice hushed.

"And what could anyone *do* in any case, if they knew what was causing it all?"

"Aunt Dawn?" Charm appeared in the arched doorway to the hallway, making the three at the table jump.

"Yes, dear," Dawn exhaled, her hand on her heart.

"Sorry!" the girl said, smiling. "I just wanted to make sure you didn't leave without saying goodbye."

Dawn frowned deeply, realizing that she and Charm hadn't even talked together, yet. Not really.

"Don't worry!" Charm waved a hand. "We have lots of time to get to know each other. I feel like we already do, anyway," she leaned around the doorframe comically, then disappeared down the hall.

Dawn looked questioningly at her friends. They shrugged.

"Has she told you anything about her seizures?"

Bethie nodded. "She showed us her medication and where she keeps it in her bag, and explained the different types she has. Seems very confident about it all."

"I promised to call Cadence once I saw her in person," Dawn muttered. A tiny bit of the chaos nipped at her periphery, but only in a fleeting way. She eyed them both. "I feel as though we have so much to say, but I've got no time. I really need to talk to my sister, and to Ed, and to Rory, Sheila and the twins, too."

They nodded. "We've got her," Connor nodded toward the hallway.

"Thank you," Dawn said, her voice a bit shaky.

"I'll be over in a couple hours," Bethie met her eyes. "Don't worry; Connor will stay with Charm."

"I need to figure things out, but I'll definitely come see

her tomorrow; spend some time with her," Dawn said, feeling guilty already for leaving.

It was very nearly dark when Charm released her from a hug on the concrete step of Connor's house.

"I'll see you tomorrow," Dawn caught the girl's eyes and held them in her gaze.

Charm nodded, seemingly accepting of Dawn's timeline, now that she was here.

"Don't..." Dawn began, but Charm cut in, rolling her eyes.

"I won't come to where you are."

Dawn hugged the girl again, feeling her sister in her niece's arms and faced again with the realization of all she'd missed. She was crying when Charm pulled away again. "I'm so sorry," Dawn cried, surprising them both.

Charm shook her head. "It's going to be alright," she asserted, hands tight on Dawn's shoulders, and Dawn walked back to the house feeling a combination of hope and regret.

As she drew closer, though, her stomach started to clench. She hugged her arms to herself as it flooded back at her in a rush: the chaos. The fear. She mused over how peaceful the house looked in the darkening night, the windows dimly lit and glowing in the soft darkness. But it only took the opening of the door to have reality rush back in. The atmosphere pressed in on her, such that she had to fight the urge to go back out again. But something planted her in place. She cocked her head, listening intently for a sound in the enduring silence.

She pondered what they'd discussed before she'd left for Connor's. Once the twins came to take over watching Shya, Sheila and Rory would head to the hospital to see John. But the place felt strange; Dawn could not sense the twins, or Sheila, come to think of it. And not Rory, either.

She toed her boots off, but climbed the stairs as she unzipped her jacket, eager to investigate as a sense of urgency shot through her. She halted in the hallway. On the floor in

Shya's room was a foot, face-down, and Dawn knew it was one of the twins, as it was clothed in colorful tights – a frequent fashion statement they indulged in. She ran the rest of the way to the room, until she saw the rest of the woman whose foot had been visible. She was face-down, indeed, and appeared to be sleeping, her long, white hair fanning out on the carpet, and meshing with another mane of white, for the second twin's head lay close, the rest of her body disappearing around the side of the bed.

Dawn didn't try to stifle the scream that escaped, but it gargled to a halt, anyway, when a throaty laughter accompanied it from the bed. She whipped her gaze up, shocked to discover that Shya sat on the edge of the bed, observing her with glittering black orbs for eyes. How she hadn't seen her first was beyond Dawn, but the sight of the twins had taken everything she had. Were they dead? Just unconscious? Hurt, somehow? She saw no blood, but now, the still figure of Shya was all Dawn saw. The eyes, impossibly dark, her chin down slightly, a shiny thread of saliva dangling from her chin.

"Oh, God!" Dawn cried, backing away, though a large part of her wanted to run to the twins, to check for a pulse, for breath, for their spirits. But still her body travelled back toward the hallway, jumping violently when the figure on the bed faked a lurch, then sat again, laughing in that deep, throaty voice that did not belong to the body it possessed. Laughing because she was scared. "Shya?" she called out instinctively, and the mirth slid from the face of her friend, and was replaced by anger.

"No!" it bellowed, and did not fake the lurch, this time, but bound across the floor to her on all fours, crashing into Dawn, teeth gnashing as they fell, and roaring, the animalistic blast following Dawn down into unconsciousness.

CHAPTER 37 – SUICIDE NOTE

Don't try to stop me dying
It just hurts even more
Makes long my exit, trying
When you stand and block the door

Don't rescue me, don't clamour
Chase my determination down
My existence lost its glamour
And holding off ensures you'll drown

For it's not just me who flounders
In an unforgiving sea
If you want your world to rebound
You must release and set me free

It's my light that tears the boundary
Letting all the darkness in
It no longer rests on balance
Light and dark, saviour or sin

It's my gift to close the portal

Put a stop to breaching veil
Let me go to join my loved ones
Let our gifts wither and fail

For though the angel's wings are gilded
With the power we inherit
Demon claws pervert its purpose
In control though I don't share it

Quiet, now, grieve not my absence
For I am already gone
Celebrate glorious resurgence
And may you prosper long

Hug your loved ones and your foes, alike
Let go hatred and regret
Hold charms and blessings up against your healing heart...
Sadness and longing, quick, forget

Do not slow my death, dear ones
Know I choose to let life go
So that many more will prosper
I'll rest in Heaven, not below

CHAPTER 38 – CACOPHONY

Waking up to two pale, identical faces over her had her bursting immediately into tears. But her relief was short-lived as images of the possessed Shya cantering across the room toward Dawn, roaring like a savage beast, came back to her, reminding her that the twins' faces looking down at her could mean the three of them were dead, just as much as it could mean they were all alive.

"Are we dead?" she asked, frozen stiff with fear. Their smiles brought back the flood of relief, but as soon as that came, the words came, too.

Once again, she'd awoken with a message, but as she sat and the words echoed in her head, she knew she was less than eager to share it.

"She's awake?" Bethie's voice came from the direction of the bed, and Dawn whirled, as much as she could while sitting, half in the room and half in the hallway, to see Bethie, her hands busy with something as she leaned over Shya, but looking back at her, concern on her face.

"How long have I been out?" Dawn breathed, her eyes on her thrashing friend, still very much conscious, and seemingly upset at the fact that Bethie was finishing tying her limbs to the respective bed posts.

"We figure at least an hour," one of the twins said. "When we came to, you were out."

The other twin, who Bethie finally differentiated as Anna by tearing her gaze from Shya to peer at her, added,

"She was on all fours in the hallway, rocking back and forth and watching you." Anna eyed the still-struggling Shya briefly before finishing with, "It was fucking creepy."

Dawn burst out laughing, which immediately quashed itself when she heard how *wrong* it sounded.

"Sorry," Anna grimaced.

"It's OK!" Jane reassured her twin, reaching across Dawn to squeeze Anna's arm.

Dawn peered from one woman to the other. It was surreal to witness such... *fear* from the twins. But then, they'd been badly shaken by the message they'd received earlier, from the demon.

"I thought you two might be dead," Dawn said, her voice barely audible. The twins peered blankly at her, both sets of near-transparent eyes jiggling in their sockets. "How did it happen?"

They both frowned, even their expressions in unison. "It was fast," they both said. Dawn nodded, understanding completely.

"What do we do?" Bethie's voice demanded attention from her seat on the foot of the bed. Dawn watched as the woman cringed every time the body of Shya thrashed. "Where's Rory?"

"He and Sheila went to the hospital, and then to get some groceries," Jane asserted as she stood, then reached out to help her sister and Dawn, each with one hand. All three seemed unsteady upon standing up.

"I'm dizzy, but not hurt, I don't think," Anna pondered aloud as she observed her arms, turning them over, dazed.

Jane and Dawn followed suit.

"Why would it do this?" Bethie wondered, now.

The three women looked at each other, equally puzzled.

"To show us it could?" Jane asked.

Anna nodded.

Dawn bit her cheeks, the words of the new poem on repeat in her head. For the first time, she had no urge to get them down, for she doubted she could ever forget them. It made her wonder, though. It was the demon that knocked her unconscious, but the words were from Shya.

Or at least made to appear so.

"Dawn?"

She realized she was frowning and gave herself a shake, peering toward Bethie, but seeing Shya instead, who'd stilled and was watching her with those black eyes, smiling. She tensed bodily. The grin was... uncomfortable.

"I need to get out of here for a minute," she replied, eyes struggling to stay on Bethie, who'd said her name in the first place. She backed up, shaking off the hands of the twins as she went. The women peered at each other, seemingly at a loss.

Dawn turned, headed for the basement, where she'd stored the notebook before leaving for Connor's earlier. She would write the words, if only in secret, for now, in hopes it would allow her to release them from her brain. She needed help with them before she shared them. She needed Mel.

Her heart squeezed uncomfortably at the realization, for though she needed the man, he'd seemingly taken himself out of the equation of The Seers.

Still, after scribbling the words and noting their continued repetition within her skull, she dialled his number. She knew he wouldn't answer, but she needed him to know she needed him.

The feeling intensified as she climbed the stairs, hearing the twins' and Bethie's raised voices. She quickened her pace toward the room. Indeed, the women were arguing, all standing now, and facing each other. Shya watched, still grinning, quietly amused. Her gaze turned to Dawn when she approached, though.

"Stop!" she cried, arms outstretched. The three women recoiled, seemingly shocked at Dawn's intrusion.

The demon laughed, using Shya's form but not her vocal cords, it seemed, for it was impossibly layered and dark.

"Do you see what's happening?" Dawn pleaded. "It's turning us against each other, toying with all of us!"

Jane's face cleared, quickly followed by Anna's. But Bethie still appeared enraged. Dawn tugged gently on her arm, then motioned for the twins to follow her, too.

Anna shook her head. "I don't want to leave her," she looked at Shya, her face reflecting her dismay as the demon grinned at her through Shya's face.

"She's tied up," Dawn coaxed, pulling on Anna's arm now, too.

Jane pressed the women toward Dawn, herding them toward the hallway.

"What is going *on*?" Dawn cried as soon as they were out of the room.

Bethie pointed at each of the twins in turn, her finger jabbing in the air. "They don't know what they're talking about!"

Jane and Anna spoke at once, both saying different versions of the same line of defence.

Dawn shook her head. "Stop! I can't even tell what you're saying!"

"It's too strong for us!" Anna exclaimed.

"And we don't know if Ed will be back in time!" Jane added.

"That doesn't mean we need to involve *her!*" Bethie cried, tendons standing out on her neck.

Dawn's eyes widened. "Involve *who*?" She knew the answer, but needed to hear them say it to believe it. But even as she awaited their reply, she realized they'd been hinting at it all along. But was it because it was the right thing to do, or because they were scared for their own lives?

The twins looked at each other, then at Dawn, inhaling before saying it in perfect harmony: "Charm."

CHAPTER 39 – TWIST

"Are you *crazy?*" Sheila voiced Dawn's reaction quite succinctly.

Dawn, the twins and Sheila were outside, so as to make room for peace within the house. The moment the front door had opened, signaling the return of Sheila and Rory (John was showing signs of infection, so would be in the hospital for at least another twenty-four hours), Shya went limp, the animation of her limbs and features falling away as though knocked out of her.

She's strong enough to banish the demon when it's important, Dawn had mused, though she knew that wasn't quite accurate. Regardless, she had no time to reflect, and there was certainly no opportunity to bounce her thoughts off her friends. Bethie had agreed to fill Rory in while Sheila joined the women of The Seers outside, which was a relief, given the apparent animosity Bethie was exhibiting toward Jane and Anna.

Animosity which Dawn could commiserate with, despite her currently winning need to appear impartial. She trusted the twins; that was not in question. But their suggestion to bring Dawn's niece to the fore of their situation threatened to tip that particular balancing point quite firmly toward anger.

"Can't you see it?" Anna pleaded with Sheila who, as a rule, agreed with the twins. But that was because she saw what they did. Their gifts were similar and the three supported each other well, a firm, triangular structure which, without all three sides, would fall.

Sheila shook her head. "In the beginning, I did, but all I

see now is how that *beast* has stolen our sister!" She pointed to the house, her voice strong. "One life is most definitely in danger, even *without* the threat of the demons. It's got her convinced she needs to finish *herself* off, rather than fight!"

The twins wore identical expressions of sad confusion.

Dawn put a hand on Sheila's shoulder, which trembled. "I know we're short two members," she started, but Sheila cut in.

"*Three,*" she countered, and Dawn stumbled over her words, disturbed that she couldn't identify, even to herself, whether she'd omitted the membership of Shya, or Mel.

"Right," she said with a nod, instead. "But why does that warrant bringing in a new member at all? I wouldn't ask *anyone* to join us now! Yes, we have a life in danger, but if we bring someone else in," she stepped closer to the twins, eying them both in turn, "if we bring my adolescent, gifted, epileptic, brand-new to me, *vulnerable* niece in, we are certainly endangering at least one more!"

"At least?" Sheila questioned, her voice reflecting sadness, rather than confusion.

"Yeah, because if she goes in, I follow," Dawn spat with such force that she, herself was shaken.

"Have you ever wondered if maybe Charm needs Shya far more than any of us do?" Anna asked, and her voice was back to soothing. Smooth.

Dawn gave her a look of defiance, but said nothing. The words seemed to tangle in her throat, threatening to choke her.

It was Jane who continued, in typical fashion, "Charm *is* more like Shya," she whispered. Sheila leaned toward the three, accomplishing quite a tight huddle. Dawn could not deny the warmth it brought her. The closeness was good though, even disregarding the cold. They needed to remember that it felt good to be a group.

"She came for my help," Dawn retorted, but the words

were weak. She hated it, but she'd already considered what the twins were voicing.

Sheila straightened, biting her lip.

Jane shook her head. "She does need you, Dawn. Of course, she does."

"But we think Shya is the only one who can help her learn to use her gifts."

Dawn crossed her arms over her chest and, despite the revelation she'd made seconds earlier, walked away from the group. She observed the tall spruce that dominated the front yard, and then her eyes were on the street in front of them, patched recently after the massive earthquake that had torn it apart. The demon was a fan of ripping, it seemed. She pondered the portal ripped into the sky of Shya's rocky shore.

She whirled back to the three women, who watched her silently. "Why does she need Shya? I can help her, even if my gifts are different. Why does she need Shya?" She swallowed painfully; such was her reaction to her own implication that Shya was disposable. She hadn't meant it that way, but that's what the words *felt* like as they came out.

Anna stepped toward Dawn. "She's not exactly like Shya, either," she said. "She's so much more vulnerable, because of her seizures. But that also means she travels between the levels with more ease than any of us do. She might not realize it, but her seizures signify her traveling."

Dawn shook her head. She hadn't been compelled to question the source of the twins' wisdom for a very long time, but now, when so much was on the line, it seemed improper not to. "How do you know?"

The twins shared a look.

"They've seen it," Sheila answered for them.

"So have you," Jane said quietly, her eyes on Sheila.

"But that's not enough," Sheila shook her head.

Anna stepped toward Dawn again. "The risk is high, but this is the highest chance of success we have."

Dawn's frown deepened. "What does that mean?"

"Lives are in danger no matter what we do," Jane stepped forward, too.

"You've seen that?" Dawn asked, her breath hitching.

They both nodded.

"You're not just scared because of the poem?" Sheila again voiced Dawn's thoughts.

Jane looked at Sheila. "We are afraid, but not because of how it tries to scare us. We've seen this for years."

Dawn's heart sped to a canter. "What? What have you seen?"

The twins joined hands. "It's not certain," Anna said, and then they both fell silent.

"It's not just you though, is it?

Dawn frowned in Sheila's direction, now.

The twins shook their heads.

"What?" Dawn gestured helplessly with her hands. "Who?"

"Ed," Sheila answered for them, eyes on the ground.

Jane went to drape an arm around her friend. "It can change," she said, and Sheila nodded.

"Wait," Dawn pressed in on her temples. "What are you saying? That if Charm does get involved, nobody dies?"

Jane looked back at Anna.

"It's the best chance we have," Anna stated. Then moved to hug Dawn, who took a step back at first, then fell into the woman's arms, crying.

"This is impossible," she said into Anna's shoulder. A

million thoughts clamoured in her brain. She needed to talk to Cadence. Needed to try and get Charm home, right? Or not? Needed to talk to Mel, that one was certain. She worked to sort her thoughts. Wondered, only for the briefest of moments, if Shya's solution was one that would give them some measure of success, too. Without jeopardizing Charm. "What do I do?" she whispered, mostly to herself.

Anna pressed her back, gently. "Remember this: even if Shya dies, there will still be one soul – that we know of – who could keep the portal open."

Dawn's eyes widened. "Shya doesn't know that!"

Anna's eyes filled with relief before she nodded.

"But I can't do that to Charm," she whispered. Sheila and Jane were coming closer, and soon they were huddled again. Dawn wondered how they must look to neighbors. She hoped for confusing, rather than crazy, but knew she had no control over what others thought of her. Finally, she knew that for sure. And finally, it didn't matter much at all. "After everything," she whispered, her eyes going to the ground, much as Sheila's had moments earlier, "I can't put Charm in danger."

Jane pressed her chin up, her soft fingers stinging cold. Dawn met her eyes. "Sweetheart, she's *already* in danger."

Dawn looked to Anna, as if to confirm her sister's words, and of course, she nodded. She looked to Sheila, hoping for something different, but she nodded, too.

"I'm sorry, Dawn."

Dawn backed away from their little circle.

The three women, arms still around each other, watched her blankly.

"Tell Bethie," Dawn raised her eyebrows at Jane as she pointed to the door.

Jane nodded.

"Where are you going?" Sheila asked.

"To see Charm," Anna replied. Jane was already opening the front door.

Dawn raised a finger. "I haven't made any decisions yet, Jane," she called. "I just want to have a conversation with the girl. We haven't even had the chance to do that, yet, and I need to get away, just for a while." She eyed Anna, then. "You should, too, now that Rory's home."

"You won't need to," Jane said, stopping Dawn in her tracks.

"What?"

"Make a decision," Jane answered, then shrugged. "You just need to be strong for her."

Dawn shook her head, not getting it. Not wanting to.

"For Charm," Jane finished, then went inside.

Dawn peered at the two remaining women, then gave them a nod. "I want Bethie to know that the rule against Charm coming here still stands."

The women nodded.

Dawn reached for her phone, thinking of Cadence, and then turned to the street and started walking.

CHAPTER 40 – FATE

"Oh, thank God," Cadence answered unconventionally, but Dawn understood.

"Hi, sis," Dawn said, a bit breathless as she walked in the cold. She shoved her free hand deep in her jacket pocket, wishing she'd brought her lined mittens.

"She actually texted me," Cadence laughed, "finally! Guess she thought she could once she'd seen you."

Dawn frowned. "You sound relieved, but not as panicked as I'd thought."

"She's with you, Dawn. How can I be afraid?"

Her hands went to her lips as tears sprung hot to her eyes.

"Dawn?"

"Have I said 'I'm sorry' to you yet?"

Cadence sighed. "Yes, honey. Now, let's figure this out together, OK?"

Dawn nodded, squeezing her eyes shut and then swiping at the tears that popped out onto her cheeks. "I can't bring her back yet," Dawn cried, hating the words.

"I know," Cadence replied, and the two words soothed Dawn more than she could've hoped. "How is your friend?"

Dawn wondered absently exactly how much her sister knew about Shya and the demon they fought. Even Charm didn't know much… but Connor and Bethie did. Still, she had no clue how she should answer the question. So, she went with a redirect: "Do you think you can come get her?"

"Huh?"

"It would be better if she wasn't here," Dawn said, then pressed her lips together because, despite the truth in her statement, the assertions of her friends rang in her head. The predictions of three gifted psychics could not be ignored.

"Dawn, you don't get it, do you?"

Now Dawn said, "Huh?"

"She's – well, to say she's determined would be an understatement. Charm believes with every fiber of her being that you're the answer to the puzzle she's been trying to piece together all her life."

Dawn shook her head. "It might not be me."

"It *is.* Somehow, it is. It has to be."

She closed her eyes again, stopping in her tracks, because Connor's house was in view and she wasn't ready to end the call with Cadence, just yet.

"Dawn... Charm is an incredible girl. But the last few years, and especially the last few months, have been brutal. She just doesn't know what to do with all this stuff that nobody in her world can relate to!"

Dawn kicked at a pebble, remembering that feeling. Wondering, too, how much more intense it must be for someone with gifts like Shya's. Shya had told her stories, and they'd made Dawn thankful for her own limitations. "At least Shya had her mother, at first," she murmured, forgetting the phone.

"What? Is that your friend?"

"Yeah," Dawn replied, a bit shocked she'd spoken aloud.

"The one who's possessed?"

She inhaled sharply. "What did she tell you?"

"Just that. That there was a dark, curly-haired woman – also very pretty, mind you – and with a boyfriend equally beautiful. And that she's been tricked, and a strong entity has her."

Dawn pressed in on her temples with the thumb and middle finger of her free hand. She gazed toward Connor's house. She was a little pissed. Connor and Bethie should have talked to her before divulging anything to Charm.

"Dawn?"

"I'm sorry. For all of this."

"Not *everything* is your fault you know, Dawnie. You still having issues with that?"

Dawn barked out an unexpected laugh. "God, I've missed you," she lamented, admitting it for the first time, even to herself, and saying it simultaneously.

"I hear that," Cadence laughed. "But hey, here we are, talking, right?"

"Right," Dawn swallowed hard. "What should we do?"

Cadence sighed. "I will come, of course I will. But not 'til later, during the week."

Dawn frowned. "Wait. What the hell day is it?"

Now Cadence laughed. "It's Sunday."

Dawn gave herself a shake. Had so much really happened in only two days?

"I could come now," Cadence continued, "but it wouldn't do any good. She won't come back with me."

"Has she always been this headstrong?"

Cadence laughed. "No! This is entirely new. I was enough for her – my understanding, my encouragement, you know?"

"What about her dad?" Dawn instantly regretted the words, but Cadence pushed on without a blip.

"He died when Charm was pretty young," she said, matter-of-factly."

Dawn gritted her teeth. Had her husband died so close to their father's death? How painful might that have been? Had her father met his granddaughter, even? And exactly how must Cadence have felt about Dawn's faulty perceptions where her relationship with him was concerned. Dawn wasn't even sure how *she* felt about it all. She'd had no time to reflect, and the issue seemed satisfied to remain shoved deep inside herself, for now. "I'm sorry, Cadence," she said, finally, repeating the sentiment, feeling lame and regretful.

"We've gotten through. Kenny has been an amazing support; he's stepped up the uncle moniker, that's for sure. Charm depends on him as much as me."

"What about," she stopped, feeling selfish for wanting news on her older brothers, too, "ah, I have a lot of questions, but they can wait, I suppose. It's my own fault they've waited this long. Let's focus on Charm."

"We have time now, Dawn. Just..."

"What?"

"Don't disappear again."

Dawn grimaced against the rising guilt. "I won't. I promise." She bit back the apology that tried to surface yet again.

"I'll come on Wednesday or Thursday. Just a few days to give her time with you and maybe your friends, too."

Dawn made a face at the phone, holding it away from her. She exhaled slowly before putting it back to her ear. "It's not a good idea, Ca..."

"She needs it, Dawn. I don't know how to make you see, except to ask you to trust me! I know my girl. Even if I managed to drag her back home with me, it would be a temporary fix."

"She's vulnerable," Dawn started, and she was interrupted yet again.

"She's vulnerable whether she's there or not."

"There are dark forces here," Dawn lowered her voice, hating even the need to say the words to her sister.

"Dawnie, have you looked outside lately? Charm can't run any more than I can. Much less! Right now, the safest place for her is there, with you and others that have some chance at protecting her!"

Dawn sighed. It made some sense, but it still felt wrong. "I don't know if I can let her anywhere near that house," she said. "Even if she meets the group at Connor and Bethie's, I don't want her anywhere near Shya!"

"I agree."

Dawn let out a long breath. "Thank you."

"But Charm may not. She's got it into her head that that woman – Shya – needs *her* help."

Dawn gestured wildly in frustration, to no one in particular, but earning a curious look from the passenger of a passing car. Her eyes didn't stop there, though; they rose to scan the strangely-colored sky. She didn't think they'd looked quite like that before Asmodeus became known to them. Not on this level, anyway.

They looked like this on that rocky shoreline, though. She shivered.

"I won't ask you to keep her from Shya," Cadence's voice brought Dawn back to herself. "So please know that I won't blame you if it happens."

Dawn tried to ignore the screaming voice inside herself accusing her until-recently estranged sister of being irresponsible. Her assumptions about Cadence in the past had been wrong. She couldn't risk that again. "Cadence…"

"You have no idea how hard it is for me not to hop in the car right now, Dawn. But I want her to live this life with some semblance of happiness. And she hasn't had that lately. I've watched her fade into this hopeless, sad person I don't even recognize anymore."

Dawn recalled the inherent joy she'd sensed from her niece earlier. She'd positively radiated it. Could she truly be that different away from Dawn?

"I'm already losing her, Dawn. Please."

Dawn felt stuck. She glanced toward the house again. It was full-dark, and well past feeling like the longest day ever. "I'm going to say hello to her now."

"Good."

She sighed. "You're alright with where she's staying?"

"Are you kidding? I appreciate them so much. And I talked to the guy – Connor. Um, nicest guy ever?"

Dawn smiled. "Yeah."

"OK; go see her. I'm going to try to be as brave as I've tried to sound. And you'll call me? Whenever, whatever?"

"Of course."

"Thank you, Dawnie."

"Thank *you.* You don't have to be this kind to me after... everything."

"Yes, I do. I love you. Never stopped."

And the tears were back. "I love you, too," Dawn cried, embarrassed, but too happy to care.

"Talk soon."

Dawn jumped, a thought occurring to her. "Wait... did Charm say *how* she thought she was meant to help?"

Cadence paused, but only for a breath. "She's always said the woman needs to see her. That's all."

It meshed so well with what the Seers women had been talking about earlier that Dawn found herself wondering if Charm's very presence *could* be the solution. Surely, once Shya realized she was not the only option for the demon that possessed her, her death wish would resolve. *Could* she see that, though? Or would it be the demon who met Charm, in Shya's body, and steal her quietly as he had her friend? "It can't have her, too," Dawn said quietly. She frowned, Cadence's words echoing in her head. "You were saying she's *always* said she needed to meet Shya. You mean since she learned about this, right? A couple days at most?"

"No, Dawn. That's what I'm trying to tell you. She's been dreaming about this woman for *weeks*."

Dawn's jaw dropped as her eyes went to Connor's house again, where a silhouette was backlit by the light coming through the open door, now. Dawn raised her hand in a wave, slowly.

"You alright?"

She shook her head, letting her hand drop when Charm waved enthusiastically back, then beckoned her forward. "I suddenly feel as if I don't have any control at all," Dawn replied dreamily.

Her sister made a loud sound – whether it was of commiseration or disbelief, Dawn was unsure. "Welcome to my world," she said, and she sounded so much like Dawn's mother, slight Southern drawl included, that Dawn felt faint as they said their goodbyes and she drifted toward her beckoning niece.

CHAPTER 41 – INTERROGATION

Charm's eyes weren't as bright as they had been earlier. Finally, she was tired.

"Are you OK?"

She nodded.

"You two go ahead and make yourselves some tea, if you like," Connor poked his head around the arched entrance to the kitchen. He looked tired, too. "Our house is your house."

"I won't be here too long," Dawn assured him, but her eyes were already going to the tea pot and then the cupboard where she knew the honey was kept.

He waved a hand. "Stay as long as you like. I wish I could join you, but I'm wiped out. Hey," he nodded toward Charm and the girl made an effort to perk up, "it's really good to have you here." Connor smiled, then waved toward Dawn before disappearing into the hallway again.

The man hadn't batted an eyelash when Dawn had caught him up on the events of the evening. It had been a relief not to have to comfort him, but sad at the same time. *Nobody should react to the consequences of possession as though they're commonplace events of the day.*

Dawn smiled at Charm. "I'm making tea. Want some?"

Charm nodded. "Mom and I have, like, a tea ritual after meals."

Dawn was already switching the electric kettle on. She looked back at her niece. "That sounds familiar to me. Our mother used to have tea after every meal, and in between, too!"

Charm rested her head on an arm as she watched Dawn bustle about the room. "I see her around you."

Dawn stopped in her tracks, milk sloshing in the jug she was carrying from the fridge to the counter. "What?"

"Why do you block her out?"

Dawn gritted her teeth, confused, but completely sure she could not handle that conversation on top of everything else. She continued to the counter. "I need to get a grip on your gifts, girl. I think I made a mistake in assuming you were an empath, like me."

"How would you have known?" Charm shrugged, then seemed to catch herself. "I mean, it's OK. There's no way you could've known." She rubbed her face in her hands as she blew out a gust of air, which ended up making a rather humorous noise, and Charm giggled childishly.

Dawn found herself to be smiling. "It's alright, child."

Charm straightened in the chair, only to reach across the table and lay her head down on her bicep again.

Dawn sighed, glancing at the clock. "Good God, it's ten already."

Charm closed her eyes. "I'm glad you're here, though."

Dawn shook her head as she poured the boiling water into the mugs she'd prepared. "I'll drink this, then go. You've had quite the busy few days."

"It's true," the girl yawned extravagantly, "and I tend to seize more when I'm tired. Mom made me promise to tell you that. I feel fine, though."

Dawn sighed again, bringing the warm mugs to the table. "I *will* come back tomorrow, you know."

Charm returned her gaze blankly, then inhaled the steam from her mug, saying, "Mmm."

Dawn pondered the situation quietly as Charm carefully sipped at her tea, then asked, "Where are you sleeping?"

Charm's eyebrows raised. "Guest room. It's really pretty! Bethie says she got some design pointers from the twins last time they were here."

Dawn's eyebrows rose, now. "I didn't know that!"

Charm smiled. "You know how popular they are, right? I really can't wait to meet them!"

"Really?"

Charm nodded enthusiastically. "Their designs are featured in the types of magazines Mom gets. And it's *so* cool that they're identical *and* have albinism!" She shook her head, a dreamy look making her features soft. "I think they're beautiful."

Dawn was frowning. It felt too close to home to have Charm already connected to the twins, or the Seers at all, even in such a secondary sort of way.

"Don't you?" Charm was regarding Dawn expectantly.

Dawn struggled to remember what they were talking about.

"Are they as pretty in person?" Charm prompted, then sipped her tea. The girl had perked up, though Dawn wasn't sure whether it was attributable to the tea or the talk of Jane and Anna.

She pondered for a moment. The twins were family to her now, but she could recall how striking they'd appeared to her when they'd first met. The women had reached out of their own accord, having asked around when they'd made their family estate outside of Toronto their permanent residence. They wanted to be *part of a community,* they'd said, explaining that their family of witches (Dawn remembered how she'd burst out laughing during that first phone conversation, and the twins had laughed, too, acknowledging the term as carrying a stigma, but did not take it back). Their family had always been proud of what they were, they'd said, but were also traditionally very solitary beings, choosing to create their own secret worlds rather than integrating themselves into their surroundings, bravely refusing to be anything but who they were. Jane and Anna's mother had taken their births as a sign that they were destined to break out of that long-established, but lonely pattern, having been born as a pair. And she'd socialized the girls, though it was unnatural to her, and helped them to navigate a world in which they were different for more than just how they appeared.

The women had determined to carry their mother's efforts into their careers, and do something that forced them to work with people while encouraging them into the public eye. They prided themselves in that they had gained respect for their interior design skills even as they faced both extremes of reactions with regards to their extracurricular activities.

Dawn marvelled, now, at how the women had occasionally used the term "witch" to describe themselves since, but Dawn – too stubborn or too close-minded, maybe – had never taken it seriously.

"Aunt Dawn?" Charm was smiling, her eyebrows raised. Indeed, the girl seemed amused by Dawn's distraction.

She shook herself lightly. "I guess I'm tired, too!"

Charm giggled.

"They really are gorgeous," Dawn answered the original question, suddenly filled with pride at the privilege of calling the women her friends. "And talented," she added, absently. "They're amazing, really."

Charm sighed. "I knew it."

Dawn inhaled sharply in an effort to get back on track. "Listen, my beautiful niece, we are both very tired and I have the feeling we have equally exciting days ahead of us, but I need to know some things before I can feel good about leaving."

"Let's do twenty questions!" Charm positively bounced in her chair. "You ask a bunch of questions, quick, and I give a true and honest answer, but fast, and we don't stop to talk about it. If you ask a follow-up, it counts as a question all on its own!"

Dawn chuckled. "Your mother do that with you?"

Charm shook her head. "Uncle Kenny does it when he thinks I'm hiding something. He says maybe it's easier to tell the truth if you know you can do it fast and nobody can interrogate you about it, as long as you're playing the game."

Dawn swallowed the lump of emotion that had reinstated itself in her throat, and nodded. "Can we follow-up later if we need to know more about the answers?"

Charm nodded sagely. "But not until at least a day later."

Dawn folded her arms. It was a clever way to get some answers quick, but she knew it would take more than twenty quick-fire questions to learn what she yearned to know about her niece. But the practicality of the idea was undeniable, especially as her own exhaustion seemed to seep into her limbs as the hot tea warmed her belly.

Charm raised her eyebrows. "OK?"

Dawn nodded. "OK!"

"Except we each only have *five* questions, or we'll be here for *hours,*" the girl rolled her eyes as only a teenaged girl could, and Dawn laughed.

"Agreed."

"Nothing is off the table?"

Dawn frowned. "Why am I feeling a bit anxious now?"

Charm laughed.

"You have me at a disadvantage here," Dawn exclaimed, afraid of the family-related questions that were sure to come.

"I promise to be fair," Charm put a palm on her heart.

The girl was clever. Dawn had intended on getting answers, and here she was bartering with answers of her own. "Who's first?"

Charm leaned back in her seat and pointed at Dawn. "Go."

Shit. She suddenly wished she'd had time to prepare.

Charm peered at the time on her phone, then raised one eyebrow in her aunt's direction.

Dawn couldn't help but laugh. "OK. What is your gift?"

"Jumping right in, huh?" Charm smiled broadly. "I'm an energy reader."

Dawn frowned. "What exactly does that mean?"

"I can see energies everywhere – live people, dead people, anything living or with a living energy attached to it."

"'See?' Like with your physical eyes or in your mind's eye?"

"Both."

"And how did you discover what you were seeing wasn't the same as what everyone else saw?"

"Mom always knew it; she assumed I was like you because I always knew what was up with people, but that was only because I could see it, not necessarily feel it like you do. I do sometimes, though. Anyway, as soon as I was old enough to realize she didn't understand what I was seeing, I told her. And we talked about it. She did research, got me talking to some people that tried to help and guide me, you know?"

Dawn nodded. "So, you see ghosts, too?"

Charm nodded.

"Wow. That is incredible." Her mind whirled with the possibilities. And several new questions. She opened her mouth to ask another, but Charm held her hand up.

"Nope. My turn!"

"What?" Dawn slapped a palm to her mouth when the word popped out much louder than she'd intended.

Charm giggled hard. "You already asked your five!"

"I did *not*!"

The girl slapped a thigh, still laughing. "You're funny. You're so much like Mom in your reactions!"

"I didn't ask five questions, though! More like one!" She thought, then admitted, "Maybe two."

Charm shook her head, inhaled and appeared to gather herself. Then she ticked off the questions in rapid-fire form, counting on her fingers as she did. "What is your gift, what does that mean, with your eyes or your mind, how'd you figure it out and so, you see ghosts, too."

"Shit!" Dawn exclaimed, then covered her mouth again as Charm dissolved into another fit of giggles.

"Follow-up questions count, remember?" Charm pointed at her, her eyes twinkling.

Dawn put her hands on her hips, harrumphing.

"My turn!" Charm clapped her hands.

Dawn stretched her arms high above her head, groaning dramatically. "Well, we'd best get to bed, honey." She patted Charm's hand, ignoring the girl's shocked expression.

"Oh, no you don't!" Charm stood before Dawn could rise. "It's my turn, Auntie Dawn, and you know it!"

Dawn scowled at her niece, employing her sternest expression.

Charm laughed.

Dawn threw her hands up. "Fine. But make 'em quick." She gestured toward Charm's seat and her niece sat, positively buzzing with excitement.

"Go," Dawn pointed, hoping to apply the same pressure Charm had on her.

The girl was ready. "Do you have a boyfriend?"

Dawn scoffed. *Trust a teen girl to go straight to love interests.* Still, it could have been worse. But as she inhaled to answer, she paused, realizing she wasn't entirely sure if she did have a partner at the moment. A wave of sadness passed over her and Charm surely perceived it, as she patted Dawn's arm, her smile melting away.

"Say, 'It's complicated'," she encouraged. "That's an answer."

Dawn nodded, then cleared her throat. "Sorry. Things are sort of..."

"Complicated?" Charm smiled again, her face lighting up with it, and Dawn was... well, she was charmed.

"Is that smile the reason for your name?"

"Hey!" Charm protested. "It's still my turn!"

Dawn shook herself, still feeling discombobulated. "This game is dangerous," she muttered.

Charm sighed. "I'll go easy on you, since you're new to this." She shook her head. "Man, Kenny'd kick your butt at this. Don't agree to play this with him until you've had more experience, OK?"

Again, Dawn was at a loss for words. Would Kenny even look at her, at this point?

"I will answer you, though, because I like the answer," Charm grinned. "My mom started calling me 'Charm' while she was pregnant with me, because everybody called my dad 'Lucky'." She laughed quietly. "She wasn't thinking about the cereal at the time. Or that one might be strange – or lonely – without the other." Her eyes misted over as her smile faded.

Now Dawn was overcome with emotion that wasn't hers. She squeezed the girl's hand as her own wave of sadness enveloped her.

"You feel it, right? You don't see it, like me, but you can

feel how I feel?"

Dawn nodded. "But my friends – The Seers – they can block it, if they want to. You can too.

The girl shrugged. "I don't mind." She squeezed Dawn's hand back, sending a jolt of something up her arm. Something… tingly.

"What was *that*?"

Charm smiled. "I don't just see energy; I can manipulate it, too."

What? How? Like Reiki, or something different? She was pretty sure she hadn't felt anything close to the energetic pulse Charm had just flooded her with, Reiki master or no. *What exactly can she do? What can this mean?* Dawn's thoughts raced.

"It's not always so easy, though," the girl focused on Dawn's hand again, and a heat gathered there. Dawn gazed at the spot, too, jaw dropping as the heat intensified until it was very nearly uncomfortable.

She looked at Charm, amazed. "You got *powers*, girl!"

Charm smiled, but her eyes were sad. "No more than you and your friends, and as I'm sure you know, it doesn't always feel like a 'gift'."

Dawn's thoughts cleared as something snapped into place. The girl was suffering. She truly did need help. She needed community, too, perhaps more than any of The Seers did. "I'm sorry, love," she said quietly, "I don't think I was letting myself understand."

The girl sent another tingly rush of warmth up Dawn's arm, making her jaw drop yet again. "Fear and love do funny things."

Dawn nodded, speechless. The girl's words were so… astute that no reply seemed necessary.

Charm cleared her throat and sat back. Dawn was slower to remove her pleasantly-tingling arm from its reach across the table.

But Charm was plowing forward. "Is it weird to feel what someone else is feeling in particular situations?" The girl was blushing; her mocha skin pinking prettily.

Dawn smiled. "Like *what*?"

"Like, if they're in the bathroom? Or while they're kissing someone!"

Dawn was laughing, now. *Could be worse,* she pondered. "Um," she let out a breath between chuckles, "probably. I mean, I don't have another basis of comparison, so it feels normal to me, but I suppose if you suddenly started feeling everyone's emotions as if they were your own, it'd be really strange."

Charm nodded, looking thoughtful.

Dawn sipped her tea. The front door heralded an arrival, and Bethie's voice was quick to call out a greeting.

"Hey," Dawn gave her a little wave. "Did you and the others talk?"

Bethie nodded, her eyes going to Charm as the girl rose to hug her. She met Dawn's eyes over the girl's soldier, first questioning, then pleasantly surprised. "Well, hello there," she patted Charm's back. "What's this for?"

Charm held Bethie at arm's length. She was Bethie's height exactly. Dawn pondered the girl's height, automatically attributing it to the girl's father, for folks weren't tall on her side of the family.

"Thought you might have had a bit of a day," Charm smiled, and Bethie nodded, dazedly meeting the girl's eyes.

"I have. Thank you, sweetheart."

Dawn wondered if anyone could resist her niece. Proudly.

Bethie looked at Dawn again, her hands still on Charm's arms and seemingly happy there. "We talked. We're still friends," she smiled. "But we've had to agree to disagree on some things," she finished, then kissed Charm's cheek, surprising them both. "Feels like I've known you forever," she smiled at the girl, who seemed unphased. "I'm going to head to bed," Bethie gave Dawn a wave, then said, "See you tomorrow," before disappearing in the direction of the bedroom.

"Jordan still sleeping in their bed?" Dawn whispered as Bethie's footsteps faded down the hall, and Charm nodded, her lips pressed together.

"Can't blame him."

Dawn nodded.

Charm sat.

"Come on, girl. You got three questions left and Auntie's tired."

Charm sat up, then fired, "Do you ever want kids?"

Why do I feel like she's going easy on me? "Never thought I did," Dawn answered, leaving out *until I met you.*

Charm seemed placated. For now. "Did you really think your Dad and my Mom were in a weird, sort of incestuous-type relationship?"

Dawn nearly choked on her own tongue. *There we go. That's more like it.* She'd expected as much, but Charm's delivery, in its completely bold-faced and unafraid expectancy, had knocked her for a loop.

Charm regarded her calmly.

Dawn gulped her tea, which was nearly cold, then did cough, having inhaled some of it in her haste. Charm stood and patted her back firmly.

Dawn cleared her throat as the girl sat.

"Well?"

"No leaving that one for another day, huh?"

She shook her head.

"Well," Dawn pondered the question. On its face, it was a direct acknowledgement of the thing that Dawn had blamed for her willful severance from her family. But there was doubt there, too, as if the girl suspected more. *And maybe,* Dawn thought, *she's right.* "Honestly," she started again, hoping against hope that the words she chose now were an honest representation of what she was feeling, "I don't know. I remember the first time I thought it, when your Mom lived with us and was taking care of Dad, too. But I don't think there was strong evidence of it. I think, maybe, that it helped me stay angry at my father. Gave me an excuse to make my own way, do my own thing without looking back. I'd been suffering with my own gift," she lamented, "and feared my sisters' – and my brothers'! – blindness to who I believed my dad to truly be."

Charm frowned, but did not follow-up.

She must be saving the last for a doozy, Dawn internalized. But the girl's lingering stare made her squirm in her seat. Cast doubt on whether she'd understood Dawn's explanation. And most significantly, pushed Dawn to say more without Charm having to say another word.

"Remember I could feel what he was feeling, too," Dawn voiced, her tone rising slightly. Defensively. "He was a selfish man. And Cadence was vulnerable."

"But you left instead of trying to protect her?"

Dawn sat back in her seat as if the words had shoved her.

The girl's own features echoed Dawn's shock. "I'm so sorry. I should never have said that."

Dawn shook her head, but stiffly. It was the vocalization of what she'd known, deep down, all along. "I was scared," she said. "I never properly dealt with my mother's death. The accident..." she tried to stop, because the words were streaming from her, now, out of her control. But they came anyway: "I've never forgotten his guilt," she admitted, crying, now. "And how desperate he was for us all to be OK, because he knew he had to make it up to us! The way he treated us all, but mostly her. The way he treated my poor mother..."

"You never forgave him for that."

It was a statement, and Dawn couldn't deny it. "It was never made right for her. And she was gone so fast – I didn't even feel fear from her, or love, or understanding that she was gone." She shook her head, seeing it in her mind as if it had happened yesterday. Feeling the way her shoulders slumped unnaturally, the screaming pain of her broken collarbones where her car seat straps had snapped them efficiently in two, but maybe saved her, too. *Surely* saved her. And seeing her mother, lifeless already, on the hood of the car, and then watching as the life drained from the eyes of the deer that had just been trying to get to the other side. "I don't think I ever got over the fact that one minute, I felt her, full and strong, if not sad. It had always been there, the feeling of my mom. Without my knowing, I'd incorporated her feelings into my life as though they were a tangible thing. And when she was gone, it was so sudden I couldn't handle the pain of that absence." She met Charm's eyes, astonished at her own revelation. "And then I felt the deer die, and it was terrible – a relief and a tragedy simultaneously – and the unfairness of that made me angry." She observed Charm's confusion and added, "The fact that I could feel everything that deer did, but nothing at all from my mother. That's what made me angriest, I think."

"At who?"

Dawn threw her hands up. "God? Myself? Mom? The fucking deer?" She let her hands lower, sending an apologetic look to her niece.

"Keep going."

Her hands found each other in her lap and held on to one another as if to find some comfort there. A sob found it's way out of her as she gave in to the things she'd denied for so long. "At *him*," she said, finally. "I was so angry at him, because it took her dying to make him stop treating everyone like shit, and it was too late, because Mom never knew it." She buried her face in her hands, feeling miserable for burdening her niece, and yet *free* by unburdening herself, she supposed. She looked up past her fingertips, another revelation clarifying itself. "And it was *so* easy for him to change. Barely an effort at all. He truly could have done it anytime, had he made his mind up to! But he didn't. Not until she was gone and it was too late."

A soft hand warmed her shoulder, and if love could be a moveable, tangible thing, that was what Charm sent flowing into her, and again she was overwhelmed with the magic of this girl who was her sister's daughter, whose first thirteen years of life had been missed by Dawn, and for what? To not have to face the very basic things she'd just admitted?

Overwhelmed, she stood, pulling Charm up into her arms and crying freely, and soon Charm's tears dampened Dawn's shoulder, too.

"I wish I could go back in time," Dawn muttered once the tears had slowed.

Charm held her at arm's length. "This is how it was meant to happen, Auntie."

Dawn shook her head, her face crumpling again, not seeing.

"I'm glad you shared this with me," Charm ducked her head a bit to meet Dawn's eyes.

"Girl, I don't care what you call it: a gift, a curse, or something else. I think you're incredible. I think your heart is. And I promise to love you – and make sure you know it – 'til the day I die."

The girl's eyes swam in refreshed tears. "I was saving the fifth question, and I accidentally used it."

Dawn laughed. "I know."

"Can I ask it anyway?" Charm's self-assuredness faded, and suddenly there was a vulnerable, if not fearful, teenager looking at her with a desperation Dawn felt like a knife to the belly.

She nodded. “Of course, you can.”

Charm sniffled, nodding, then let her hands drop and sat. She gestured Dawn toward the chair across from her, and Dawn sat, nervous at the girl’s obvious effort to compose herself. And nervous because she knew that whatever her niece asked of her in this moment, Dawn would have no choice but to grant. For love.

Charm met her eyes with a fearful intensity and asked, “Will you help me find a teacher?”

Dawn nodded without hesitation, feeling like a wet sheet left out to flap in the cold wind with no knowledge of when she’d be reeled in again.

“Then you have to let me help Shya.”

Dawn blanched, though she was unsurprised.

Charm reached for Dawn’s hands over the table, and Dawn reached back, letting the girl grip her flesh with a fervor fuelled by hope and need.

Dawn nodded, feeling like she may vomit, and forced herself to say, “Fear and love make us do strange things.”

Charm nodded back, then smiled.

CHAPTER 42 – STUCK

After that night, Dawn and Charm indulged in each other's company at every chance, which was surprisingly often; progress with Shya – or indeed with any of The Seer's goals – had slowed to all but a stop.

Sheila, in fact, had returned home for the workweek. It wasn't without regret; the woman was determined as they all were to bring Shya back, but without direction, none could predict when that might happen. She'd promised to return at the end of the week. And before leaving, she'd pulled Dawn aside, insisting they make a pact to get in touch if either of them heard from the men in Tibet, for even Ed had grown silent.

The twins stayed, but spent more time at the hotel, working remotely via video chats and conference calls, and spending an equal amount of time doing "research," though Dawn wasn't entirely sure what they were researching. The occasional glance at their open laptops, whenever Dawn and Charm went to see them, revealed little, but what it did show was dark, indeed. Articles on possession, black magic, the demons of Hell, interspersed with theoretical writings on portals, the psychology of the possessed and those who tried to exorcise them… it was all topical according to the situation, but Dawn failed to glean the ultimate goal of their searching. And they were keeping the answer between themselves, for now.

At Shya's childhood home, things were much the same, if not further stymied by frustration. John had returned home from the hospital, but the time away seemed to have changed him. Rather than wallowing as he was before, seemingly mired in the muck of apathy that consumed the house, he had determined to take on some consulting work. Apparently, his scientific background had been sought out by a Canadian company mandated to study the evolving global situation. John would not reveal what he knew about the cause – which was everything - but seemed grateful for the excuse to leave – and stay away. Dawn could see the blank look steal over his eyes after about an hour at home.

Rory could have used a sabbatical, too, but he remained by Shya's bed. To which, incidentally, Shya was now strapped. It was soft material that tied her limbs to the posts, but the measure, though necessary, was one that Rory hated.

Shya hadn't risen, though. Not since the straps were applied, though Dawn wasn't convinced the two were related.

But for Dawn, the presence of her niece was enough to transform the somber visit into something unexpectedly wonderful. While she was away from the house, that was. And while she wasn't wondering about Ed. And Mel – who hadn't said a word since that text on the night they'd arrived in Tibet.

Charm took all of that away. She was clever, funny, and bright, and seemed to want to be beside Dawn at all times. Dawn hadn't allowed her to the house, yet, but then Charm hadn't asked. She'd gone with Dawn to see the twins at The British several times in the days since Sheila had departed, and that was another element of surprise; the twins were immediately fascinated by the girl and drew her into their mysterious world in such a way that Dawn was left feeling rather like a third – or fourth, as it were – wheel. But that was alright, too, because when the three were huddled together, Dawn would stretch out on one of the beds in their shared room, and sleep.

She slept much better at The British than she did at John's home. Though Shya hadn't had another incident since the last terrifying one, Dawn couldn't seem to stop listening for it. She would lay on the pull-out in the basement, eyes wide and staring blankly into the darkness, tired but frightened that if she let herself fall asleep, the demon would know and Shya would be fuelled into consciousness again, whether for the demon's purposes or her own.

The two were difficult to distinguish, these days.

And so, bereft of ideas for how to proceed, the group had agreed that they needed to wait. Wait for Ed, and maybe even the Bodhisatta, to be able to control the manipulation of the portal, or to act as portals, themselves? And Mel, to plan and to guide them, though none were certain if that would happen. And in some way, for Charm, who seemed serenely confident that she could help, but hadn't articulated exactly how, and nor had Dawn pushed the girl, for the girl's involvement still felt wrong to her logical self. She'd spoken to her sister several times over the weekend, and just twice since the workweek started for her, and now it was Wednesday and Cadence was waffling on whether she'd show up on the weekend. Charm would not commit to returning home with her, and kept asking for more time. Dawn had to bite back her comments on that, and when she was successful, she found herself in admiration of the relationship between the mother and daughter. In the end, despite the risks, Cadence seemed solely focused on Charm's happiness, as long as Charm and Dawn kept her well-informed. And Dawn discovered that Charm naturally inspired that sort of give and take: she could reason with the best of them and had an uncanny knack of poking at just the right soft spots in a person's armour to achieve her goal, though not maliciously so. Somehow, it always made sense to Dawn. And the girl's capacity to manipulate any situation was an impressive consequence of her gifts. Of course, she could sway a person! To her, what was unsaid read as plain as spoken words in the energies of her companions. *Why not use that information?* Dawn reasoned. After all, it was only human nature to respond to the elements we perceive, whether it was limited to tone of voice, or with the benefits of body language. A person's aura was only one more piece of the puzzle, to her talented niece.

And so, they all seemed to be waiting for *something* to happen. Something to change, something to call them into action. And in the meantime, Dawn was getting to know her niece. And not only trying to understand the girl's gifts. They'd ventured across the border to shop at the Ottawa malls and drink café coffees and enjoy meals away from everyone else. Dawn loved the girl, undoubtedly, and as they spent time together, she found she *liked* her, too. It was bittersweet to find the connections between the girl and Dawn's siblings... and Dawn, herself! Her mannerisms, her humour, even the way her family said certain things with a tinge of a southern drawl unique to them, it seemed, as it was Dawn's parents who'd brought that to Canada and perpetuated it, it seemed, with gusto in the way they spoke to their family.

While Dawn kept busy with her niece, she effectively avoided the parts of her life that felt uncertain. Ironically, her blossoming connections with members of her family seemed a solitary comfort in her life, while everything else seemed to float, untethered and without direction.

She knew it couldn't last, but felt at a loss for how to change it in a way that would be beneficial. They'd all agreed they couldn't try to retrieve Shya on their own again, and the notion of adding Charm to the mix, especially when even Sheila had departed, was foolish. At least they all agreed to that, to Dawn's relief. Going home didn't feel like an option, either, even if Charm came with her. Home was a step back. Back to where the shadows were freely inhabited by ghouls, to where Shya was indefinitely *gone,* and to where Mel's absence would be most keenly felt.

So, they waited.

They saw the strange skies, perceived the dark presences that flooded through the tear in the barrier between life and that part-life that was Shya's Hell. And they exchanged glances that said, "We have to deal with this, and soon." But still, they waited.

And the inhabitants of Earth spiralled in a sucking vortex of despair, increasingly overcome by fear as conspiracy theories and legitimate, study-based theories abounded. The government was not silent on the matter, but they were maddeningly vague, so citizens turned to social media and the news coming out of foreign countries to try and fill in the gaps. Suicide rates were at a steady, record-breaking high, with young people succumbing with shocking frequency to the depths of melancholy inspired by the insurgence of darkness into the living world.

There were those, though, who stubbornly carried on, going to work, then trudging home to eat dinner in front of the television. Employing blinders to block their peripherals while the promise of a solution remained elusive. And who could blame them? That was perhaps the most menacing outcome of the situation in its entirety: options were few. Either carry on, pasting on a smile and doggedly practicing the "business as usual" attitude that government-backed psychologists peddled in daily addresses and sponsored advertisements, or fall, peering horrified into the roiling clouds of the transformed sky, and then everywhere else, in search of a reason. In search of hope and, finding none, either determine to keep trying, or to leave it all behind. And the shadows of demons were especially good at disguising signs of hope as further signs of what many had dubbed the apocalypse.

And, depending on your definition of apocalypse, one would be hard-pressed to deny the accuracy of the label, Dawn thought.

She wondered if Mel, despite his knowledge, had simply joined the ranks of the melancholy and now sought to find a handhold before he fell entirely.

So, determining to wait was not an easy task for the Seers that remained in Aylmer with the possessed. It was a frequent task, yes, but one ruminated upon every time they made it, and all the time in between, too. Indeed, Rory lamented the choice at every pass. His drive, though strangled by their limitations, persisted, and Dawn, for one, was glad. It seemed so easy to give up in those times, which undoubtedly was a purposeful side effect of the breach between the levels.

But she was determined that their stagnation was a temporary thing. She reassured herself – and anyone who would listen – many times each day. And then she carried on, choosing to live, but without the benefit of blinders.

She and the rest of The Seers could not unknow what they knew. Their gifts took that privilege away. And there were others who knew, too, others around the world who sensed the breach and sought their own answers. Others who knew The Seers and reached out, asking *why.* This was especially true for the twins and Sheila, all of whom practiced their craft and had clients and friends who trusted their insight. And Dawn knew the women didn't lie. But because they loved Shya, they omitted details as appropriate.

Dawn thought it was so painful because nobody knew when it would change. Which, she'd been told, was the most agonizing element of depression. And now, it was a collective race that was depressed. So, she focused on the positive. Which translated, in truth, to grateful gazes toward her beautiful niece.

And then, Wednesday night, when Dawn went to bed after a particularly heated discussion with Charm regarding how much school, exactly, she was willing to miss while they floundered in indecision and lack of solution, Dawn did something different. She didn't mean to, but it happened, anyway. She fell asleep right away. Not that restless, semi-conscious sort of sleep she'd been maintaining, but a deep and complete unconsciousness. And she dreamt. Not of Shya, or that world she remained trapped in, but of the ghost that clung to her and guided her until Asmodeus stole her up.

Or at least, that was what Shya thought had happened.

CHAPTER 43 – REVEAL

She panicked as soon as she realized she was deeply asleep, and dreaming. Her immediate reaction faded, however, as she acclimatized, for this place was not the rocky shore she feared, but seemed quite the opposite. There was a vast space around her, misted over in such a way that it felt as though she was inside of a cloud. Soft, quiet, and most importantly, *safe.* She remained on alert, even as she allowed herself to turn in a slow circle. Looking for something – anything – that could signal subterfuge and shock her into waking. But there was nothing. Just fluffy, floaty white on all sides, as far as the eye could see. For a while.

And then, there was something. Dawn was feeling nearly comfortable by the time the blob of an object appeared before her, far into the distance. And even then, she was not startled, for the greyish blob blended seamlessly into its soft surroundings – just a darkening element of the fog. And as it came closer, for it was, Dawn was sure of it, it became more solid. More a shape of its own, with another shape atop it. A person. And she wasn't afraid, because it was slow, and whatever presence was there emitted only hope and calm. Dawn knew the demon was tricky. A part of her urged her to run. But it was a very small part, and it was overshadowed with a comforting feeling that Dawn doubted could be accomplished by a spirit so malevolent. And by that presence and the calm it pressed ahead of itself. She was reminded of Mel's gentle, soothing touch, and then that of her long-dead mother, and the realization was very nearly painful.

But it was not Dawn's own mother that approached her, now, on what she could see was a steadily-moving bed; her sailing vessel in an ocean of clouds. It was, of course, Shya's mother.

Dawn had seen pictures of the woman, but recognized her as Shya's mother first because for one incredible, joyful second, she thought it was Shya herself, returning to them on the very bed the ghost of her mother had been trapped on.

Still, her disappointment was fleeting when she recognized the older woman whose looks were so much like Shya's. Dark waving curls to her shoulders, wide eyes both wary and curious (an expression that had seemed permanent on her friend's face as she both struggled and thrived with her gift), and a long graceful frame dressed in a flowing white gown, which nearly made Dawn laugh, such was the cliché of it.

The smiling woman – Clara, Dawn remembered - was directly in front of her, now, eyes sparkling.

"Is it really you? Clara?"

The woman nodded.

"And not *him*? Asmodeus?" Dawn whispered the last, determined to confront the beast directly if indeed he was hiding behind the visage of the beautiful ghost.

She shook her head.

Dawn frowned. "Why are you – Shya said you were trapped. And the last time *I* saw you, some nasty things was happenin'!" she tried to smile, but the memory of the woman, whose current fair expression of herself had been quite the opposite, as she'd vomited and inhaled the vomit quite violently, impeded her.

The woman shook her head, and Dawn noted wisps of light and colour that her movement left. Shya had spoken of this in group: how ghosts sometimes moved as if in watercolour, or oil, leaving smears of the forms they took behind them.

"What? You're not… sick?"

She shook her head again, her dark curls leaving dreamy wisps about her head.

"You're not… trapped?"

"No," the woman said.

Despite the fact that she'd already lined up her next question (Why can't you speak?), the sound of Clara's voice made Dawn recoil as she gasped.

She reached out, her face eager. "It's alright!"

Dawn nodded, putting her hands on the wooden foot of the bed in a show of trust. "I don't understand," she whispered.

"The demon clouds her vision!" the woman said, and it echoed around them as though several of her had spoken.

Dawn fought to remain where she stood, focusing on Clara's mouth, which moved in that watery, delayed sort of way and even now tried to catch up with the words.

"She sees everything through the veil," the woman continued, her voice overlapping over itself as she trailed off, but her eyes said the rest. Her eyes said she was desperate.

"What can I do?" Dawn asked, raising her hands to her sides and letting them fall.

"Show her," the woman crawled to the end of the bed in the opposite fashion her speech had employed, moving too fast, too halting, too jerky to make sense.

Dawn took several steps back, that time. And she felt a pull behind her.

She was waking.

"Show her what?"

"That I *choose* to be with her!"

Dawn shook her head, now. The woman was fading. "How can I do that when you can't?"

"Lift the veil!" Clara was leaning over the footboard now,

straining to get her message through as Dawn began to fly backward. It was fast; the woman and her bed were swallowed by the mist, her final words barely there, but painfully clear in Dawn's ears as she bolted upright on the pullout, a shriek dying at her lips. "Show her Charm," the woman had said.

And there were other words swimming around in her head. Other words she knew she had to write, but instead, she breathed, slowly.

And then buried her face in her hands and cried.

CHAPTER 44 – TRAVELING

There was a knock at the door.

Dawn was still reeling, her hand between her breasts where her pounding heart threatened escape, but the sound was undeniable. She sucked in a breath, eyes going to the stairs in the darkness.

It came again.

She jerked her hand to the end table where her phone lay and pressed the on button as she brought it in front of herself. 3:33AM. She swallowed hard. The significance of the time did not escape her, but there was no time to contemplate, for the knock came again, and it was bolder, this time, and offensive in the dark quiet of the night.

And there was an answering sound that time: a guttural laughter, throaty and strangled, that Dawn knew belonged to Shya's possessor. She rose, quickly, and darted to the stairs on instinct. Knowing that the knock and the laughter signaled a coming together of something she'd been avoiding, even passively. And when she opened the door, her suspicion was confirmed, but not like she expected.

Charm stood on the step in her nightgown, her feet bare on what must be a very cold ground, for it was snowing. The first snow of the season, beautiful as it floated in great, soft clumps around her niece, lit by the streetlight behind her like a halo. But her face bore no expression of peace, no glad tidings spilled from purplish lips as they would have from an angel. Instead, the girl looked frighteningly pained.

Dawn wanted to pull the girl inside; to wrap her in blankets and pull thick socks over her feet, but as the laughter sounded again, making the skin on the back of her neck prick and burn with awareness, she wanted the opposite: to push her niece away. To follow her into the yard and to take her away from the demon that held her friend.

But she could do neither, because something was off. Something was *wrong,* and she saw it more plainly as Charm struggled to speak. No air passed her lips. Instead, a thick, white foam oozed from between them, and she convulsed, her arms jerking wildly and her eyes rolling back in her head until her amber irises were gone.

Dawn reached for her with a yell as the girl fell back, and she should have been able to grab a slip of her nightgown at least, to pull with all her might so that Charm landed more softly, but she didn't. She couldn't. Her fingers swished through Charm as though she was a manifestation of the air itself, and then she was, fading as she landed with a *whoosh* on the thin covering of snow and was gone with barely a sigh.

Dawn came a voice in her ear and Dawn jumped. It was Charm's voice, Charm's breath that tickled her skin. And she was in trouble.

Dawn wasted no time with shoes or her jacket; her earlier disapproval of her niece's bare feet was forgotten. Later, she'd be thankful she'd always worn socks to bed, for though her feet were damaged by the frenzied run to Connor's house, it would surely have been worse without them.

She wasn't thinking of any of that then, though. She pushed aside that menacing voice from the second floor as the laughter grew louder and ever more fanatical. She refused to be moved by the eery mirth it portrayed as she lit upon the stair and slammed the door behind her. She didn't feel the cold wetness of the snow on her soles, nor the harsh grit of the pavement once she'd run past the newly paved section of road.

She failed to realize that Shya had run just as she was running now, towards Connor's with but one mandate driving her.

She only flew, her feet slipping sometimes on the slushy, wet, new snow, and nightshirt flapping around her in the cold air of the night. And when she had to stop, because the door between herself and Charm was locked, she screamed in frustration and pounded on it, knowing then how Shya had run straight through Ed to get to where she needed to be, because if the door didn't open very shortly, she meant to do the same to it.

But Bethie was there, then, pulling her housecoat around herself and looking suddenly haggard, as if all the healing she had done since Jordan's return to them fell away at the prospect of Dawn's early-morning visit. But Dawn didn't care; she pushed past the woman, shrieking, "Call 911!" and ran for the guest room. Her heart throbbed against her ribcage. Her pulse pounded in her ears. Jordan's waking screams assailed the air. And then she was there, and Charm was on the floor, her body stiff and spasming as foam ran from her mouth. One arm reaching in front of her for some invisible thing - *for me,* Dawn thought, *for me!* - and the soles of her feet bright red and bleeding.

CHAPTER 45 – THE CHOICE

All is twisted in the mire
The land of hate and rage and fire
With shadow creatures oozing there
Between your toes and in your hair
It's hard to breathe and time runs slow
Light intertwines around its foe

Sky of contradicting hues
Sunset orange and navy blues
A streak of blinding light that tears
Such good, so unwittingly shared
Or taken by the darkest one
The King of Demons has his fun

He throws slick stones along your path
Sends crashing waves to drown his wrath
Disguises truth with shadowed veil
Sets love adrift without a sail
Digs ever deep in gurgling sand
Grows you roots and cuffs your hands

But daughter, you must not believe
That all there's left to do is grieve
You mustn't let him fool you, love
There is still light of good above
He's got you where you've deigned to stay
He's sketched your world in hues of gray

Take heart, daughter, unshield your eyes
Close your ears to wicked lies
Gaze beyond your suffering
Lift your voice my love, and sing
Reach beyond what he shows you
Your reality so darkly skewed

I am here, but I do not rot
I am not unwillingly caught
The visage he has made you trust
Is just the surface, merely crust
Retreat; don't give it all to him
Don't heed his lies of guilt and sin

Don't give the greatest gift you own
Not eyes to see, not light strings strewn
Not what the demon wants of you
Not what you're entreated to do
It all is pale when held against
Your *life,* my love, in present tense

You're convinced that it's all undone
What door is torn won't be torn down
All's lost unless the light is gone
Snuffed out when withered shell is done
But without you, he'll need another
And no, he cannot use your mother!

There are more souls that shine, like you
And if you go, they'll be trapped, too
Stop – don't add that to the weight
Of all you've taken on to date
Just live, dear girl, and we will find
The right way to leave it all behind

CHAPTER 46 – REDIRECT

"The demon skews *everything!*" Jane exclaimed. Her sister nodded enthusiastically beside her.

"What are you saying?" Dawn asked, feeling perilously close to the line between discussing and arguing. "Are you telling me the demon projected Charm onto our doorstep to alert me to her situation?"

Jane rolled her eyes.

"How kind!" Dawn threw her hands up.

Anna put a gentle hand on Dawn's forearm. "All we're trying to say is that we can't understand everything right now! Regardless of what we know, regardless of what gifts we have! We can't be confident of any conclusions. The demon..."

"Skews everything, yeah, yeah," Dawn waved the words away and turned, walking a couple steps away from the twins. A bodily effort to retreat from the line they all tread so close to.

"It started with you," Anna added. Her voice was quiet and smooth, and even that return to normalcy brought tears of relief to Dawn's eyes.

She turned. "What?"

Anna smiled, but Jane stepped forward. "Since when have you been able to travel through time and space in order to embody the physical form of *anyone,* much less that of someone whose existence you hadn't been aware of?"

Dawn frowned.

Anna stepped in beside her sister. “Or communicate directly with ghosts?”

Again, Dawn waved the words away, making a face. “How do we know that wasn’t just a dream?”

Both women cocked their heads to the side, studying Dawn intently, before saying “Was it?” in perfect unison.

Dawn rubbed at her face furiously. “No!” she answered, finally, the word bursting from her.

“We’ve been learning about possession; about the demons. There’s a theory that in order to come through in the living world, these dark entities have no choice but to change things,” Anna gestured with her hands as she spoke.

“What, like that hole in the sky?” Dawn chuckled sardonically. “Isn’t that enough?”

Both women shook their heads. “More than that. They need to interact with us. Frighten us. They use that fear to gain power in the living world.”

Dawn frowned at Jane. “What does that mean?”

“It means that boundaries get blurred,” Anna stepped forward. “It’s not just the rip in the veil between life and death; it’s that the entire border is stretched. The natural and the supernatural mingle!”

Dawn sighed. “So, you’re saying our gifts are enhanced? That it’s easier now to cross that border?”

The women nodded, but then both held up a finger. Anna smiled at Jane in a rare acknowledgement of their duality, and Jane gave her an appreciative nod before saying, “Not necessarily ‘enhanced,’ though.” She looked at her sister again. “More like,” both women looked at Dawn and finished with, “*changed*.”

The chaos in Dawn’s mind, as usual, found itself loosening the knots it was in as the intuitive womens’ words asserted themselves as truth. She raised her eyes to them again. "So, when Charm was on the step?"

They nodded. "We think her seizures make the boundaries even more fuzzy. She was having a Grand Mal seizure, which Cadence said hasn't happened in some time." Jane gestured toward Charm's hospital room, whose door was closed as both Charm and Cadence tried to get some rest. Cadence had arrived at mid-morning, and besides a rushed embrace, she and Dawn had had very little time even to discuss the situation. Dawn had not, however, been able to ignore the new lines on her sister's pretty face, and the softer contours of her body. Her heart had galloped in her chest, too, when she recognized her mother in Cadence's adult expression. And since that first, rushed greeting, Dawn found she was plagued by that old, familiar ache that settled into its spot over her heart, where it had lived for so long before Charm cast it away. And she was forced to admit, again, that despite her blossoming relationship with her niece, she still had a mess to clean up with the other family members she'd shunned for so many years.

"Wait," Dawn rubbed at her face again as she paced in the narrow hallway. "What about her feet?"

The twins regarded each other soberly, then looked back at Dawn. "We don't know," they chorused, before Jane took over again.

"The demon..." she paused to smile at a passing nurse, then stepped closer before opening her mouth to speak again.

Dawn held a hand up. "Skews things," she finished for her friend, whose eyes cleared as a small smile touched her lips. Dawn shook her head. "So, how does this help us? I mean, it just feels even more – uncertain, to me, considering all that!"

Anna touched Dawn's arm again, and this time, she welcomed the warmth. "We have to have faith," she said. "We believe that this irregularity gives us new opportunities. We just need to figure out how to take advantage!"

"Pfft," Dawn shook her head as she chuckled. "You two

are going to have enough faith for all of us," she muttered, her eyes going to Charm's door again. She pointed to it before speaking again. "How?"

The women regarded her, stunned.

"Charm might as well be lost to us, like Shya is!" Dawn's voice rose, though she hadn't intended it to.

"She could wake up anytime!" Anna tried a smile.

"This isn't unheard of after such a serious seizure," Jane added, but confusion still ruled her features.

"But right now," Dawn jabbed her pointer finger at the floor, "she's... well, we don't even know where she is, do we? How, without Sheila, or Ed, or Mel, or Shya, or *Charm!*" she jabbed her finger in the direction of Charm's room again. "How do we even begin to comprehend the situation itself? And you want us to figure out how to use whatever new abilities we don't even know we have?"

A nurse popped her head around the corner, her face stern. Dawn raised a palm, nodding. "Sorry." The woman touched a finger to her lips before disappearing around the corner again.

The twins were both reaching for her, with a look Dawn knew too well. It said, *I know you don't understand. Let me help you.* But Dawn was full to overflowing with enough information for the moment. She backed away, shaking her head, then turned and kept going, her eyes on the elevator at the end of the hall.

The twins did not call out. They, above anyone else in the group, seemed to know when to give people space, and in the moment, Dawn was grateful for that, at least. So, when she heard light footfalls coming up behind her as she pressed the button for the elevator, she was confused, but refused to glance behind. It was Cadence that stepped in beside her, though, and Dawn immediately embraced her, her tears finally flowing freely as her sister's presence seemed to break the dam she'd been working so hard to hold strong.

"Come on," Cadence whispered when the elevator door opened, and Dawn allowed her to lead her into the mirrored box. She even raised a hand and waved – to the twins, Dawn assumed, but she did not look.

It wasn't until Cadence had led her to the small, grassy courtyard between two buildings of the campus that she fully looked at her sister again, but all that accomplished was a resurgence of tears. Only that time, Cadence cried, too. Dawn was surprised to find they were sitting on a bench when they both came up for air. The two gazed, rather dazed, at each other before Dawn voiced her confusion. "How the hell did we get *here?*" And then they were laughing, leaning on each other as they did, until they were sighing lightly and wiping at their eyes.

"Oh, Dawnie, it's so *good* to be near you again," Cadence exclaimed, squeezing Dawn to her in a sideways hug.

"Cadence, I'm so..."

The woman shook her head. "You already said 'I'm sorry,' Dawnie." She ran a cold thumb over Dawn's damp cheek. "Trust me, you have tougher customers than me to make up with," she gave a laugh.

Dawn pressed her face into her palms and sighed.

"It's OK," Cadence patted her back.

After all these years and so much ignorance, she's still taking care of me. The tears threatened again, so Dawn gave herself a shake and sat up straight. "How is she?"

Cadence smiled. "She'll be alright. Trust me."

"Has this happened before?"

Cadence looked out into the little trees that had been planted around the boxy little yard. "Sort of."

Dawn turned toward her sister, balancing half-on, half-off the cold bench. "Please, Cadence. Be honest."

Candence lowered her head. "She *always* sleeps the day

away after one of these monsters." Cadence shook her head.

"But?"

Her sister met her eyes. "But she usually wakes up first."

Dawn nodded, her eyes going to the saplings, this time.

"I mean, she's always groggy, but I think this is the first time she's stayed unconscious, you know?"

Dawn nodded again.

"But, Dawn," Cadence squeezed her arm with both hands until Dawn met her eyes again, "she *is* going to be OK."

Dawn fought against the urge to scoff.

Her sister noticed and laughed. "Dawn, you've been gone a long time. A lot has happened."

Dawn put her face in her hands again.

Cadence pulled them away, laughing. "No, silly! I'm not trying to make you feel guilty! I'm sure you have enough of that to last a lifetime."

Dawn met her sister's eyes again.

"I'm trying to tell you that I *know* she's going to be OK."

Dawn's eyebrows arched as she began to comprehend. "You got it, too?"

Cadence laughed. "Not like Charm, or you, even. But in our efforts to support Charm, we found ourselves exploring our own intuition, and both of us found that maybe we got a little of Great Grandad's gift, too."

Dawn's smile felt unfamiliar, but good. But just as quick, she frowned. "You said, 'our' and 'we'. Do you mean you and her father?

Cadence shook her head. "Lucky would have been enthusiastic if he'd been here to experience it all, but he died before we started." Her eyes lowered as she searched in her pockets for something. Dawn figured she'd pull a tissue out, but she found her wallet instead, and opened it to a photo, which she tilted toward Dawn, smiling. "That's Lucky. Lewis was his name, but he was always 'Lucky' to the people who knew him."

Dawn found herself smiling into the hazel eyes of a handsome man with Charm's smile. "He's really handsome," she whispered as the emotions attached to the photo touched her, then eased into her chest. She looked at Cadence. "You loved him so much."

Cadence turned the photo back to her own view. "Still do," she whispered back.

"Where did you meet?" Dawn asked, suddenly eager to learn more, now that she'd seen the man's face. "And how did he – I mean, you don't have to tell me anything, but…"

Cadence tucked her wallet back into the deep pocket of her plaid woolen jacket. "I'll tell you everything," she patted Dawn's hand, "but not today."

Dawn hiccoughed, then nodded. "Of course." The two sat quietly before Dawn broke the silence. "If not Lucky, then who did all this 'exploration' with you?" She asked, but before Cadence answered, she knew. Her eyes widened, because in the moment of her revelation, she also realized that Cadence had said "they" had discovered their own gifts. "Kenny!" she exclaimed.

Cadence nodded. "Freddie and Jason, too, though they're less interested in developing it."

"Wow," Dawn breathed. "And they made fun of me so much," she giggled, some sort of retribution asserting itself at the realization. A thought came to her and she looked at her sister with wide eyes. "Do you think Mom…?"

Cadence paused, frowning at Dawn, then said, "Dawn!"

Dawn frowned.

"Please don't tell me you shut her out, too."

Dawn recoiled.

"The woman you missed so much... whose death changed *everything...*"

Mortified, Dawn blinked. Charm had said something similar, but she hadn't thought about it again.

Cadence shook her head. "You haven't been punishing us, have you?"

Dawn couldn't speak.

"You've been punishing yourself."

Dawn shook her head, but only because it seemed to be her only option.

"Oh, honey," Cadence hugged her sideways again. "You can feel her better than any of us," she muttered.

"What about Charm?"

Cadence exhaled loudly. "She can see Mom's energy, of course. But she never knew her in life. It's *you* who needs to acknowledge her. Why haven't you?"

Dawn stared at the ground, and for the first time in weeks, her mind was a complete blank.

"Maybe that's a story for another day, too," Cadence patted Dawn's knee.

Dawn shrugged. "I need to write the book, first."

Cadence looked confused for a moment, but then her face cleared. "You don't even know, yourself, do you?"

Dawn shook her head, but already that well-practiced wall of denial was erecting itself, making her feel safe. Cadence sighed.

"Anyway," Dawn said on an outbreath.

"Were you and the twins arguing?" Cadence deftly changed the subject.

Dawn shrugged. "It's funny; The Seers are like family,"

she caught herself and shut her mouth, eyes going to her sister, estranged for many years, until now. Cadence smiled and waved her onward. Dawn cleared her throat. "We're very close," she said, but it didn't feel any better than the last, so she just kept going. "We disagree often! But it's rare we can't find our way to seeing eye-to-eye. I feel like we're falling apart," she admitted, and her stomach did a sick turn.

"Where are the others?"

Dawn chuckled, but it was sad. "Sheila's coming back tomorrow night; she had to work for the week. Ed and Mel are in Tibet."

"What?"

Dawn laughed for real, that time. "Long story. And Shya... well, you know about Shya."

Cadence nodded and kept her head down as she picked absently at a hangnail. "What's she like?"

Dawn smiled. "She's amazing."

Cadence met her eyes. "Do you think she's with her? Charm?"

Dawn grimaced as the tears returned and took her sister in her arms.

"She *will* be alright," Cadence said, her words muffled against Dawn's shoulder.

And Dawn nodded, remembering the twins' words about having faith. *Maybe that "fuzzy border" will help Mel and Ed, too,* she thought, and Cadence pulled away.

"What?"

"She's talked about Ed, too," she said. "What's his gift?"

"Ed's a portal," Dawn murmured.

"A what?"

"A door between *there* and *here.*"

Her sister's eyes lit up.

"I don't know when he'll be back," Dawn was quick to explain, lest her sister's hopes rise too high. "And he was still struggling with it, last we saw each other. Still learning."

Cadence nodded. "I hope he learns fast."

CHAPTER 47 – SURGE

The atmosphere hummed in Sheila's room at The British. Dawn breathed it in as the twins brought their returned friend up to speed. That thing that had been missing from the group dynamic – Mel had called it their "mojo", but Dawn always thought of it as a sense of confidence and power that they gained when they were together, regardless of their individual self-perception - had rushed back in, and while Sheila's return had seemed to herald it, Dawn knew there were other factors involved.

For her, it was the frank, difficult, and sometimes humorous discussion she, Cadence and the twins had had over Charm's hospital bed. Jane and Anna took to Cadence almost in the same way they had to Charm, weakened only by the fact that Cadence couldn't relate like Charm could, intuitive or not. But the three got along like wildfire in crackling straw, and while Dawn was quietly proud of both elements of her family, she was absolutely thrilled with the response she felt from Charm.

The women talked while Dawn *felt.* Her niece was surely listening on some level because her emotional reactions were perfectly timed with those that had gathered around her quiet form. Dawn felt joy, excitement, fear, frustration, the whole spectrum of emotions that accompanied the discussion. But most importantly, she felt *something.* She felt from Shya sometimes, too, but Charm was so much more present than the spirit of her friend. If Dawn had voiced Charm's reactions for her, the girl would have been a lively participant in the conversation. And the women did inquire, after some stretch of silence from Dawn, and smiled and laughed when Dawn told them her interpretation of Charm's contribution.

To put it plainly, when considering the option of somehow bringing Charm to find Shya, Charm was all in.

None of them hesitated to entertain the possibility of rescuing Shya completely, but they were quick to acknowledge, too, that without their group in full force, it would be difficult. For now, the goal was to wake the woman up from the stupor the demon had her in. To make her see she was not alone. To make her know it was not her fault. And to prove to her that her death would not accomplish her intended goal, because there were others that shone like her. And the demon was a determined bastard.

Dawn roused from her thoughts as the windows shook. She peered out the window and saw the beginnings of a storm, multitudes of snowflakes whirling in the fists of the wind. She realized the other women were silent, too, and looked toward Sheila.

"Reminds me of that thunderstorm," she said, smiling weakly at Dawn and then toward the twins. "Remember? When we were all here talking about Jordan's exorcism?"

The twins nodded.

"I'm glad you're back," Dawn returned the smile. But what she really wanted to know was whether she'd heard from Ed. Her stomach turned at the thought of asking, though.

"What is it?" Sheila frowned.

Dawn shook her head. "Just thinking about all the loose ends," she murmured. The twins came to sit on the queen-sized bed, either end of which was already occupied by Dawn and Sheila. They all giggled a bit as the bed creaked.

"It feels better now, though," Anna patted Dawn's knee and she nodded, then looked out at the chaos of the weather again. The snow was illuminated against the dark night rather beautifully by the outside spotlights of the historic building that was The British Hotel.

She'd nodded, but the swirling flakes felt more akin to

the state of things for the group.

"Has anyone heard from the guys?" Sheila broached, and Dawn had her answer.

She shook her head. "I wish we knew what was going on."

Sheila tittered unconvincingly. "Do you think they're being held prisoner?" She smiled, but much like her laugh, it was weak. "Maybe they know too much to be let go, now!"

Dawn looked to the twins for a hint of quiet knowing. The women often appeared unsurprised at the turn of events or reassured when the rest of them were floundering for answers. And sometimes, they could be swayed to share their predictions. But tonight, their lips were thin and pressed tightly together.

Dawn, however, was not in the mood to let them keep anything to themselves. "Ladies," she said, and was relieved at the sense of authority she'd managed to convey in her voice. Encouraged, she went on, "this is not the time to hold anything back." Both women lowered their strange, pale eyes.

"She's right!" Sheila raised her eyebrows, nodding.

"We don't know what's happening right now," Anna nearly whispered.

"But you know something," Dawn stated.

The women shared a look, then Jane continued. "We've seen Ed at the shoreline."

Dawn frowned.

"What does that mean?" Sheila was frowning, too.

The twins both shrugged. "We don't know," Anna said again, "which is why we haven't shared."

"So, wait," Dawn raised a finger. "*When* will Ed be there? Where Shya is?"

"The future," Jane nodded, then shrugged again. "That's

all we know.

Dawn chuckled. "You're right; that's not much to go on."

"But it's something," Sheila countered. "At least we know he's alive, and that he *will* be there! To help, hopefully."

The twins nodded absently. "He *is* stronger."

Dawn slapped her own thighs in frustration. "How do you know *that*?"

Anna shook her head, but Jane spoke, "You, more than anyone, should know that. Just reach out and connect to him."

Dawn shrank back. They were right. Sheila gave her an understanding smile. There was a bit of pity in there, too, and it rose Dawn's hackles. Still, she kept silent.

"You can do the same for Mel," Jane pressed.

Dawn shook her head.

In a rare show of exasperation (though it was becoming more common, of late, Dawn thought), Anna shook her head. "Dawn, if you worked as hard on developing your gift as you do at denial, you'd be a force to reckon with."

Again, Dawn was stymied. She knew she'd be white as a ghost if her chocolate brown skin would allow it, for the blood drained from her face and she swayed a bit, dizzy.

"Come *on,*" Sheila gently smacked both of the twins then crawled between them to give Dawn a clumsy hug. It made her laugh, which was a welcome relief. Sheila pulled back enough to meet her eyes. "We all have issues, sis. And just so you know, you don't have to face them alone. At least there's that."

Dawn stifled another laugh, even as her eyes grew hot with tears. Sheila laughed and hugged her again, purposefully knocking her off-balance and making the twins shriek as they nearly toppled off the bed.

I am *blessed,* she found herself thinking as they all worked to gain some semblance of order.

"Is Rory with Shya?" Jane looked at Dawn, as Shya's family home was her home base.

Dawn nodded. "And John, actually."

"And Cadence is with Charm," Anna added.

Dawn nodded again. "Cadence said she'd been fluttering her eyelids last time we talked. That's very good; the doctors think she'll wake up, soon."

Sheila put a hand to her heart. "I'm so glad."

"Me too," Dawn whispered.

Jane smiled. "And tonight, just before you sleep, you're going to try and connect to the guys in Tibet."

Dawn raised her eyebrows. "I don't remember saying that." She tried to remember whether she'd told the twins that the time between wakefulness and sleep was the easiest when she wanted to connect to someone's energy. Surely, she had?

"Just energetically," Sheila said, her eyes pleading.

"Just to get a sense of them," Anna finished, her eyes positively steady on Dawn's. "Just so we can make some decisions around timing, here."

"That's a lot of 'justs.'" Dawn regarded her quietly. They hadn't established a time for trying to bring Charm to Shya, probably because the girl was still recovering from her seizure, not to mention unconscious. But also, because they all wanted the two far-flung members of the group to be present when they did. The more support they could gather, the better their chance of success. But time was a commodity now, and they all sensed it was running low.

She had to do it. Gathering any knowledge at all from their friends (and loves?) meant more than her avoidance of Mel's continuing silence. Taking a deep breath and holding it, she nodded.

"Good!" All three women said it in unison, and after a short, surprised silence, they all laughed together again.

Jane rose and stretched. “Let’s go,” she said, and started for the door.

“Where?” Sheila cried out after her, as Anna rose to grab her sweater.

“Tea,” Jane smiled, gesturing to the side window and toward The British Café, which resided in another historic building on the other side of a courtyard that joined the two associated businesses.

Sheila clapped her hands and rose, retrieving her suitcase in a flutter of movement and finding a warm hoodie.

And Dawn, willing to defer her bedtime task indefinitely, stood, eager to join them. So, the four drank tea and played rummy with the café’s cards until bedtime could be pushed no more.

CHAPTER 48 – SEEK

She found Ed immediately. It was so easy, in fact, that she instantly regretted avoiding it for so long.

And he felt good. Better than good. She was hesitant to believe it, but no matter how she searched for that odd pressure-pain in his chest, she couldn't find it. She sighed, and her ears pricked at the sound of her own breath.

The house was silent. John had stayed up late with Shya so Rory could retire early. He'd finally given in and started sleeping in another room (his old one, in fact). He loathed being away from her, but the reasons *not* to lay in bed with her had finally outweighed the reasons he'd been compelled to do so for so long. He'd been tied up, knocked out, left entirely only to wake and find Shya had accomplished either hurting herself or part of the house. And finally, he'd been unable to find a way to configure himself around her bindings. On the first night she had them, he'd lain on top of one of the wrist straps and eventually drifted off, only to wake to the sound of crashing thunder, his face pressed by the strap so close to Shya's, the tips of their noses nearly touched. And the worst of the experience was *not* that there was no thunderstorm to speak of.

The worst, he'd said, was being face to face with Shya's possessor, whose eyes were glittering black and whose smile stretched her face in a grotesque exaggeration of glee.

So, that first attempt to sleep while she was tied down was, in the end, the last.

Understandably.

She refocussed, ready to find some answers in Ed's comportment, distant as it was. But after a few frustrating minutes, she realized that though she could connect to her friend with ease, either he or someone else had erected a wall around him. Distance was the only thing she could establish. He was still very far away. Oh, and he felt good.

She balled a fist, knowing she'd have to try Mel.

It was strange to feel afraid to connect to the man, after he'd succeeded in teasing her out of the shell she'd taken years to build and reinforce. After he'd made her love him! Hell, she'd warned him of her impending proposal before he'd left, and there'd been no answering hesitation in his eyes. None whatsoever.

But now...

She closed her eyes, inhaling deeply. Drawing in the boundless energy around herself, around the world, making up the universe itself. She let it fill her, coursing through her with warmth, with joy, with power. And then she reached, a vast length of awareness through time and space, for the man whose spirit she knew so well.

And she found him.

And even more, he was unguarded.

She thought he might be sleeping. But there he was, smart and sure and quiet. Inquisitive, determined and doggedly sure that if we could all just *learn,* our problems would be easily surmounted. And then, there was the guilt. The fear that he would never be enough. The belief that he'd failed Shya, failed the group, failed Dawn.

There was something else. There was a new excitement. A new project? A new love? Dawn gasped at the hurt it inspired in her. At the bell of sadness in her chest and the little voice that admonished her for finding him this way, without his permission or knowledge. She burned with shame. She felt... unwelcome. But as the waves of sorrow eased back a bit (they'd surely be there later to ruminate upon), she had the presence of mind to wait before she pulled away. While she was reaching, and in the light of their need for guidance, she thought to extend her mission to the people around her friends. The monks? Other seekers? The Bodhisatta?

The Bodhisatta.

She was so close, and when Dawn's energy touched hers, she reached right back, and for the second time in as many days, she heard a disembodied voice beside her ear. But this time, it said, "Hello."

She bolted upright, gasping for breath. Shutting the connection down.

Had it been *her*? The one who was teaching Ed? The portal? Did she know about Dawn? Had she been reaching, too?

Dawn shook her head.

Did that accomplish anything?

She lay back, drained all of a sudden. It felt so nice to sink into the warmth of the bed, even with the odd, raised line in the mattress where it would fold to become a couch again. The air was heavy and warm, and she was being lulled into rest and despite everything, she wanted to give in.

There was a creak on the stairs.

She turned her head, not breathing. The only light that shone was that of the streetlight filtering in through the front door window, but it was enough to see a pair of bare feet and the bottom hem of a nightgown standing at the top of the stairs. Just below the landing.

Shit.

Her eyes were frozen on the unmoving shape, hoping it was a trick of the light. It was the narrowest of views, being the top step beneath the entryway. Just a triangle between the railing and the basement ceiling. She couldn't move. She waited. The feet were still. But then, there was something else… a dripping sound.

Dawn grimaced, confused and afraid. Her lungs burned with spent air and cried out for a fresh breath.

Drip. Drip.

She opened her mouth, either to call out *hello,* or to exhale, or both, but before she could complete her action, the stairs were flooded with light. Dawn jumped with a sound of surprise, then pushed herself against the arm of the sofa-bed, eyes riveted to where the spotlight shone. A spotlight whose presence was odd, in and of itself, for it shone directly on those feet – and they *were* feet – while the remainder of the basement languished in continuing dark.

And then the feet were lifting as if by a set of invisible, giant hands, and then they were fed through the space between the ceiling and the stair railing, where the woman's body flopped like that of a doll's, in midair. Dawn tried to scream, but nothing would come out except a strained hiss of air. Like in a nightmare.

Shya's head hung limp to her chest, her hair hiding her features, and Dawn could see now that she was suspended at the wrists, where glistening strands of red had been ripped from her arms and they were what was dripping, drip, drip, droplets of blood from shredded wrists whose veins were taut, rising past the dark line of the ceiling to the floor above, presumably. Horrified, Dawn covered her gaping mouth, which still tried to scream, and failed.

A sudden, thin note of music strained from all around, making Dawn jump. An accordion? *Yes,* she confirmed as the music swelled, a singsong circus tune with gay and jangling notes, and Shya was moving with it... or being moved, the veins stripped from her arms, jostling her along to the beat. Her head bounced and lolled. Her blood ran in rivulets down bony arms and pooled in the hollows of her armpits before continuing downward, soaking the sides of her nightgown until the music halted and Shya's head snapped up, making Dawn jump back again. Her hip collided painfully with the wood of the sofa arm, but her eyes remained on Shya's slack features. Eyes rolled back, jaw yawned open, cheekbones sharp in mottled skin.

Oh, God! What she dead already?

"Shya!" She cried, her voice found, finally, and her friend's head snapped to peer at Dawn that time, but the eyes were glittering black and the smile unnaturally large. The music started up again.

Dawn whimpered, repeating words of denial over and over again, stopping only when Shya's legs were suddenly spread taut, then gouged at the insides of the knees, then violently wrenched as more strings of red were torn from them, knees to ankles, and sucked up to where the others went, to some sick puppet-master above.

Next, she danced.

Arms and legs jerking with sharp pulls of her strings, bouncing to the clang of the chaotic circus tune, blood pooling in dark puddles below suspended feet. But her eyes… her neck was stiff and her head unnaturally steady as the rest of her jostled violently about. Eyes on Dawn. Black, glittering eyes.

Dawn shrieked.

And that time, she woke, bolting straight out of bed and rolling to all fours, adrenaline fuelling her as she half-crawled, half-bear-walked to the stairs. The blissfully empty stairs. She didn't know she was aimed for the door until she was yanking it open, nor that she would vomit painfully when she stepped out onto the snow-covered cement step in her sock-covered feet for the second time in as many days.

But she was unsurprised when, at the notion she was being watched, she gazed up to the picture window and Shya's slight form was there, smiling and waving, her eyes dark and on Dawn. Dark and menacing. Dark and *knowing.*

She sank to the ground as the house awoke behind her. As Rory spotted Shya and shouted, "Oh, God!" and "Help! John! She's fallen!" But John was already pulling Dawn upright when Rory called. He brought her inside hurriedly, then took the stairs in twos to retrieve his daughter, whose puppet-master had afforded her escape, yet again.

CHAPTER 49 – READY OR NOT

"It's clear to me," Jane asserted. "We can't wait any longer."

It was no surprise that Anna nodded. Sheila followed, then Cadence, and Dawn had expected all of that. But it was Charm who gave her pause. The girl was sitting up in her hospital bed, sipping apple juice through a straw and peering at the twins with wide eyes. But she turned to Dawn before she nodded, too.

Dawn raised her eyebrows.

"I won't get better," the girl said, quietly. She was still a bit slow-moving, having only been awake for a few hours. But Dawn felt her spirit plain as day, and knew the girl was doing well. "That thing is affecting me, too," she voiced, now. "I know I won't get better 'til this is done."

Dawn frowned but nodded. She couldn't deny the truth that rang in Charm's words.

They were all quiet for some time. Dawn's thoughts raced. She'd told her friends about her efforts to connect with Ed and Mel, but that discussion was left with loose ends in light of Dawn's "dream" and Shya's latest escape from her confines. Rory and John had taken her limp form back to the bed and redoubled her restraints, but that had ended in a fight, with John stating a desire to have Shya put into care, where professionals could better manage her. Rory, of course, had shouted that there *were* no professionals in what was ailing Shya; that even Dawn and The Seers, with all their gifts and foresight, could not profess to know the answers, and the men separated. Loose ends again, leaving Rory in despair at Shya's bedside and John leaving hours early for work – a job Rory had taunted as being "ridiculous," given what John knew.

Dawn had been relieved on many levels when Cadence called to say Charm was awake. Her niece was *not* trapped with Shya, as they'd all quietly feared, and she was showing all signs of returning back to her regular state of health, so there was that. Both monumentally important. But it also meant Dawn had an excuse to call the women at The British. An excuse to leave the house with its oppressive atmosphere and uncomfortable silence since the events of the early morning hours.

Now, they all congregated in Charm's room, which Cadence had managed to change to semi-private rather than the ward Charm had been on. Her insurance would have covered a private room, but none were available. Charm didn't seem to mind her neighboring patient, but the young woman who occupied the bed closest to the door surely wished she had a private room, given the chaos that Charm's company brought. Regardless, she appeared to sleep through the majority of their ad-hoc meeting, which allowed them all to talk a little more freely.

Dawn shook herself back to the present when she realized all eyes were on her. She smiled weakly. "Sorry; what?"

Charm giggled.

"Why don't we just do it now?" Sheila appeared to be repeating herself.

Dawn let out a blast of a laugh, but it petered out immediately. *She's serious!* Dawn felt her eyes widen. *No way.* "Do *what?*" she asked, refusing to believe the woman meant what Dawn thought she did.

Sheila crossed her arms with a huff.

Dawn tried to laugh again. "I'm sorry! I was thinking! And there's no way you mean the thing I automatically assumed!"

"We were talking about trying again," one of the twins said. Dawn had to look hard at both of the pale women to discern who was whom, causing more guilt to set in. Had she even established their identities when they'd first sat down? She couldn't remember.

"Jane's wearing my coat," Anna said, discerning Dawn's confusion. Sheila's answering sigh made Dawn think that, too, was a repeated statement.

"I threw up," Jane said.

Dawn snapped her eyes to Jane's. "What?"

"At the hotel," Anna jumped in. "She just rolled over in bed and barfed, and her coat happened to catch it. Not a drop on the carpet!" She shrugged.

"When?" Dawn was still trying to catch up.

"When you did," Sheila murmured. "What is going *on* with you?"

Dawn shook her head, feeling entirely discombobulated. Cadence and Charm each laid a soft hand on Dawn's arm. Dawn peered about, confused.

Jane reached across Charm's legs. "I only mentioned it briefly. I was dreaming – about a puppet?"

Dawn gasped. "How did I miss that part of the conversation?"

Jane smiled kindly. "A lot is happening, and you're the only one of us at ground zero, so to speak. It's alright that you're feeling overwhelmed."

Dawn nodded gratefully, then met Sheila's eyes. "I haven't been sleeping well." *That* was an understatement. "I'm sorry."

Sheila's eyes welled with tears. She shook her head. "No, I am. I've been so stressed with work and being away, and then not knowing what's going on with Ed and Mel… and Shya's getting worse! And we have no idea what to do!" The woman gestured helplessly as tears spilled onto her cheeks and her voice rose perilously high. Cadence glanced surreptitiously toward the sleeping woman, whose name was Peg, if Dawn remembered correctly. She bit the insides of her cheeks at the smile that threatened to render her entirely insensitive. Shoved down the revelation – which she realized was not funny - that she could remember the other patient's name, but none of the conversation that should have meant so much.

Anna threw her arms around the woman, whose face was bright red, tears shining on ruddy cheeks. Dawn gulped, realizing how spent they *all* were.

Jane leaned toward her again. "I know it sounds crazy to go – there – again, but what else can we do except admit defeat?"

Dawn frowned as she gazed into the silvery eyes of her friend. She hadn't even considered defeat. Oddly, though, there was something in her that questioned whether she'd already accepted it, without knowing. "The demon is messing with us," she muttered.

The twins nodded solemnly.

"We have to try," Charm spoke up.

Dawn looked at her niece, whose eyelids drooped, revealing her fatigue. She then peered incredulously at Cadence, who was looking on with tightly pressed lips, and then at Jane. "What do you mean?" She gestured to Charm with a thumb, chuckling. "She's certainly not participating!"

"I *have* to!" Charm whined. Cadence rubbed her daughter's feet absently through her blankets but said nothing. Dawn saw the struggle plainly on her sister's face, though. "Isn't that the whole point?" Charm continued, gesturing with her apple juice such that droplets flew around her in an arc, landing on all of them.

Cadence chuckled softly. "Calm down, sweetheart."

Charm looked blankly at her juice and then laughed, too.

"Sorry," she smiled at each of the women in turn.

Dawn let her smile show, finally, as Sheila giggled through her tears. Only the twins retained their composure as the group laughed, and Dawn used that as an anchor, breathing deeply to try and regain her composure.

"At this point," Jane said, and they all hushed, "we have to do *something*, and I think we know that we can't wait for anyone. Ed and Mel included."

Dawn shook her head, but not to refute her. It was because she saw no other option. They were all looking at her expectantly, again. She realized that despite everything, she was still their leader. She slid her gaze to Charm's again. Charm seemed suspended, breathless as she waited. What Dawn said, however, surprised them all. "Where were you?"

As expected, Charm frowned.

"What do you remember?"

"From the coma?" the twins chorused.

Dawn's eyes were still on Charm as she nodded. "Yeah, the coma, but before that, too. What did you see before you had the seizure? During?"

"She never remembers any of that," Cadence said, a hint of defensiveness lacing her words.

Dawn smiled at her sister, then looked back to Charm. "Do you remember anything? I have to know."

"Why *now*?" Sheila wondered aloud.

"Because we're trying to decide whether to usher my niece into Hell," Dawn said evenly.

Sheila sat up straighter, nodding once. "Yep; that makes sense." She shook her head, eyes on the bedspread but further than that, too, before peering at Dawn again. "It really *is* fucking with us." Her hand flew to her mouth as she remembered Charm, but Charm was already giggling. Sheila looked to Cadence. "Sorry."

Cadence shook her head. "I'm the outsider here, and even I can see how... messy things are. I think your language is appropriate.

The statement silenced them all for a moment.

Dawn lowered her chin at Charm, asking again, wordlessly.

The girl furrowed her brow. "I only remember one thing."

The second patient in the room rolled over, sighing. Dawn observed Peg's face as she blinked her eyes slowly, then looked back at Charm with a new sense of urgency.

Charm shook her head, struggling. "It was like, light. Lines of it, but with balls gathered all along the lines. Like patio lights, or Christmas lights, except *all* golden and glowing, even the strings in between." She raised her eyes to Dawn, a question in them.

"What else?"

"Nothing. Oh. The light was coming from me; from my chest, and it sort of had me stuck in one place, it seemed. Didn't feel *bad,* necessarily. Just sort of – trapped."

The women of her group all wore the same expression of fear and awe. Jane spoke first. "Is that all you remember? You saw nothing else, like where you were? Or where the light was going?"

Charm's face cleared. "Oh! It was going to the sky!" She shook her head. "Weirdest-looking sky ever, and that's saying something, considering how strange the sky has been lately," she gazed out the window. All eyes followed.

"It's aliens," said the woman in the other bed, and they all jumped. Hands flew to hearts and smiles lit on their faces as they turned to the woman. Peg. She shrugged. "Makes about as much sense as the other theories out there."

Dawn looked back at Charm, wishing it were aliens.

Wishing the changes were down to anything but Asmodeus and the insurgence of his dark army. She took Charm's hand in her own and squeezed. "OK," she said. The women around her turned sharply to face her.

"OK?" Jane asked, sounding relieved and afraid simultaneously.

Dawn nodded. "But not today. We wait until Charm is released." She looked at Sheila. "We use whatever energy shields you can erect," she went on. Sheila nodded enthusiastically. Dawn looked to the twins, now. "And you two are to be solely focused on grounding Charm; keeping her here." They nodded, too. "You three are *not* to get pulled into that place, like last time. You have to be vigilant of that at all times."

"And what about you?" It was Cadence who voiced it, so Dawn turned to her.

"I bring her in," she said.

Charm squeezed the hand she still held, sending a frisson of warmth and tingles up Dawn's arm.

Dawn patted the hand she held and smiled into the amber eyes of her niece. "We go in together, and we come out together."

"Maybe with Shya?" Sheila broached, as a question, which seemed entirely appropriate.

"We aim to make Shya realize she's not the only one who can keep the portal open," Dawn said, something in her mind clicking as she considered the warmth Charm had sent up her arm, using energy. "Anything besides that is cake."

"But we'll try?"

Dawn rolled her eyes at Sheila. She hadn't done that in a while, and she was proud of that effort, but it felt appropriate, now. "Of course," she muttered. Sheila smiled big. "But that's not the goal. For now, we'll settle for connecting with Shya and getting the message across that she should stop trying to kill herself. And getting Charm out safely." She bit her lip, considering. "Do you think we can figure a way for Charm and me to be… removed from the situation? Even a room away?"

The twins looked at each other for several, silent seconds, then looked back at Dawn.

"Maybe?" Jane said.

"You've been there when we were *home*, with Ed, remember?" Sheila's tone was elevated in her excitement.

Dawn nodded. "I just want it to work. I want to help Shya and keep Charm safe. We all need to agree on the best plan." She looked at her nodding friends. They all jumped as Dawn's phone buzzed. Grateful for a distraction, Dawn let go of Charm's hand to retrieve her phone from her jacket. Her eyes widened when she saw who the text was from.

Sheila leaned into the twins and they fell into their huddle, planning already. "If only we could have some way of knowing when the demon wasn't looking," Sheila said.

"We might," Dawn breathed, then held the phone out to the women, Mel's text enlarged on the screen:

Mel: Hi, love. I miss you. Been learning a lot. Hopefully, I'll be of more use to the group. Can't talk details, nor can I predict when I'll be home, but I can say this: you were right about my ability to use my gift remotely. Tell me when you read this, and I'll show you.

Sheila looked up, eyes wide. "Ask him about Ed!"

Anna put a hand on her friend's arm, then looked at Dawn. "Tell him you've read it. I want to see what he means."

Dawn nodded. She texted Mel so quickly that autocorrect messed up some of the words, but she didn't care. He'd understand. Her heart soared as she pushed "send". He'd said he missed her. He'd reached out, despite the obvious difficulty in doing so.

He still loved her.

A wave of heavy calm rolled over her. She smiled,

surprised at her physical response to the relief she felt. But then she regarded her friends and family and gasped. They *all* slumped in their seats, their faces slack. Jane's arm, which had been on her lap, fell to the side. Dawn, whose eyelids begged to be closed, looked to Cadence, who was smiling a dopey smile, her chin resting in her hand as she put her elbow on the bed.

Dawn looked to Charm through quicksand air, and gaped, her jaw drooping open in slow motion. The girl was fast asleep, a thin trail of drool spilling down to her chin.

"Holy shit!" Sheila exclaimed. Her voice sounded distant, as though muffled by water. Dawn managed to look her way and saw that Anna, too, had succumbed and was actively sliding down in her seat, with the floor as her unconscious destination. Sheila was holding a hand in front of her face, studying it. It seemed right that she appeared the most alert, Dawn thought. The woman had always been boundlessly energetic.

The air suddenly lightened, and Dawn could see the effect right away: Anna woke and pushed herself back up in her seat, peering wide-eyed at her twin, who was smiling broadly.

Cadence sat up, too, mumbling, "What was *that*?"

Charm snored on, her current state of recovery her obvious downfall.

Dawn met Jane's eyes. "Mel," she whispered, smiling.

Jane nodded and smiled back. "Seems our professor has found a way to take advantage of the situation."

Dawn nodded, remembering their conversation about benefitting from the current state of the world by enhancing their gifts, somehow.

Mel had done it.

Her phone buzzed again. She raised it slowly, still feeling dreamy, and laughed at the text.

Mel: Did it work?

"Hell yeah, it did," she muttered as she texted the same back to him.

And then Sheila was gesturing toward the phone. "Ask about Ed!"

Dawn nodded, but her phone buzzed again before she could.

Mel: I can't say anything more – not about me or Ed; I was given permission to do one test, and that was it. Have to sign off. I do love you. I hope you've been holding on to that. You can trust it, Dawn. I promise.

She peered at Sheila, tears swimming in her eyes. "He can't say anything about Ed," she said, her voice shaky, "but they're both fine. I know it."

"But when will they..."

Dawn met Anna's eyes and shook her head. Anna sank back in her seat.

"What does this mean about what we've decided?" Jane voiced what they were all wondering.

Dawn looked at the sleeping Charm, then at her sister before answering. "We still have no idea what to expect from them. I think we have to carry out the plan. Show Charm to Shya."

"Especially considering what she saw while she was..." Sheila trailed off.

They all sat quietly until Cadence piped up. "Can someone please explain why we all nearly passed out a minute ago?"

A flurry of words spilled forth as they delighted in explaining to Cadence that Mel seemed to be developing his gift of calming. To put it mildly.

Cadence looked at Dawn. "Can he do that to the demon?"

It had been Dawn's first thought. "I don't know, but once we know when we're going back in, we can ask him to try."

Sheila's eyes lit up.

"This could be good," the twins said in unison.

"I hope so," Dawn said, and she was trying for cautiously optimistic, but failed. She was downright excited.

CHAPTER 50 – BREATHE

Rory looked sadly at the unconscious Shya, seemingly lost in his thoughts, or perhaps not thinking at all. His beard was coming in with ferocity, as though all it had been waiting for was some sort of consistent complacency before it surged forth with gusto. He was thin, his cheekbones standing out beneath the mesmerizing blue of his eyes, and Dawn had noticed the way his pants hung off his hips. He withered in tandem with his love, but somehow maintained his undeniable handsomeness and charm, even as he withdrew ever steadily into himself.

John was standing, chewing a nail, eyes on Shya, as well. Dawn had insisted he be part of the conversation, but the man seemed ready to bolt at the first indication they were done.

Neither, however, had said a word.

The Seers had agreed that Dawn would broach the subject of another attempt to connect with Shya alone. Dawn didn't mind. The less chaos, the better. And truth be told, she wasn't eager to have anyone in the house who didn't need to be. Somehow the air had grown even more oppressive. Dawn's head ached when she was there, like it did when a pressure system was rolling in, only breaking when the skies opened up, as though the release of the rain signalled the balloon in her head to deflate, finally. And it smelled. Shya was changed regularly, and her teeth were brushed twice a day. Her bed was clean, or it *should* have been, as Rory was fastidious about it, changing the sheets more times in a week that any man Dawn had known had done in a lifetime. It seemed to comfort him, taking care of her in such ways. But regardless of their efforts – and Bethie's, too, who gave Shya sponge baths, having taken over when Rory started to break down over the changes in the possessed woman's body – the sheets seemed to mildew beneath the body of the sleeping Shya. And Shya herself seemed to ooze an odd stench that would hit visitors now and then, like a whiff of a breeze from some swampy, mouldering place.

But it was more than that. The hints of the scent from her seemed to hang in the air, permeating any freshness let in through cracked windows. And it was acrid, reminding one of nostril hairs being singed by a leaping flame if the gas was turned on too long before lit. And there was something else, vague but pervasive, beneath it all. Rot.

It was difficult to be around for very long, but more than that, it was sad. It was *wrong* for that smell to drench the beautiful woman who had never offended as such when she'd had her faculties about her. Like all of it, it was just one more element that wasn't fair.

Dawn chewed her bottom lip nervously, her eyes flicking from Rory's fixed ones to Shya, and back. At first, she'd been fine with the silence, even grateful for it. She had much to think about, after all. But now it seemed it would never end, and though she was in no rush to retire to her pull-out in the basement, she was in danger of becoming convinced they'd never resolve the question.

Which was, "*Are you alright with trying this again when Charm is released from the hospital? Even without Ed and Mel? Even just to try and wake Shya up, just a little?*"

John seemed to have left it to Rory straight away, having shrugged and stood, retreating to the corner where he remained. And Rory just stared at Shya, Shya whose weight loss detracted from her own intrinsic charm, unlike Rory's. Whose cheekbones jutted further beneath shuttered eyes, which, when open, were either lifeless or a glittering, solid black. *Which one's worse?* Dawn wondered absently.

"Rory?" She broached, her voice quiet.

He didn't respond for several seconds, then rubbed his

face slowly with his palm, beard bristling, before turning his face toward her.

"You don't have to be a part of it."

He looked insulted. "Of course, I do."

Dawn nodded. Of course, he did.

Rory shook his head. "I just don't know if it's worth it." He looked to Shya again. "All this time, I've been sort of counting on the next effort being *it.*"

Dawn sighed. "Waiting is... dangerous." Flashes of Shya's night wanderings: John's hand spurting blood as his face drained of color, Shya smiling that glittery-eyed smile as Dawn puked up her terror on the front walk, post-puppet dream. She shuddered.

"And this is safe?" He raised his eyebrows in her direction.

She frowned. "No. But how long can we just do *nothing,* Rory? We have no idea when Mel and Ed will be back... and Charm is being affected. And Shya..." she broke off, peering desperately toward her friend.

"Shya wants to die," John spoke up from the corner, making them both jump. "Sorry," he added as Dawn put a hand to her heart.

Rory shook his head, jaw flexing as he considered. "At least now, we're not failing," he whispered, and his lips trembled as his eyes filled with tears.

Dawn gently took his hand. "That depends on your definition of 'failure'," she said, smiling sadly. He turned to her, his eyes beseeching hers to convince him. "It's certainly not getting *better,* Ror," she added.

He pressed his lips together. "I don't know what to do anymore," he said, his voice shaky, and then his head was in his hands and she was holding him, her hands rubbing his upper back in listless lines. Back and forth attempts at comfort.

"I want you to try," John stepped forward.

Dawn looked up at him, surprised.

"We can't just let this go on!" he gestured helplessly. Rory's head rose to look at the man who'd been his mother's husband for a short time, and would now be his father in-law, if he had any say in what the future held for Shya and him.

John squatted by Rory's chair and looked up at him pleadingly. "Trying and failing is better than just... watching her fade!" He gestured toward Shya, paused, then looked back at Rory. "We'll hate ourselves if waiting ends in her having the time to keep trying to end it," he cried, a tear escaping to his own stubbled cheek, "and succeeding!"

Both men regarded the other, and then John was pulling Rory into an awkward hug, with Rory leaning down and John having to go to his knees so as not to fall. Overwhelmed, Dawn put her arms around them both, her tears flowing as though not to be left out. When they pulled apart, they all looked at Shya. Perhaps hoping for her input. Wishing for it, more like. But the woman's silence persisted.

"When?"

Dawn looked at Rory. "Charm is doing well. They're talking about releasing her as early as tomorrow."

"She's up for this?" John's brow furrowed. "She's so young," he added, but Dawn needn't have been told.

"I don't know," she smiled through her tears, "but she's not well right now, and *she* is sure she has to try. We're going to try being in a different room, she and I." She frowned, unsure.

John sucked in a breath and held it, pressing his lips together as he looked at Rory.

Dawn looked, too. Rory shrugged. "We have to try. Let's try. Let's try and make things better, if not end them completely."

Dawn nodded. "OK."

John stood and shoved his hands in his pockets. "I don't know if I can..."

Dawn touched his arm. "It's alright, John."

He nodded, then put a hand on Rory's shoulder. "It's funny. I never wondered why I couldn't *feel* like a father figure to you. I wanted to, you know, but you were like Shya; you two seemed to have your own little bubble of existence, like she and her mother had. It was too easy to just... stay distant."

Rory was frowning up at Shya's father. "What about now?"

"Now, I feel blessed that you'll be like a son because of Shya, not because of any relationship I had with your mother. I do love you, and I love her so much it breaks my heart." He pressed a hand to his mouth, then looked at Dawn. "Thank you for working so hard for her."

Dawn nodded, feeling a little like the man was saying goodbye. "You alright, John?"

The man nodded. "Just feeling guilty over not being around," he muttered.

"You're here now," Rory said.

John nodded, then chuckled. "I quit that consulting job."

They both peered up at him, surprised again.

"You two were right; it's ridiculous for me to be there. Would've been better to start building a new housing lot!"

Dawn laughed. "So, you'll be around more, then."

John nodded. "Lou's back from her cruise, too, and she wants to come and see everyone, meet all the 'psychics'."

Dawn and Rory exchanged a look.

"I told her not yet," John added hastily.

They were all quiet for a moment.

"So, it could be tomorrow?" Rory looked at Dawn

questioningly.

Dawn shrugged. “When Charm asks to do it, we’ll call the twins and Sheila, and I’ll text Mel and Ed, hoping they’ll read it and be able to be with us, at least in spirit.” She paused as her stomach did a flip. “And then we’ll do it.”

Rory sighed. “I’d like to think I have realistic expectations, but I won’t lie: if this is the ass-end of any involvement we’ll ever have with that fucking monster, I’ll consider myself the luckiest man who ever lived.” He rubbed one of Shya’s blanketed feet.

“I hear that,” Dawn sighed, her stomach turning another somersault at the mere thought of a future without Asmodeus in their lives.

But then she thought about the dark hordes that had seeped through the tear in the boundary and wondered what would happen to them when the portal closed. She thought about something her mother used to say with a surge of melancholy.

It don’t matter none if the meal is done, there ain’t no fun ‘til the dishwasher’s run! She smiled a bit wistfully, but then it melted away as she realized the mess that would be left after they brought Shya back. Or even if they didn’t.

Especially if they didn’t.

CHAPTER 51 – ROADBLOCK

"Dawn."

One of her brothers was calling her from downstairs. *Am I late for school?* She wondered, rubbing her eyes and then stretching. Her eyebrows knitted as she yawned. Her brothers were never the ones shouting up the stairs. She frowned, then froze. Something was off.

"Wake up," the voice said again, but louder, almost in her ear. and Dawn realized that though she'd recognized it, the voice indeed was *not* a brother.

She clutched her blanket as her heart thudded in her chest. "Who's there?" She hadn't cracked her eyelids yet. Not a brother's voice. Not her childhood home, either, for the smell was off. No instant coffee scent to permeate the air, no arguing siblings, no strained conversation as her parents readied themselves for work, colliding a thousand times during their mundane tasks as if in reminder that all was not well.

But there was something: the familiar, sickening scent she'd learned to expect in what was her temporary home. The stink of rotting flesh.

She bolted upright, her eyes darting around the still-dark basement, looking for *him*. For the source of her wake-up call. For Mel.

But he wasn't there.

It *had* been his voice. That she knew.

Her eyes adjusted as she peered frantically about, no

longer looking for Mel, whose presence she could not feel, but looking instead for anyone else that might be lurking in the corners or hanging over the stairs. And though she discerned no human figures, she did see something. The shadows were oozing.

Her breath caught.

Her thoughts went automatically to the dark mass she'd seen behind her TV as Mel packed in the bedroom. These shadows were bolder than that, though. They slithered on the floor and crawled along the angled join of the wall and ceiling. *Why now?* She wondered. Her face stretched into a grimace. She tried to remember the last time she'd seen the dark presences that had infiltrated the living realm, and couldn't.

Had she seen any since that time at home?

"It made you look away," the voice came again, softly, and she let out a squeal, pulling the blankets up to her chin.

"What?" she cried breathlessly. "Mel?"

"It's not your fault."

She stood, then, throwing her blankets to the side in one swish of movement and speed-walking toward the stairs. Mel wasn't there; not physically, anyway. But the shadows were. She turned halfway up when she realized a hissing noise was following her. And before she could think about it, she looked into the dark room and they were seeping from the walls and corners and blackening the floor, a congregating darkness that hissed and rattled as it moved.

She ran.

She wanted to call the twins, or Sheila, or Cadence, but she'd escaped before thinking to pick her phone up, and no way was she going back. She paused on the landing, frantic for solutions, whimpering when none came. She peered up the stairs and into the dark kitchen, listening for any hint that Shya was behind her rude awakening, but heard nothing. Her head swiveled as her panic rose: dark kitchen, her hanging jacket, the stairs going back down. And then two things happened that forced her into action. First, the stench of rot intensified, and she was instantly gagging, each breath an assault to her senses. Second, her eyes stopped, riveted on the stairs to the basement as darkness continued to seep toward her, first obscuring one step, and then two.

Breathing hard, she stepped into her ankle boots, grabbed her coat, and opened the door, sliding through it without another thought. Wanting only to get out. To not see.

But she'd been wrong, and Mel's disembodied voice had been right. She didn't know how she was seeing them now and not before, but they were everywhere: black shapes of hate that flowed and coalesced, only to disappear behind a tree, under the step, beneath the ground as the dark slowly eased from pitch to grey. She put her hands over her mouth and cheeks, her eyes still darting here and there as the shadows danced a slow waltz in the night, disappearing in the light from the tall streetlamps, then coming together again on the other side.

Dawn was shuddering, not breathing, holding back a scream. And then she felt it around her ankles, just like she had on the rocky shore; the sucking quicksand of the dark creatures. Little demons at her feet, pulling. She screamed, then leapt to the walkway, where she landed wrong and slid on the thin sheen of frost, pitching forward to her hands and knees before springing up again, running, not looking behind her.

But she slowed at the end of the driveway, where the new pavement glowed like molten lava at its edges, illuminating the dark patch of the road that reminded her that there'd been an earthquake strong enough to tear a hole in the ground. Reminding her of the demon's power.

She whirled, her breath siphoned through a tensely constricted throat, wheezing. She'd had what the doctor called "pre-asthma" as a child but had never had a full-on attack. She wondered now as the sun peeked up over the trees to the east and a wave of dizziness made black caverns in her vision if that was what was happening now.

Her eyes landed on John's car. She could drive to The British, get Jane and Anna and Sheila. Or go to the hospital to find Cadence and Charm. Adrenaline rushed through her and she sprinted to it, then looked toward the front door. She'd need to go back in. She'd need to find the keys. She let out a sound of frustration, her eyes darting around again, and stopping on the trunk of the massive pine on the front lawn, where a shadow that had been peeking around at her disappeared behind the tree, leaving her making small grunts as she tried to take in breath, panicking. Thinking about how tall it was. Wondering how she hadn't seen before.

It made you look away.

Mel's voice had said it first. Just what hadn't she seen through the veil the demon had erected around them all?

She backed away, eyes on that spot on the trunk where the head of the creature, larger than her own, and with ears as pointed as one of those stone gargoyles, had eased behind it.

What now? Think, *Dawn!*

She tripped backward over the edge of the walk, falling back and into the car, which prevented her from hitting the ground.

It peeked again, and that time an arm slithered around the trunk first, followed by the tip of a pointed ear.

This can't be real!

Her chest heaved. Maybe it *was* a dream. But what did that mean in these times, anyway? Weren't their dreams interwoven with reality, now? Wasn't all she'd doubted proven?

Did not the dead weave their paths around the living?

She blinked, her head turning this way and that until it landed on the fence to the back yard. Without thinking, she ran, but her legs were heavy, and the ground tried to suck her down. And she wasn't breathing well. Every muscle screamed for oxygen. She wrenched the fence toward her, then stumbled in, absently wondering at her goal. What could she do differently in the back?

It was darker in the yard, shadowed by the house as the sun tiptoed up the ladder of the sky. The ground was wet and the air cold and damp, and she turned on the spot, finding the oozing demons in every crack and crevice and moving like water under the deck, a horde.

She sank to her knees and was reminded she was in her nightgown; her lower legs and knees protested as the stinging cold sank its teeth in. The gate was opening again. Or closing. Had she shut it behind herself? She didn't think so. Her heart thudded painfully. She couldn't breathe.

She fell, and the world was fading to black before she closed her eyes. Before she was well and truly out.

But she didn't shut down entirely, for rather than falling into blissful unconsciousness, she was transported to another place entirely. But not all of her; she floated, vessel-free, and looked down upon the people in a stark, downtrodden land, simpering in the grips of an impossible heat. Wandering with blank stares through the stalls of a colorful street market, where vendors fanned themselves in their complacence and goods fell into the path and floundered there, forgotten. In an alley a man tugged a rubber tourniquet with his teeth, making the skin of his wasted arm fold and pucker, before injecting himself with a syringe. Dawn saw the site with impossible clarity as all else faded and the brackish brown liquid was fed into a vein, where it flowed, too much, it overwhelmed and searched, it surged and it shocked and it halted his heart and he died, smiling, died, with relief in his heart.

Dawn shrieked as it faded; the scene eased away, and she flew through a mist. She thought of the dream in which she'd seen Clara, her sickbed approaching through the clouds.

But then she was somewhere else. A frigid land, white and vast, just one shape on the landscape. She zoomed in and it was another man, dead in a black and frosted pool of blood, blank eyes staring endlessly at a barren sky streaked through with a single, jagged-edged tear.

She was whisked away again, to a set of a news channel, where co-anchors argued before they went on, one threatening to tell the truth and the other stuck in inaction, refusing to back her.

To a hospital overrun with attempted suicides and its morgue with the dead, its administrators drowning in their desperation.

And she knew that, dream or no, what she was seeing was the truth.

Then she was in Shya's house, in a room she hadn't seen. It was John's, and he was quivering on the bed, eyes squeezing shut, the tendons in his neck straining to hold the glinting blade that had damaged his hand away from a wrist that fairly begged for it, smooth and unmarked, teeming with warm blood.

Shya's sickbed was next, and Dawn resisted the sight until she could feel the presence so intensely it stung. When she opened her eyes, she was in her body again, sitting by the bed, and Shya was upright, sitting cross-legged and smiling glittery-eyed at Dawn. Her feet were free of their restraints, but her arms still reached taut and at awkward angles, to the post. Her right arm appeared to be bent unnaturally at the shoulder as it strained against the angle, making Dawn cringe.

You are my sunshine, it sang. Dawn recoiled from the guttural voice, her chair nearly falling backward with her in it.

My only sunshine,

The thing's eyes fluttered. Dawn leaned forward again.

You tore a hole in the skies so grey, it chuckled wetly, then laughed in a throaty, breathless tone that had Dawn's hackles rising.

The lids fluttered longer this time, and Dawn could see

Shya's eyes between blinks. *She's trying to escape!*

You'll never know, dear, the thing smiled again, having regained its hold over her friend. *How much I L O V E you!* The demon spelled out a word Dawn wasn't sure it could've articulated any other way, but any satisfaction gleaned from that was gone when its smile stretched up in Shya's cheeks, her lips splitting and bleeding. Blood between her teeth.

"Stop!" Dawn cried, standing.

The eyes turned completely then, and Shya's green-eyed gaze surfaced, hollow and beyond exhaustion.

"Shya!" Dawn screamed, then stuttered in her efforts to tell the girl what she needed to know before she was lost again.

"Kill me!" Shya cried, voice faint and echoing as if travelling from the shore her soul was trapped on.

"No!" Dawn gripped the footboard until her fingers ached with pain. "It won't work!"

Shya frowned momentarily, then she was fluttering again, and the eyes that fought to shove her spirit down were *angry,* now.

"There's another!" Dawn screamed, but she was filtering in and out like static, and the demon was winning. "No!"

Shya's head snapped back with an audible crack, making Dawn gasp, and then it lowered in another quick movement and regarded her, black-eyed and enraged.

I don't need this one anyway, it belched in a crackling, singsong voice that took Dawn to her knees, eyes on her friend as her head was wrenched violently again, but twisted to the side that time, eliciting a sickening *snap,* after which Shya's head lolled lifelessly to her chest.

Dawn was clawing at the footboard to stand up, now, screaming "No!" over and over, and "Rory!" But her friend's body was sinking down, withering and drying out so thoroughly that her wrists slipped from their restraints. And in the blink of an eye, she was on her hands and knees, her head turning grotesquely until she was regarding Dawn sideways and upside-down with a lifeless gaze, then bursting forward in a crawl across the bed and reaching for her. And Dawn tumbled backward, landing hard on something cold, lungs aching for air and sunlight dazzling her eyes.

She was in the back yard again.

She sat up. "Shya!" she cried, then hastened to her feet as the sound of the gate opening – or closing – filled her ears again. Or still. Had it been a blip in time, only? She considered the possibility that she was on some never-ending loop; one that brought her in circles around and inside the house to watch her friend be killed repeatedly. To find her desperate father fighting against his own blood's desire to spill. To watch the thing take her.

She ran toward the corner of the house, but he came around it before she got there, making her skid on the wet ground where the sun was melting the frost.

"Ed!" she cried, and she leapt into his arms, then went limp, letting go as she cried on his shoulder. His muscled shoulder. Ed was still Ed, but there was less of him.

She pulled away slightly, but he still held her tight. Her feet dangled above the ground. She looked into deep brown eyes and whispered, "Mel?"

He shook his head.

Dawn whipped her head toward the house, suddenly needing to see Shya. "Oh, God!" she cried as her dream – if that had been what it was – came back to her.

Ed was shaking his head. "She's not dead," he said quietly. He set her gently on her feet, then put his hands on her shoulders and slid them a few inches down, leaving a trailing warmth that was almost soothing. "I can feel her." He squeezed her upper arms. "And we have to do this now," he said, so sure and clear that Dawn was left with no option but to nod. "If Shya dies, we aren't just losing a friend – a *family* member –

that we love. The world loses her family's gift."

Dawn's eyes threatened to pop out of her skull as her thoughts whirled painfully.

Ed's eyes welled with tears. Dawn observed the details of his face that were new… that had been buried in flesh before. "And she'd say it was for the better!" he exclaimed, letting his hands drop and taking a step toward the fence. Then he whirled, continuing "But it isn't better, Dawn. Her gift – it is divine. It is *known.*"

"Known?" Dawn managed one word. Her lungs still hurt, and the cold air wasn't helping.

Ed nodded. "It helps maintain the balance."

She felt simultaneously confused and enlightened. "We need to call..."

He was shaking his head. "No time."

"But Charm!"

"Don't worry!" he raised his voice, making her cringe, and then apologized. "I'm sorry, Dawn, but we have to go in. *Now.*"

She nodded again, and he turned, and they ran around to the front of the house.

CHAPTER 52 – HERE I COME

Dawn managed to gather herself, at least partially, as she followed Ed around the house. Watching him hitch his pants up in a fight against gravity. *How?*

He glanced back at her. "I haven't worn pants since we arrived in Tibet! Need to go shopping."

Dawn shook her head. "What the *fuck,* Ed?" She gripped his arm as they rounded the last corner.

He stopped on the step, his hand on the door handle. "We don't have time for this!"

She threw her hands up. "We don't have a chance in there!" she was yelling, now, and it felt good, despite the shortness of breath.

He had the nerve to appear confused.

"That thing has her completely brainwashed! And there are... *things* in the basement! And *we* weren't strong enough! Jane, Anna, Sheila and I! It kicked our asses! Are you trying to tell me that whatever you learned in Tibet made it so just you and I can save her?" She panted, leaning forward slightly against the tightness in her lungs.

"I'm trying to tell you I can close the portal. And we're not alone."

She peered, dumbfounded, into his eyes. Dumbfounded, and angry. She shook herself, fighting tears. Fighting the angry words that still bubbled up and yearned to burst forth.

Gritting her teeth, because if there truly was no time to explain anything to her, she'd be damned if her own need to be in control tipped the scales of this fight into failure. She met his eyes again. "I don't know what to do," she whined, completely shocking herself.

Ed pressed his lips together, his eyes going hard. "We have to go in."

She sniffed and wiped a tear away, nodding, and then she was pushing on his back as he opened the door.

On the landing, she looked around the tower of a man, struggling to see the stairs to the basement. Needing to know if they'd been entirely obscured by the advancing dark scourge. They were clear. "Can't tell what's a dream and what's real," she muttered, but Ed was pulling at her jacket sleeve as he mounted the stairs to the main floor. She followed, thinking of Mel. Thinking of the three Seers just a scant five-minute drive away with a pang in her heart. Thinking of Charm at the hospital. Feeling as though she was just arriving at the top of the most harrowing drop of a rickety rollercoaster and seeing the situation she'd been trapped in with clear eyes for the first time.

CHAPTER 53 – WAKE

Anna sprung up in bed, screaming. Her hands were at her throat. Her lungs burned and sucked in a massive gulp of breath as soon as her scream died out.

She looked around the room, which was just starting to show some signs that the dark was waning, just beginning to fade in the encroaching light of day.

She sprang out of bed and bolted to the door, calling, "Jane!" as she stuffed her feet into her shoes. Then she turned and looked toward the bed by the shuttered window. Her heart skipped a beat, then thudded painfully against her sternum. She could see the huddled heap of her sister's form beneath her covers, but she couldn't feel her.

She couldn't feel her twin for the first time since conception, and perhaps further back than that. Her fingers went numb, and lights burst before her eyes as a faint threatened to take her. And then she lurched, crying out her sister's name again. Leaping onto the bed and on top of her, pushing her into the mattress and then dragging the covers down, then pressing on her again and again, screaming "*Jane! Jane, oh God! Jaaaane!*" as she took in the peaceful countenance of her mirror image.

Suddenly Sheila was beside her, frantic. "Anna! What's wrong?"

Anna paused, her wide eyes burning, for she hadn't blinked since her eyes had met her sister's face. "I can't feel her!" she mumbled, her voice unrecognizable to her own ears.

Sheila seemed frozen to the spot.

Anna whirled to face the woman. “I can’t feel her!” she cried at the top of her voice, her face a mask of terror.

Sheila sprung into action, racing to the side of the bed, where she knelt, putting her ear to the face of her unmoving friend as a strange sense of calm eased over her. “She’s alright,” she whispered, knowing. Feeling a shallow breath against her ear. She peered up at Anna. “She’s deep, but she’s alright.” She silently thanked Mel for the soothing energy.

Anna sat awkwardly, her straddle over her sister failing to prevent the act, so her butt landed on her sister’s legs. Undone, she wailed, her face turned up to the ceiling.

Sheila gripped her hand and squeezed it. She was saying something. Anna’s wail died as she looked down at her friend. “Reach out for her, honey,” the woman said. She placed a palm on Jane’s cool forehead and squeezed Anna’s hand again. “You *can* feel her.” She turned to meet her eyes. “Just try.”

Anna had never had to *try* to connect to her sister. The idea was as foreign as existing without her. But, desperate, she tried.

And there she was. “Jane,” she breathed, falling forward, her head on Jane’s chest as she filled with relief. “She’s not gone,” she cried, and Sheila smoothed the woman’s still sleep-tousled long, white hair. Jane’s heart thudded against Anna’s ear, a glorious beat that urged her own pounding heart to slow down.

Jane awoke with a violent intake of breath, and tried to bolt upright, but was instantly pressed back into her pillow when her chest met her twin’s head. And then Sheila and Anna were embracing her and crying. All Jane could do was yell “Stop! Stop!” breathless, until the women backed away, their faces a mess of emotion. “Get off!” Jane pushed her sister enough so she could wriggle her legs out from under her, then stood, nearly knocking Sheila over, and collapsed to her knees. Sheila's hands were on her shoulders. Slowing her down. She swiped them away and stood, then went to the door.

"What are you *doing?*" Anna cried, once again distraught, heart racing.

Jane looked at the women as if they'd each grown a second head. "We have to *go!*" She cried, motioning toward the door, and the women exchanged a look of shock and remembrance.

Each were already dressed to leave, their jackets thrown on over pyjamas, boots on but undone.

"Come *on!*" Jane motioned frantically for the women to follow her as she raced out of the room, and, newly fuelled by the urgency their dreams had planted within them, Anna and Sheila surged forward to join the apparently revived Jane, whose own dream had nearly dragged her too far down to be rescued. But they *had* found her. They had brought her back. And all three were rushing to find Shya, too.

When Anna told the story later, Dawn would shake her head and say, "Thank God."

CHAPTER 54 – BACKFIRE

"Shya!"

Rory's scream made Dawn's blood run cold. Ed stopped in his tracks, and she ran around him, towards the panicked voice. She glanced over her shoulder, crying, "Ed?"

Ed raised a single finger. *Wait.* He looked to his right, his jaw hard.

Dawn shook her head, then kept going. She found Rory in the room where Shya should have been, her restraints binding him to the bed and a look of terror on his face.

"Where is she?" He bellowed when he saw Dawn.

She stopped, frowning, then turned. Remembering that it was John's room just before this one, where Ed had stopped. Remembering what she saw in her vision. She ran again.

"It wasn't her!" Rory was shouting after her, but he made no sense, and she knew where she was going now, so she didn't slow. She fell when she tried to round the door and nearly slammed into Ed, who, despite having lost a bunch of weight, still made an excellent wall. She hit the floor hard and grimaced, her hand going to her hip. She felt as though she was in a constant race to catch up to events, and floundered in that feeling on the floor, aware of the sludgy air, part of her wanting to just stay down.

It's doing this. Asmodeus.

Determination hardened her features. She pressed up to

standing, and Ed's hand was on her forearm just as she sucked in a breath to shriek at what she saw. A warmth flowed into her arm, stealing the scream away, and strangely, loosening the grip some invisible force had on her chest, just for a moment. Making her tired. "Stop that!" she demanded, eyes accusingly on Ed. Dawn hadn't a clue how Mel's abilities were working through Ed, but in the moment, she didn't care. *If the man can't be here in person to do some good, I'll be goddamned if he's going to slow me down.* Ed absently let her arm drop. The confidence he'd bounded into the back yard with seemed to have gone as he turned his eyes back to the scene on the bed.

She looked too, her mind racing, searching, begging for an answer. Anything to stop it.

Shya was there, on her back, and it appeared as though she were still unconscious, but her face was obscured by the figure of her father whose back was to Dawn and Ed. He was on his knees, bent over her, his arms jerking, working on Shya, and he was breathing like a beast, guttural and frenzied. And there was blood.

Dawn forced her legs to move, her eyes on Shya's body, which jerked to and fro as her father worked. She pushed with her mind, screaming silently for her feet to carry her faster, but seemed helpless to do anything but walk. Nonetheless, she saw soon enough.

She saw the glint of the blade, first. Silver in the light that shone in early morning rays through the curtain. But he was done with it, and it dropped, spattering blood on the sheets. In his other hand was Shya's arm, palm-up, and split in a neat, oozing line from inner elbow to wrist. Dawn's hands flew to her mouth as visions of a limp Shya, hanging from the veins of her arms and legs, assaulted her.

She tried to scream, but there wasn't enough air, and now John's fingers were easing into the wound at mid-forearm, and she looked at his profile. He was smiling, bouncing on his knees in apparent excitement, as though Shya was a gift he'd been dying to open. She turned to stare at Ed, who was frozen to the spot, sweat running in rivulets from his temples to his jaw.

And it hit her.

They'd been waiting all this time, depending on the return of Mel and Ed. Easing their fears by reassuring each other that they'd be able to fill in the blanks of the mystery that was Shya's salvation. But Ed didn't know, either.

And Mel wasn't there. Her heart hardened against the man and his unexplained absence in that split second, without giving her mind a chance to do anything about it.

Dawn turned back to the sickening scene before her, her heart racing painfully, now, and finally, she was able to make a sound, but it was a small one. A whimper.

John was pulling his fingers from Shya's arm, slowly, and they were tangled, interwoven with tendons and veins, wound together like the roots of a tree. She sucked in a breath, the scream rising in her like a flood from a burst dam, and the body of Shya's father turned its head to smile at her, black eyes glittering, corners of his lips stretched to his cheekbones. And she leapt with a primal scream, with no plan but to attack the beast, her voice curdling into a choke as the demon raised a hand and she stopped in midair, her chest constricted and her legs pedalling as though through quicksand.

A sound from the door revealed her inability to move her eyes in their sockets, but peripherally she saw Rory stumble around the door, as she had, but not falling entirely, because he was slow. One hand rubbing the opposite wrist. Freezing as he saw, his features going slack.

"It's too late," a guttural voice came from John, but it was *wrong,* for he was still smiling that grotesque smile; a demonic Joker, painfully gleeful, and the words merely spilled from the gap in his lips. "She's already served her purpose!" It cried, ecstatic, then broke down into a fit of phlegmy giggles through the still-frozen visage of Shya's father.

Dawn twitched, needing to see the other hand. Had he severed her veins? No, but they were straining in his grasp, and the wound had made a dark puddle for her arm to lie in.

The laughter disintegrated into a choking sound, and then a sickening gag, and Dawn watched as the man/beast's eye changed, flickering, as Shya's had fought to do in her vision, but faster, like static. John's eyes, then the demon's, then John's again in quick succession. The only movement in a still-frozen face.

"Ed!" Rory cried from the doorway, and Dawn was aware that Ed jumped, stirring finally from his state of shock, and Dawn fell as the outstretched hand of the demon dropped, crashing half on the bed and half off, her knees striking the floor with a hot jab of pain from each knee, but she wasted no time. Her eyes were still on the fight in John's eyes, watching the two souls flutter, noting the slow lowering of the other, tangled hand, the sound of tendons snapping back into place, obscured in a deep and gaping line of blood. She leapt again, reaching, crying out with the effort it took with a chest that was still strangely tight, as if it were in a vise. And just before she touched him, Rory screamed at Ed again from her left and Ed moved, but he couldn't stop anything, now. She touched the possessed man, and her body fell like a stone on top of Shya, while her spirit was sucked down into the familiar vignette of Shya's rocky shore.

CHAPTER 55 – CRASH

Her landing was not soft. Her ankles twisted as her feet found crevices in the rocks, her knees hit the stones with devastating ferocity, but Dawn was no longer a slave to her physical self, nor to the heavy atmosphere of Shya's childhood home. Knowing that, she got straight to it: she scanned the shoreline for Shya's tree first, and seeing it was gone, looked to the glowing horizon for Clara's sickbed rowboat. She moaned when she discovered that gone, as well, heart squeezing enough to steal her breath. She peered at the sky and found it changed as well; the portal swirled slowly and had shrunk in upon itself, but the black hordes still floated to what remained of the golden-edged void.

Dawn gasped, a memory surfacing, and scanned the sky again, but this time for the strings of light. *Shya's* light. They were gone, too. She observed the empty shoreline. *No tree, no light.*

But then she was squinting, because the shoreline wasn't empty, not entirely. There was a boulder, larger than the rest. A moving stone, one part larger and seeming to cradle the smaller. Dawn moved forward, feet slipping on the rocks, eyes ever on that huddle, and as she advanced it changed; it clarified. It wasn't one, but two. It wasn't stone, but two women, one cradling the other and rocking. Crying over her until she perceived Dawn, at which point she drew her gaze up from her daughter and toward Dawn. She shimmered, fuzzy at her edges, but beautiful and whole, though dead still, yes. Dead but not tortured. Dead, but here by choice. "She won't wake up," the woman cried, and then lifted Shya's right arm, limp and splayed apart. "The bleeding stopped! I was sure she'd bled enough for it to all be gone, but *she's* not gone!" She peered up at Dawn, her features contorting, watery. Hinting at dissolving.

Dawn bit the insides of her cheeks. If she fainted now, surely Shya's chances would fade, as well.

"She needs to wake up!" Clara wailed, shaking her daughter as she screamed. Shya appeared lifeless, her skin absurdly pale in the odd light of this otherworld, and the dark wells beneath her eyes too deep. Her head lolled as the ghost of her mother tried to wake her. Her lips were pale, nearly blue.

Dawn squeezed her fists even as her chest constricted more. *What is happening?* She pushed the question away.

Clara screamed again, seemingly giving up on Dawn as the answer, and howling up at the unnatural sky. And Dawn, feeling a failure again, ten times over, overlapping, layer upon layer, cried, too, but quieter. She looked desperately up and down the water line. *Why no tree?*

Did the demon abandon the tree to take John? To kill Shya as they watched? To defeat them even as the portal suffered? She wrung her hands, eyes darting to the horizon, then to the tear in the sky, then to the women. The girl and her mother. And then she peered down at herself because she was damp, and there it was: a line of blood across the fabric of her jacket. Her eyes went to Shya's arm. The lines matched. *She* was staunching the flow. Her body was pressing on that arm, back in John's room. She flew to the women on the wings of the tiny triumph, sliding down at the last second and skidding on her ass until she could touch her friend. She'd touched the demon to be transported here; perhaps this was their way back.

But nothing happened.

Shya's skin was cold and still, thick and still like rubber. Dawn shook her then, too, looking up at Clara, who was muddied now, her figure barely discernable. Slipping in her despair. And then, they were bathed in a light, and Dawn shielded her eyes, the raising of her arms tightening the vise around her torso, making stars dance in her eyes. And when it didn't fade, she looked, and a sun was burning in the sky. Instead of the portal? She squinted, trying to see. The portal *had* been replaced, but that was no sun that filled the hole.

She whirled, looking back to where she'd come from, recalling her escape – she and her friends' – through a portal of their own, Rory pulling them through. And there they were: Rory, working to restrain the struggling John down on the floor, Shya, obscured by Dawn's body, and Ed in the foreground, his arms raised slightly at his sides and his chest glowing, impossibly bright. His face a mask of effort, teeth bared.

"He's closing it!" she cried out loud, and Ed looked at her, she swore he did, and then she knew it because she felt his relief and his joy, but his chest dimmed at the change. He grimaced but tried to say something before refocusing. Dawn leaned forward, desperate to hear, and he tried again.

"If I close it now, she'll die! She has to wake up! Wake her! Bring her out!"

Dawn slumped, newly defeated. "How?" she cried out and saw something else: the twins and Sheila were spilling through the door and clamouring immediately to help. Jane knelt beside Rory, her hands on the fighting body of John, and closed her eyes. Anna was moving Dawn roughly; Dawn felt the movement in a secondary way, instantly nauseated and lurching forward, hands on her midsection, refusing to vomit when she needed to stop her, stop Anna from moving her, for Dawn was staunching the flow from Shya's arm! But Sheila saw and tore a sheet from the bed, wrapping Shya's arm tight and sure.

And then, they all paused. And looked toward her.

Dawn peered back at Shya, willing to do anything just

to not fail once more. Willing to give herself, if only she'd be of use to the demon. She cried out again as she touched Shya's cheeks and jiggled her shoulders. And then she froze because there was a presence behind her. A guttural laughter. And her eyes widened as a shadow fell upon them, reaching high, branching out into the sky and rooting deep into the ground and then emerging, slithering tentacles of roots surrounding Shya, wrapping around her too fast for Dawn to wrench them all away. Wanting to pull her down.

"Nooo!" she shrieked, her hands going to her ears as if to block it from her senses. Whirling again to tell Jane to stop, now. Whatever she'd done to John had released the monster! Her chest squeezed again, and sparks of pain shot through her shoulders to her fingertips, so she could say nothing.

But she saw.

She saw Charm burst through the door, IV line flying behind her, and Cadence not far behind, and Charm didn't stop: she ran, her face drawn in concentration, and then turned and leapt, and burst through Ed's swirling mass of light that was his chest to crash painfully to the ground beside Dawn.

Dawn inhaled to say something, but Charm took her in and held her tight. Whispering, "It's alright" into Dawn's ear, and then pulling away to focus on Shya.

Cadence roared her despair in the room the rest of them were in, and Dawn looked, eyes disbelieving. She'd done it. Charm had burst through, just like Shya had, and Ed was still standing.

"Get ready," Charm was saying, and Dawn met her eyes.

"For what?"

"She doesn't know me, Auntie. She trusts you. You have to take us out!"

The tree crackled and boomed as it continued to grow. It loomed, dark above them, and Dawn gaped up at it until Charm yelled her name. She gripped her shirt between her breasts. It hurt to breath. It hurt her heart to beat. It hurt to *live.*

Charm gripped Shya's upper arms tight and closed her eyes, blowing out a breath and then inhaling deep again. And then she did the thing she'd done to Dawn, but Dawn felt it via Shya. Because she was an empath, and perhaps useful in that one way. She felt the blast of tingling energy like a shock of electricity, tremored as Shya gasped into consciousness, was bathed in joy when Shya recognized that Dawn had come to save her.

To take her home.

And that was how she knew to stop Charm, to cut the connection before Shya was knocked unconscious again and to take a hand of each of them into her own and pull, envisioning the room behind her as if it was just a fall away, meeting Clara's eyes as they solidified in the ever-hazy form that reached in tendrils for her daughter, trailing in wisps as Shya was pulled toward the realm of the living.

And flipping her middle finger to the mountain of a tree as it howled after their retreat.

CHAPTER 56 – HEART

She watched them, all in a flurry of activity around her; John was leaning on the bed, helping Anna put pressure on the wrapped wound of Shya's arm as he sobbed. In relief or regret... Dawn couldn't be sure. Rory was holding her, sitting behind her and crying into her hair and Jane was looking on, from the corner of the bed, her face confused. Dawn felt her uncertainty. Her anger. She'd trusted Mel's energy. She'd let him work through her, and yet it had resulted in the demon's freedom.

Dawn understood the feeling.

Charm was sitting on the bed, her eyes bright on Shya and a hand on her foot, no doubt feeding energy to the woman until the ambulance arrived and she could be fed the blood she needed, too.

Ed was in the hallway, pacing, on the phone with 911, peeking in each time he passed, as if to make sure she was still there. Still back.

And Shya in the middle of it all, a bit dazed, but conscious. And herself. Empty of demons. And something else.

She met Dawn's eyes and her face hardened. "It's not over, Dawn," she said, and though it was quiet, her voice stopped the din of the rest of them. "That bastard has done so much damage," she whispered, and a tear leaked from her eye. "We have to make it right."

Dawn, who was on the floor, still, supporting herself with arms that were numb, and contemplating the possibility of her own death, given that the intense pressure in her chest had, if anything, only worsened since they'd all returned, nodded gratefully.

"After we're healed," Shya finished, her eyes impossibly knowing, but then it was not impossible at all, considering their gifts.

The rest of them turned to Dawn, their faces suddenly concerned. None had considered the fall of their leader, and that was alright, Dawn thought.

Shya was back.

She heard the wail of a siren and let go a little, falling back as things went black, ready to rest.

Finally.

Watch for The Seer's Series Volume 3:

Seer Sisters

Fall, 2021

BOOKS BY THIS AUTHOR

Rose's Ghost - The Trilogy

Viktor and Rose Maplestone built their house in the woods as a hideaway, but their safe haven became a prison when those left behind failed to join them, proving to be lost or killed. When Rose and Viktor join those who've gone before, there is one left to solve the puzzle of his ancestors. But Greyson isn't alone; he has help from living friends and the ghosts of family.

Rose's Ghost

She just wanted her baby back. Rose's Ghost is the first book in a series of three about a family's connection with a tormented ghost, still desperate to gain back the child she lost.Rose remains tethered to her family's property, beseeching those who reside upon or around it to help in her quest. But somewhere between her death and the haunting of Maggie Ridgewood's family, Rose's reality has become darkly skewed, and her efforts to find her child threaten to alter the lives of those whose help she enlists – or end them.

Heather's Grave

Rose is at rest, but the haunting of the Ridgewood family continues in Heather's Grave: Book 2 of the Rose's Ghost series. Maggie is relieved to have found peace in the Ridgewood family home, having solved the mystery of Rose Maplestone. But with the onset of new adventures as she and Jack prepare for their new addition comes more ominous change. Max is forced to admit his anxiety stems from more than regret over his role in saving Alice Ridgewood from Rose's ghost. His body is sick, too. And the tragedies of the Maplestone family didn't end with Rose, for after all, the child she lost was a secret in life – her existence unrecorded and unacknowledged - except by those who'd witnessed it all. And as her desperation to honor her child grows, Rose determines to help Maggie in the strangest of ways – raising questions around her intent. Does Rose mean to help, as she's vowed, or do her methods force an ultimatum instead, wherein the life of Maggie's child depends on the finding of hers?

Dmitry's Shadow

Greyson is grateful for the peace he's found with the help of his friends, but all is not yet well; the questions of his ancestry remain. Why did Viktor Kotova flee his home country? Who was left behind? Amidst rumours of a family connection with the mafia and the suspicious circumstances surrounding his grandfather's death, there are ghosts that linger, insistent on the solving of the Kotova family puzzle. So, Greyson and the property of his family home - once abandoned and then demolished - remain haunted, and like his mother before him, he enlists the help of those who reside upon it.
But Max and Maggie are fighting demons of their own, and Charis finds her world rocked by the dark patches in her vision. Will they be able to pull together and face the truths of a buried past? And will the answers they find bring long-awaited closure to a man whose life is just beginning at the age of seventy-four?

Asylum

From the creator of the Rose's Ghost series comes another thrilling tale: Asylum proves to be a ghost story that stands on

its own.
We follow Bailey O'Connor on an exciting urban exploration trip across the border to discover the secrets of a long-abandoned institution for mentally and physically handicapped children. But there's more than just mystery darkening the crumbling buildings they discover, and Bailey finds herself lost within them with the help of those who linger.
The search for her is mounted during the day while her own search takes place in the dark. Are the rumors true? The whisperings of experiments performed on the innocent and vulnerable? What secrets lurk within the few impenetrable buildings on the site? Most importantly, can the truth be uncovered before the property is leveled and its secrets are buried forever?
Told in Dale's unique voice, readers both familiar and new will appreciate an engaging cast of characters and a compelling story that is hard to put down.

Constance & Enzo's Tea Time With Peyton

From the author of the Rose's Ghost Trilogy and Asylum comes a thrilling new tale featuring familiar characters...
Peyton's come a long way from the awkward twelve-year-old girl we met in That Summer, but her incredible gift is still wreaking havoc with her life. In her ongoing quest to find others like her, she's unknowingly left a trail of breadcrumbs to her front door – for commiserating friends and desperate souls, alike.
But she couldn't have predicted the lengths one visiting stranger would go to take advantage of her ability to talk to the dead. She's never been good at predicting the actions of people, dead or alive, But this time her weakness - combined with the all-encompassing need of her captor - results in her disappearance.
Her advantage? Those who love her will do everything they

can to find her and bring her home, including the recruitment of two uniquely qualified women. Will Margot - a pioneer in the world of science and the supernatural, and Charis - a sometimes reluctant, but highly gifted psychic - succeed in using their own special talents to see clues the police simply can't?

Chrysalis

In Chrysalis, we explore the quiet underworld of an ultra-conservative Canadian city. Our unlikely hero, Trey, is an energy-seeing, cross-dressing sex worker on the precipice of a life or death decision, but when a friend goes missing, he finds himself distracted from the business of self-destruction.
Desperate to find his missing colleague, twenty-four-year-old Trey finds himself part of an unusual group, from a deranged kidnapper to a devoted cop, all focused on a missing girl. And when confronted with these Canadian people, dealing with both human and Canadian issues, we find ourselves suspending our judgement on characters we'd often prefer to look past.Through it all, we witness Trey's chance at transformation – will he be able to set himself on a new direction in life as he finally begins to understand that being different doesn't necessarily mean you don't belong?

Spirit Talker

The first book in a new series from the author that brought you the Rose's Ghost Trilogy and Asylum.

Shya's no stranger to events of the paranormal sort – the women in her family have passed down their strange gifts for as long as they know. But the early loss of her mother has meant far less guidance for Shya than they'd both hoped for, and now she finds herself floundering as she faces darker elements of the spirit world.

She's grateful for her friends in The Seers group... at least they take her seriously, and even provide insight she couldn't have gleaned herself, thanks to their incredible collection of supernatural gifts. But none of them are prepared for the fight that looms ahead, and it's not only a possessed child's life that hangs in the balance – the demon wants Shya most of all.

Will The Seers succeed in saving both souls when Shya's gifts are turned to work against her?

Join Shya and The Seers on an adventure that will have you in its grips and leave you wanting more.

Bird With A Broken Wing

A fourteen-year-old girl living in a rural community of Nova Scotia, a group of neighborhood kids, and hours spent exploring or just hanging out in the woods and on the train tracks along the river.
Bird With A Broken Wing brings us back to a time when the best thing about evenings and weekends was heading outside to find your friends - but there is nothing typical about Margot's new friend, Wren. And the new family at the bottom of the hill knows why.
Just as she tries to accept her feelings of being perpetually left behind, Margot discovers some of the different faces of love in the most unexpected way.

That Summer

Twelve-year-old Peyton is dealing with an Asperger's diagnosis and a summer spent away from her parents. Everything changes for her that summer, but it takes some new friends - live and ghosts alike - to get through it all. In the end, she not only learns that being herself is her best option, but that she can make a positive difference in the lives of others, too.

www.ingramcontent.com/pod-product-compliance
Lightning Source LLC
Chambersburg PA
CBHW072126250626
47159CB00007B/2581